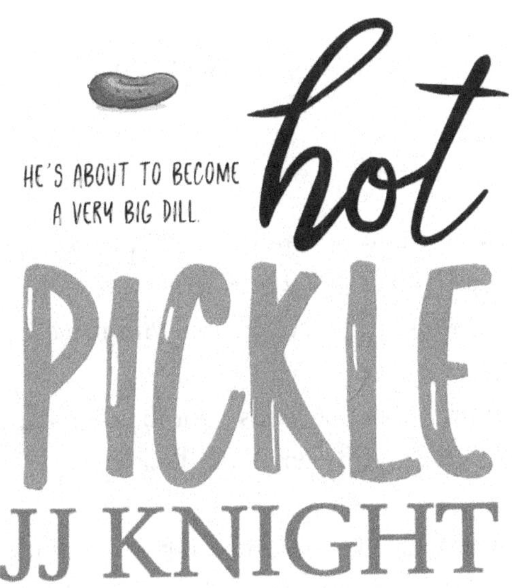

The *USA Today* bestselling author of

Single Dad on Top
The Accidental Harem
Big Pickle
Uncaged Love
Fight for Her
Reckless Attraction

Want to make sure you don't miss a release?
Join JJ's email or text list.

ABOUT THE PICKLE SERIES

★ ★ ★ ★ ★ "Funny, romantic, sexy, sweet. And lots of pickle jokes! JJ Knight wrote a real winner!" *New York Times* bestselling romance author Lynn Raye Harris

★ ★ ★ ★ ★ "This book was adorable. Smart, sassy and sexy!" Alphas Do it Better Book Blog

★ ★ ★ ★ ★ "Laugh-out-loud hilarious, and it's a fantastic, fabulous read that you absolutely don't want to miss!" Book Addict Blog

★ ★ ★ ★ ★ "From the first Page I could not stop Laughing. This was my first JJ Knight book and will not be my last." Nadine from Deeply Love Reading Book Blog

★ ★ ★ ★ ★ "This was a fun, hilarious, upbeat book! It definitely got me out of my books slump!" The Smut-Brarians

★ ★ ★ ★ ★ "The steamy sexy content, friendly banter, and pickle entendres successfully kicked my enjoyment up several notches. I remained engaged from the first page through the last." Reader Edyn Book Blog

★ ★ ★ ★ ★ "This is a fun romantic comedy that had me rolling on the floor with laughter. The witty banter and LOL shenanigans were genius. Pick this one up, it's a hoot!!" The Eclectic Reader

★★★ HOT PICKLE ★★★

I'm rock hard.
No, not like that.

When that happens, you won't need me to tell you.

I'm a competitive bodybuilder, ready for my very first contest. And winning requires more than killer workouts and stage presence.

It's all about the tan.

My training partner Franklin uses the best in the business — Camryn Schultz. She understands the career killer of a badly placed white spot.

She's also his sister.

So when the craptastic tan I'm given for my first competition requires an emergency patch, Franklin knows exactly who to call.

The thing is, when Camryn's hands hit my skin, more than a few muscles spring to life.

I'm about to head on stage in the tiniest Speedo imaginable and parts of me no longer fit.

What I need to do for my friendship and my future on the circuit is to walk away.

But when my best friend's sister has her hands on my hard body, there's no way this Pickle is going to get anything but *hot*.

Edition 1

Casey Shay Press
PO Box 160116
Austin, TX 78716
www.jjknight.com

Paperback ISBN: 9781938150913

1

MAX

S o, I'm naked.

    In a tent.

The tent only has three sides.

Aaaaaand…it's in the middle of a parking lot.

But that's not all.

A woman blocks the fourth, open side of the tent.

She's a willowy bottle-blonde with a tight black shirt that says "Ride 'em Shiny."

And she's hosing me down.

Now, you may wonder how a man arrives at a scene like this in broad daylight.

I've got nothing but time to explain as the woman tells me to spread my legs. I take a wide step, arms in the air, trying not to flinch in the spray.

I'm happy to tell you this story. It will distract me.

So, first, you have to be *rock hard*.

Hey, now. Get your mind out of the gutter.

Actually, don't.

I like the gutter.

But right now I mean muscles.

Pecs. Gluts. Biceps. Lats.

To reach tent-in-a-parking-lot level, you'll work out every day for at least a year, probably two.

Your diet will be strict. Lean meat, measured carbs.

You'll go through bulking periods to put on muscle, then a cutting phase to burn the fat out of the creases.

On the last day, you'll have to dehydrate so your skin pulls tight and every sinew is revealed. And you will eat like a maniac, infusing those muscles with carbs so they'll plump out.

Then, and only then, will you find yourself in a tent behind an arena, butt naked, getting a spray of tan and oil before you go on stage to compete in a regional bodybuilding competition.

That's where I'm headed next.

You with me?

Well, not with me.

Your eyes might be bugging out if that were the case.

But you can picture it, right?

Me. Naked. Muscles. Oil.

Is your mind in the gutter again?

Good.

The spray is cold and brown, like being pelted with chocolate milk.

Which is kinda…gross.

That might have melted your lady boner.

Sorry.

Well, unless you like licking chocolate milk off—

"Take a quarter-turn, honey," the woman says. "Got to get all the pale bits."

Pale bits. I'm not exactly pasty on a normal day here in sunny California. But for the lighting and the stage, you have to be dark for your muscles to shine.

Plus, there are parts of me where generally the *sun don't shine.*

"Turn again," the lady says, and now I'm facing her, all the goods on display. She works like a pro, her gloved hand shifting the dangling parts aside so she can get my thighs.

As she bends, I spot dozens of people milling around the parking lot. It's a big regional competition. People peer in, and I guess I'll have to get used to it. If women can stick their heels in stirrups and pop out a kid in a roomful of onlookers like my cousin Greta did, then I suppose I can shut my trap about getting gawked at by strangers wandering by my tanning tent.

I am, after all, expected to put my body on display. The tight competition trunks don't cover up much more than this woman's pale blue glove.

"I'm gonna put a finish on it," she says, and I stifle a wisecrack. I'm sure she's heard them all. For now, I'll keep my crusty remarks to myself.

The woman sprays another pass, then steps back to assess me. "Lookin' good, baller," she says. "Make a slow turn so I can do a final check."

I do as she says. Good thing I'm not shy.

"All right. Give it a sec to dry. Don't touch anything you don't have to, and don't scratch any itches!"

She clips a towel over the opening so I can stand

there without an audience. I let out a long breath. I'm dying of thirst.

I got to eat a huge breakfast this morning, part of making sure my muscles aren't "flat" for the big day. It was heaven, honestly, after the dieting of the last ten weeks. Four orders of French Toast, three sides of hash browns, and six scrambled eggs.

Unfortunately, I only got to drink half a cup of black coffee with it.

Prejudging is in a couple of hours, but the evening show is when the audience will arrive. I will probably eat carb loads several times today, but I won't be able to take more than a few sips of water until it's all over. Otherwise, I risk bloating my hard work.

I touch my chest. Damn, I'm dark. My arms look like they come from someone else's body.

It seems dry enough, so I slide my posing trunks on carefully, trying to avoid too much pressure on any one spot. But they're tight, and it's like a wrestling match to get them in place.

Nobody tells you about this part, not even my best bud and training partner Franklin. And I thought he'd told me all the bad shit.

I finally manage to get the tiny blue trunks in place, and everything tucked in. I snatch up a loose hoodie and slide it on. Next, baggy sweatpants to avoid rubbing the tan, but keep my legs warm. It's not cold out, but Franklin warned me that letting my muscles use their glycogen stores to keep warm will lessen their bulge when it's time.

I'm trying to do everything right.

I slide into my slip-on shoes and shoulder my bag to head out of the tent. The woman gives me a wink as I lay a tip in her hand. "Good luck, baller."

I mumble my thanks and take off. After that show of flesh, I could use a beer. But I won't be doing that anytime soon.

The parking lot's a circus. Tents for supplements and weight systems line up in a row, banners whipping in the wind. Men pose with women in bikinis dangling on their arms.

There's skin everywhere. Bronzed, shiny, bulked-up bodies are on display in every direction. They aren't competing, obviously. You can separate us by what we're wearing. The marketers don't need to protect their tan or keep their muscles warm. They're selling stuff and trying to show off what it can do.

I wave off several who approach with samples and swag. I was supposed to meet Franklin five minutes ago. His prejudging is in less than an hour. He wants to give me a pep talk and make sure I look the part.

I fish my badge out of my bag and flash it at the guard sitting by the back door. Then I'm inside, air conditioning flowing over me like a Bahaman breeze.

The pre-staging area is a madhouse. Some weight categories are already headed to the stage, so tricked-out bodies turn sideways to avoid bumping into each other and messing up their perfect oil. The air is full of tension and angst.

I spot Franklin grabbing his pin at the registration table. He's prepped and ready, a loose towel across his shoulders, slip-on shoes, and red board shorts. He does the physique category rather than classic, so he gets long loose trunks that almost reach his knees. Not like my tiny bit of stretch. His tan is glossy and perfect.

He's a regular on the regional circuit. When I first started, he was a beast compared to me. But during this last bulking phase, my muscle mass developed beyond his. I'm glad we're in separate classes and don't compete against each other.

I spot an empty bit of wall out of the way of the crowd, a place to stand and wait until Franklin leaves the line. The sea of bronzed humans fascinates me.

I don't think I would've taken up the call if I hadn't reconnected with Franklin. We were roommates at UCLA as undergrads, but lost touch after I started running my family deli.

When I felt the excess of too much pastrami on rye, I asked around for a good workout joint. Franklin had been the one to recommend Buster's Gym. Thing is, it's an old-school, free-weights place where once you start pushing hard, you need a qualified spotter to work in pairs.

He was already competing and needed someone more reliable than his current training buddy. Even though I was a wad of flab compared to him in those early days, I got bitten by the fitness bug and soon both of us were hitting the weight room five or six days a week.

When I started putting on muscle, it became a bit of an obsession. Franklin motivated me to push as well as kept me in check. He reminded me there was life outside the gym, and after my brother Jason screwed up his own franchise good and hard by ignoring it, I knew I needed to find some balance between my workouts and my business.

Today is the day I will test that balance.

I don't expect to compete anywhere near the top. But there's always the possibility I'll get up there and knock everybody dead.

I don't know how I'll manage my business if that happens, but I guess I can only do what Grammy always says and crunch that pickle when I get to the jar.

Franklin leaves the desk and spots me. His stride is confident as he threads his way through the crowd. I hope this is his night. He's waited a long time to qualify for Nationals and the journey to a pro card.

He holds out his arm for a fist bump, because even a handshake can impact the smoothness of his oil and tan at this late stage, "How are you feeling?" he asks.

"A little nervous I'm gonna screw up."

"No way. Amy is a great posing coach. Don't let the nerves get to you."

He surveys my face and hands. "You're good and dark."

"Just got my last round done."

"You carb up this morning?"

"Yep."

"You have more carbs and some weights to get your pump before you go on?"

"I do."

He smacks my shoulder. "I think you're going to do great. You're a natural. Let's take a look at that tan."

I unzip my top.

Franklin frowns. "She was in a hurry. I see some areas where it could've been blended better. Take that off."

In any other situation, having two people examining each other's mostly naked skin would mean something else entirely. But here, it's happening all across the room. Women adding bronzer to the cleavage of other women. Dudes kneeling in front of other dudes' junk, adjusting the fit of an elastic band.

Franklin tilts his head. "It's probably good enough. Turn around, though. Your rear lat spread is where it's at. You don't want to have points deducted after all the work you've done on it."

He's right. My back is my strong suit, according to our posing coach. It's where I'll have an advantage.

I turn and hear a sudden intake of air.

Franklin's voice could peel paint. "I don't know what the hell she did, but you've got a white line going down your spine."

"What?" I turn my head as far as it will go, like a dog chasing its tail.

"The spray has to dry before you relax a pose, or it will pull the color. It can even wreck an old tan." Franklin says. "The most amateur tanning artist should know that."

My gut twists. Pro Tan had me wait. There was a timer in the pod. I remember that now. Miss Ride 'Em Shiny had rushed me through. "How bad is it?"

"Enough to blow the score on your rear lat."

Well, shit. "What do I do?"

"Let me see if I can track down Camryn."

"Your sister?"

When I turn around, Franklin already has the phone to his ear. His eyebrows are drawn together, and his expression is murderous. I want a mirror to see how bad this is, but despite all the people preening in the room, there aren't any.

I watch Franklin, tempted to pull my jacket back on, afraid of feeling ridiculous. How can I go on stage like this?

He finally speaks. "Yes, I know I'm supposed to text you. I was afraid you wouldn't look at it."

He pauses. "My buddy Max is doing his first show today and some crap-tastic amateur gave him a spine line."

The squawk in his ear is so loud he pulls the phone several inches away from his head.

When it quiets, he says, "Over by registration," and shoves the phone in his bag.

"So, your sister can help?" I ask.

His jaw hardens for a moment, and I have no idea why. I've never met his sister. Maybe they don't get along.

He leads me over to a quiet corner. "She's a pro among pros, and booked solid today, but I can't let you go up like that."

"So, she's coming?"

"She's going to squeeze in a three-minute patch job on you." He walks behind me again and grunts in irritation. "Bro, next time you need a tan, sign up in advance."

"I got the first two done by Pro Tan like you said."

"And who did this horrid last-minute job?"

I don't want to say the name. But Franklin's in my face. He probably feels like he blew all the time he's put into me.

"Ride 'em Shiny," I finally admit.

Franklin spins away, his hands on his head. "Ride 'em fucking Shiny? Do you know who their primary clients are?"

"No." My voice sounds as stony as I feel, but my gut drops when Franklin utters his next two words.

"Porn stars."

2

———

CAMRYN

I might be short, but I'm hard to intimidate.

The woman in front of me is over six feet tall even before you account for her three-inch heels. She towers over my head like she's ready to devour me whole. I'm five-two. My rainbow sparkle Converse do not help with the height differential.

And this woman is pissed.

"I have been your client for two damn years," she hisses down at me. "And you're saying you can't give me ten minutes right now?"

This woman could break me in half. No doubt she could bench press my measly body weight when she was ten. She wears a sunny yellow competition bikini over her even, deep-black skin, her hair swept up in a burst of perfectly arranged white braid extensions.

Her false eyelashes blink at me as if I don't have the mental competence to understand her problem.

I steady my breath. "Tanisha, you are one of my star

clients, and you know how much care I put into every single competitor on my list. But competition day gets booked solid. You didn't even tell me you were competing today, or I would've left a big spot for you."

I pull a brush from a sling lined with tools like a soldier carries bullets. "Let me blend your jawline a touch." I run the soft bristles over her skin. She doesn't need any fixing. She just needs me.

"Let me see your shoulders. You know those are what get you points." She turns and I run the brush in all the shadows.

"There," I say as she makes her way back around. "You are perfect. You have the Camryn stamp of approval."

Her eyes mist a bit, and she touches a finger to the corner of her perfect lashes. "Thank you, love."

"Book me for the real deal next one, okay? Send me your calendar."

She leans down for an air kiss, then I hurry for the door.

I do feel bad I can't do a final prep on her. Women in particular have extra needs on competition day. Cleavage shadowing, extra taping. Blending their face makeup into their neck and shoulders.

But even though I'm careful not to overbook, today is especially crazy. It's the first regional competition of the season, and everybody's stressed-out, dehydrated, and on edge.

It's my job not only to make them look good, but also to keep them calm, and most importantly, avoid letting them psych themselves out.

I feel like an absolute misfit among the bronzed and oiled skins. My complexion is incredibly fair, and even though I am known for my perfect tans, I rarely apply one to myself. I'm like the handyman who never fixes his own sink. Or the gardener whose rosebushes always need pruning. I'm bathed in chemicals, oils, and bronzers all day long. When I'm alone, it's nice to escape it.

I glance at my phone. This was supposed to be my five-minute sandwich break before attending to the next set of clients preparing for prejudging.

But no, my brother Franklin has called me with a charity case, a new training partner who apparently thinks any tan will do for competition.

It's unlikely I will be able to do much other than fill in some splotches or blend a stripe. If it's an overall hack job, I won't be able to fix it. No time.

I haven't met this new partner. I know they've been training together for a while, but I have to limit my time with my brother. I love Franklin, but he's got the mother of all big-brother complexes, and he tries to control more of my life than he has any reason to.

Hopefully, his friend isn't the same alpha, over-bearing sack of machismo. If both of them try to tell me what to do, I'm going to have to walk away.

"Camryn!" squeals Amanda Johnson, a trainer who sends me lots of referrals. She's fit and perfect in a hot pink exercise bra and matching cheetah print yoga pants. She likes to be seen.

I notice a fine white line in the crook of her elbow and a subtle streak across her shoulder. She should have me do her tans, but she doesn't like my rates. Still, she looks good. Her green eyes sparkle as she gives me a quick hug. "I don't want to keep you from your busy day. Did you finish up on Sean?" He's one of her clients.

"I did. He looks great. He's probably already getting out there, right?"

"He's all lined up. We're hoping third time's the charm!"

She tweaks my hair, pulled back in a ponytail so it doesn't get caught in my work. "Love these auburn streaks. It's glorious."

I can't even thank her for the compliment before she's off. I try to hurry, but I'm stopped three more times by clients. I try to give each of them the right amount of attention while also making clear I need to move on. The sandwich will have to wait. I have zero time to help out Franklin's friend before I locate my ten o'clock.

The sharp scent of chemicals and oils in the air makes me feel buoyantly alive. This is my scene. I started out doing tans and brow waxes in a low-end nail salon where I was paid by the hour.

But I studied and trained and decided to be the best at one thing only. It was Franklin's idea to start catering to the bodybuilder crowd. I could command higher prices there, and during competition season, I can make enough money to last all year. Suggesting it was one of his finer moments.

I'm my own boss, and I love what I do. When one of my clients wins, I feel like I had a part in that. Six of my bodybuilders have earned their pro cards. Of course, traveling to shows all over the world means they have to leave my client list, but maybe one day I will have a great rapport with someone who hits it so big they can afford to take me along.

I grew up in L.A. and have never left it, but I have dreams of other cities, glitzy dressing rooms, and the biggest show of them all—Mr. Olympia.

I enter the main registration area, and it's a madhouse. The physiques are about to go on stage, including my brother. Classics are starting to filter in for registration and weigh-in. I'm not sure if this friend is in the same class as my brother or not. I guess I'll find out.

Searching this crowded room is a lot like someone from Munchkin Land trying to see through giants. I mainly get an eyeful of well-oiled backs and beefy biceps.

I pause, not sure I'm ever going to be able to spot my brother without standing on a chair, when one of my clients known as The Behemoth spots me craning my neck.

"Sweet Camryn," he says, taking my hand in his two enormous bear claws. His head is bald and shiny, and as perfectly tanned as his face and body.

I completed his look early this morning even though his competition isn't for hours. He likes to strut around the grounds and talk to all the competitors, old and new. He's in his fifties, which shows in the crinkles around his eyes, but you wouldn't know it by looking at his body. He's never hit the big time, and probably never will, as his symmetry is off. But he's a friendly beast, and most everyone loves him.

"Big B," I say. "Do you see my brother in all this chaos? I'm trying to find him."

The Behemoth scans the room. "Yeah. He's in the far corner."

"Thanks."

"I'll take you to him."

The Behemoth clears the way as we cross. I spot tons of people I know, clients of mine, trainers who refer them to me, and people who are on my waiting list. Everyone wants to curry my favor. Since I've sent so many people into the pro level, I'm something of a good-luck charm. Everyone wants to tweak my hair and shake my hand, hoping the pixie dust will rub off on them.

As we approach, I spot Franklin standing next to a tall man who looks like a deer caught in headlights.

He's awfully handsome, though, and his anxiety is apparent in his how he bites his extraordinarily kissable lip. He's in dark gray sweatpants, a jacket clutched in his fist.

It always amazes me that these outrageously built men can get completely paralyzed by the idea of going out on stage. They could break a log over someone's head with ease but ask them to step in front of an audience and they turn into timid frogs.

But this one. He's something. His dark hair is cut short on the sides, flipping across his forehead in the front. I already want to run my hands through it.

My heart squeezes for only a second, then I remind myself that the last person I would ever want to be interested in is a friend of my brother.

He bounces on his feet, full of nervous energy, worried he's screwed up.

And if Franklin is right, he has.

I guess I'll have to save his damn day.

3

______

MAX

When the registration crowd starts parting, I wonder if there's some bodybuilding celebrity entering the room. People smile. Others wave. But everyone seems to know whoever's coming.

Franklin says, "That's her. Come on."

She must be tiny, because even as people step away, I don't see her. There is, however, some giant brute of a bodybuilder pushing the crowd aside.

I follow Franklin until a diminutive woman steps out of the masses.

And my heart turns over. She's like nothing I've ever seen before. Her hair is long, almost to her waist despite being pulled into a ponytail, alternating in streaks of rich brown and deep mahogany red.

Her eyes are the ever-changing gray of storm clouds and fringed with dark lashes. If she wears any makeup, it's too natural for me to see it.

I tighten every muscle in my body involuntarily, real-

18

izing that even in my outrageously fit state, I pale in comparison to many of the bronzed gods throughout the room. And judging by their interest in her, she can have any one of them she wants.

She's dressed in a no-nonsense black tank and gray yoga pants. She might not be muscular like the other women, but every inch is toned. In this room of dark shining skin, she is a perfect pale moon.

Only when Franklin lets out a feral growl do I realize he's practically challenging every man who might be looking at his sister. Thankfully, his angry gaze targets the crowd and not the best friend behind his back.

I blink a few times to clear my horn-dog expression and give her a quick nod. "You must be Camryn," I say, since Franklin is too involved in his glaring matches to introduce us. "Apparently, I screwed up."

Franklin snaps to attention at that. "Ride 'em Shiny," he tells her.

Camryn shifts her weight to one hip, cocking it out in an *are you kidding me* stance. "How bad is it?"

"Turn around," Franklin orders.

I'm holding everything tight and suck it in even harder as I pivot in a half-circle, my jacket and bag clutched in my fist.

"Good Lord," she whispers.

This lets the air out of my sails, and I relax my muscles in defeat. "Can you fix it?"

Her voice is sharp. "I have exactly negative two minutes to get to my next paying client, but yes, I can fix it."

My manners tell me to let her off the hook, to learn my lesson and take the loss in points. But before I can say a word, her finger presses against my spine.

"Back into your rear lat pose," Camryn barks. "Don't let up until I say so."

Her tone could make a drill sergeant stand at attention. I tighten back up. The spread of something creamy cools the middle of my back.

"You've got at least six pale blotches back here. When you step on stage, they'll blast like headlights if we don't fix them." Her fingers trail across my shoulders, and an airy floral scent hits my senses. I take her in, the smell, the touch, the memory of her face and luscious hair.

It's a total sensory assault.

I stay fixed in a hard flex. Every muscle burns, but I can handle it. It'll get a hell of a lot worse when I'm on stage and have to hold position until the judges finish their comparisons. I have this terrible need to impress her, even if I'm way down the list of winning candidates in this crowd.

People move around us, a few pausing to comment on her work. Camryn shifts to my side and a soft breast brushes against my bicep. Her eyes flit up to meet mine, and I'm a goner. Hook. Line. Sinker. I can barely swallow, and if my mouth was dry before, it's the floor of the desert now.

"I'm going to work on your neck while the back dries. It's a mess," she says.

I stand there, chin up, feeling every inch of her near me. It's been a while since I've dated anybody. First it was the deli taking all my time, then my fitness obsession. I'm constantly running to New York for one thing or another, and recently I had to head to the French Riviera to knock some sense into my brother.

I could stand the company of a woman in my life.

Maybe this one.

Something clunks the back of my skull, and I realize it's the round end of a brush. "Stop sweating," Camryn commands.

I feel a trickle on my temple. She's right, but how am I supposed to stop? Standing this close to her is making me perspire like a man on death row.

Franklin comes around to my front. "They're calling my class. I have to pump. Knock 'em dead, Max. Camryn will fix you right up."

"You too, man. I'll be cheering from the side when I'm done here."

Franklin's eyes quickly dart to his sister, then me, but he gives me a quick nod. "See you after."

Camryn's work feels even more awkward with Franklin gone. I can't squelch the feeling that I'm overstepping. And if he knew what I was thinking, he'd crack my jaw.

I shift my head to look back at her. "I'm sure what you've done so far is plenty. It's my first time to compete. I'm not expecting to place or anything."

The brush thumps the back of my head again. "Listen here. This entire room has seen me working on you. You have no choice but to let me make you as perfect as everyone expects my work to be."

I think about the sea of people greeting her. She's a regular, obviously. "You're that good?"

She rounds my front and those stormy gray eyes meet mine. My knees waver. I'm so sunk.

But her voice could cut steel. "Whatever you're thinking of, I'm twice that."

I grunt out an obliging laugh. "So I should shut up and let you do your work?"

"Exactly."

While our eyes stay locked, everything around us fades away. The people, the noise, the pushing and shoving and angst and anxiety.

Something flows between us, an energy that threatens to knock me off my feet. I tune into every detail about her, the long lashes, the upsweep of her hair, one spiraling tendril lying close to her ear. I could stand here a million years, taking in her face.

Someone greets us, and Camryn seems to shake herself, nodding hello, then dropping her gaze to a funny belt that holds a dozen brushes. The moment is over.

I want to say something smart and bold, but I can only point to an empty loop. "You're missing one." It's probably a boneheaded, obvious thing, but my mind feels erased. What else could I say? I think I love you? Where have you been all my life? You must be an angel because I'm in heaven?

Nothing runs through my head but bad pick-up lines.

Camryn pats a small zipper pouch on her hip. "I

keep the used ones in here until I can clean them. I have a good system."

"Conscientious. I like that."

Her phone buzzes. "That's my next client, no doubt wondering where I am."

"Like I said, I'm sure you've done a great job."

She pulls out a brush, her eyes on the end as if she's considering bonking me with it like before. "We haven't even looked at your legs," she says. "You're heavyweight, right? So you have an hour until you go on stage?"

"That's right."

"Come with me. My next client is always well prepared. I'm more or less there to give her confidence. I should be able to do a quick bit on her, and then I can finish you before your warm-up."

She twirls the brush in a small canister. "And we can work as we walk. Go. Toward the hall to the left."

I do as she says. Somewhere in the back of my head, I think about how I should be running through my poses, warming up slowly, and getting my head straight for this first appearance on stage.

But if Camryn's right, my tan will hurt my chances. And besides, I couldn't leave her if I wanted to. My gaze is superglued to her, even as she glides a brush along my biceps while we walk.

It's wild watching Camryn work the crowd as she passes through. She greets everyone, slow and easy, as if she has all the time in the world. But she never stops, never gets drawn into a lengthy conversation. And her attention stays on my skin, her brush, the never-ending application of shadows and fill.

We duck into a small side room where a darkly bronzed woman in a gold lamé bikini squeals upon seeing Camryn.

"I'm so glad to see my lucky charm," she croons.

The two women air kiss. "Dahlia, you look divine," Camryn murmurs, and it's the warmest voice I've heard from her so far. "I'm going to emphasize these glorious triceps a touch more. This is where your points are. You're gonna kill them with these."

Dahlia closes her eyes, her long fake eyelashes resting on her cheeks. She visibly relaxes as through Camryn's words are a drug to her anxiety.

She's good. Really good.

"Let me get those cheekbones," Camryn says, stroking something a shade darker along the woman's face, and then something shimmery on the line above. Dahlia looked good before, but now her face is absolutely chiseled, like a Grecian statue.

"Run through your routine for me," Camryn says. "Show me everything you do, and I'll make sure there isn't a flaw on you."

Dahlia shifts and turns, rolling fluidly through the poses I'm familiar with, minus the two women aren't required to perform.

Camryn flutters her brush across the indentions in Dahlia's skin as she moves.

When Dahlia sweeps into her final side bicep pose, Camryn stands back, tapping the blunt end of her brush on her cheek.

"One more thing." She leans forward to add one more stroke along the woman's abs.

Dahlia catches me looking and gives me a big wink. "Is this *your* man candy or can anybody take a lick?"

Camryn tucks her brush away. "He's my brother's training partner."

Apparently, I don't even warrant a name.

"He looks nervous." Dahlia's voice drops into a low purr.

Camryn steps away, looking between the two of us. "I'd introduce you, but Dahlia, you've only got ten minutes to get to pre-stage."

They air kiss again. The whole thing has been incredible to watch. I wonder if Camryn's at all perturbed that Dahlia came on to me. If she is, I can't tell.

Dahlia passes so close to me the gold fabric of her bikini top brushes my arm. "I could eat you for lunch."

I flash a wry grin. "Probably not enough carbs for a good pump."

Dahlia's perfectly arched eyebrows lift in surprise. "A sense of humor. Do find me later." Then she's out the door.

In any other circumstance, I might have given that woman my name, number, and the combination to my safety deposit box.

But now I've met Camryn. Nobody can hold a candle to her.

Plus, the way she watched our exchange makes it clear she expects me to try to hook up with Dahlia.

And I don't like being predictable.

"All right, Romeo," Camryn says. "Get out of those pants and let me see what other disaster awaits. I hope you've learned your lesson. Stay away from any company with a last-minute slot on competition day. Every reputable tanner is booked at least two weeks out."

"Understood."

A man enters and announces the stage check for the women competitors. The room quickly empties.

Camryn waits for me to shed my pants. I almost trip over them, anxious and unsure. Damn, but she's getting to me. I toss them on the floor with my bag and hold out my arms.

"Tell me the damage."

Camryn makes a slow walk around me, tapping the end of a brush against her cheek.

"You smeared it here when you put on your trunks. You should always wear them for your final-day tan to avoid this." Her hand smooths something low on my ass, and everything in my body goes warm.

My eyes blink shut, and I try to concentrate on something other than her touch. I run through my poses, picturing myself on the stage.

Something bonks my nose, and I open my eyes to see Camryn standing there again. "I have your back acceptable. You shouldn't lose any points."

Before I can even get in a *thank you*, the end of her brush pokes my chest. "But we have to do something about these abs. You have a light patch below your navel in the critical area from belly button to…" She hesitates. "Below."

I don't know what she was going to call it, but apparently, it's a word she doesn't want to use around me.

I can't stifle my grin. "You saying my happy trail is too bright?"

She rolls her eyes. "I'm saying the lack of consistent color won't do you any favors with the judges."

"Do with me what you must."

Okay, now hold up.

I have to pause the story here.

Because this, my friend, is where things get awkward.

As I look down, my best friend's little sister gets on her knees in front of my junk. Her eyes flit up to my gaze, and those lashes about kill me.

She starts moving her hands along my belly, her fingers spreading something creamy on my skin.

My brain is no longer on this competition. It is not on my poses, or carbing up, or doing my pump, or where I need to be in half an hour.

I'm high, like I've taken a shot of heroin straight to my veins. Every bit of energy in my being is focused on the motion of her hands.

I look down at her duotone hair, the hint of cleavage in that yoga top, and her perfect lips, mere centimeters from my competition trunks.

My *swelling* trunks.

Oh, shit.

She's right there.

And these trunks are *small.*

Like, my-toddler-nephew-could-wear-them small.

I have to be tucked a very precise way to fit.

And things are moving.

Growing.

Shit.

I try to divert my thoughts. Corpses. Zombies. Rotting limbs. The entire cast of *Walking Dead* stomps through my inner vision.

It's working, but not enough. I'm closing in on half-mast, and the elastic band of this these tiny trunks is about to pull away from the very belly she's working on.

"How's it coming?" I ask, then wince at the word I've used. *Coming.* Really? Another rush of blood shifts from my brain to the parts of me I don't need to be using right now.

"Almost there." Camryn's gaze lifts, and she's so damn beautiful, and she's in such a compromising position, that this is it. Full mast. I can feel the cool air hit the tip.

Oh, *fuck.*

I whip around to face away from her.

What do I say? Do?

My mind locks up.

"Max? You okay?"

Great. I have a name *now*. Now that my cock has come out to play. Did she see?

I blurt out the first thing that comes to mind. "I think I sweated. Can you check my back and see if I messed up your work?"

Hell, yes, I'm sweating. My hairline is drenched.

"Seems okay," Camryn says. "And I need to finish that patch in front."

She hasn't seen. She doesn't know.

My only goal, the only thing in the whole damn

world I care about, is getting this dick in place before I turn around. I have to stall.

"Uh, what about the back of my neck?"

I frantically try to shove my dick back in the shorts. *Stop this,* I warn it, and feel lightheaded when it springs right back out. *Oh my God.* How do I make it stop?

"It seems fine. Max, are you sure you're okay?" Camryn tries to move around front, but I turn with her, keeping myself carefully out of view. Except now, of course, I'm facing the *door*.

"I'm fine. Just nervous. I'm sure my abs are fine." Sweat pours from my hairline. A trickle runs down my back.

A man enters the room, making Camryn's head turn. I take the moment to snatch my jacket from the floor to cover my stupid turgid junk. Why now? Damn it! Fuck!

"Male heavyweights on deck," he says. "Head to the staging area."

"That's me," I say. "Can you send me a bill?"

Camryn grabs my arm and forces me to turn. I pin the jacket to my belly with my arm. I'm not going to let her take a single peek.

"What the hell is going on, Max?" She glares at me, and entire constellations shoot out of her eyes like an angry ambush of stars.

"Just nerves. You'll bill me?" I try to sidestep away from her, but she easily moves in my way.

"That's it? Bill me? When I saved your damn bacon?" She snatches at the jacket. "What are you doing touching this to your skin? That oil is too fresh to—"

She stops talking abruptly. "Oh!"
I glance down.
And yeah. That's it.
All the goods.
Standing straight at attention.
And my best friend's sister saw every damn inch.

4

CAMRYN

Well, that's impressive.

I can't drag my eyes away from Max's rather exuberant body part.

I've seen my fair share of male junk, both in my business, and outside of it.

But this one has my attention.

Long. Thick. A beautiful blue vein pulses along one side.

It's like it's happy to see me.

But, it's not for me.

He's a client.

And a friend of my brother's.

And a total stranger.

I take a few steps back. This boy needs some space.

He smacks the jacket in front of his crotch again, and I wince at what the pressure of the fabric is surely doing to his newly oiled belly.

The runner has left and the room is empty, so I close the door and twist the lock.

Max turns to the back wall, staring up and out the high windows, possibly wishing he could fly out of one right now.

I find some words. "So, Dahlia got to you after all. You wouldn't be the first."

Max grunts. "Hardly."

"Not Dahlia?"

No answer.

Wait.

Is he saying *I* caused this?

It's not like a man has never had a reaction before. You get all up close and personal with people's skin, and things can happen.

But nobody's ever flown out of their trunks.

I'm not sure how to help, but I say, "You'll be fine before you go on stage. The nerves will draw the —"

"I know."

"Is there anything I can do?"

His body is held so stiffly he could be made of granite.

Stiffly.

I swallow my giggle.

To be honest, I'd take a Max statue in my living room. Especially in his current...er...state. My mind quickly drifts to an image of *that*, and then I have to push the thought away. The man is in distress.

I need to focus.

"I could talk about fire ants. Spoiled eggs. Bathtub mildew."

He groans.

"I've got plenty more. Sour milk. Roaches in a cereal box."

He holds up a hand. "Okay, okay. I've got it. I'm nearly there."

Nearly. But not all the way.

"You might have time to take it to its conclusion if you want me to step out. There *is* a lock."

His head turns slightly, his jaw set. "This is one hell of a conversation to be having with my training partner's sister."

I have to bite my lip to avoid laughing. "Would it be better with someone else?"

He shakes his head. His back looks good. Max may not realize it, but he's already above two-thirds of the competition. If he can hold it together on stage, he has a shot at placing. I've never seen someone arrive at their first competition in such perfect shape.

And I would be lying if I didn't say a few sparks weren't flying in my girl parts.

Thankfully, it's not so obvious as his.

"Should I go?" I ask.

"That might be helpful," he said. "Apparently there's something about you I can't resist."

"Oh." Now that's something. The newbie god has a weakness.

Me.

I feel like Meg in Hercules.

More sparks.

I take a few slow steps toward the door. "Well, it was fun. Interesting."

"Thanks for your help." His voice is monotone.

"All right, see you around."

I unlock the door and slip out.

The halls are quiet, so I take a moment to lean against the wall. My heart is hammering an awful lot over someone I just met.

But *whoa*.

For a moment, I entertain a fantasy about going back in there, sliding those trunks right down, and straddling him in the ultimate one-off before sashaying away. I can almost feel those muscles under my hands again.

Max is a rare specimen of a man.

And he preferred me over Dahlia.

That's new.

I haven't dated anyone in a while, not since Malachi, who I helped fly up in the bodybuilding ranks before he ditched me for the next *anyone* who could help his career.

That was a bad scene.

And a broken heart.

But that was last season.

Max is now.

He has the most perfect rumbly voice.

And a great sense of humor.

I *have* already touched a lot of him.

And seen even more.

Yeah, I've seen plenty.

I'm more than sparking. It's a straight-up ache. I'm not a one-night-stand sort of girl, but I could play one for a day.

My hand is on the door handle when my phone buzzes.

Right.

Work.

I'm at the top of my game.

And it's competition day.

Shoot.

I shake my head at what I'm contemplating.

Pull it together, Camryn.

I take a deep breath and move down the hall. It's mostly empty. The majority of competitors are either in prep, on stage, or are sitting in the seats to watch the other classes.

I need to head to the other dressing rooms and tackle my last two clients prepping for prejudging. Then I will have about two hours before it all starts again for the evening show.

I won't have a chance to go see Max on stage, sadly. I couldn't even carve out time to see my brother.

But he'll be around. All day.

I thumb through my paper schedule as I hurry to my next client. I'll be done with everyone by the time the heavyweights go on for the evening show.

It might be fun to watch this Max fellow when he can't see me gawking. Mostly naked. In the spotlight. Posing just for me. Well, and a thousand other spectators.

I haven't thought about dating someone since last year's disaster.

Maybe it's time I did.

5

MAX

I made it.

The competitor in front of me bounces lightly up and down to stay warm as we all wait for our turn on stage.

The hall leading to the steps is narrow, so I can only see a few people in front of me. Twenty bodybuilders are queued up for my category. It's a good showing. I'm trying to focus.

By the time I got my jets cooled and left the room where Camryn had fixed me up, I was tight on time. I barely managed to cram some rice cakes down my gullet and start pumping hand weights to make sure my muscles were as defined as possible.

Even now, as we wait to go on, the competitors who are farther back in the line constantly drop to the floor for more push-ups to avoid going flat.

I run through the poses over and over, the *thump, thump, thump* of the bass driving the beat from the music in the main arena.

I'm not as nervous as I thought I'd be. Maybe all my panic got used up with Camryn.

Or maybe compared to *that* scene, this is nothing.

We move forward, and the stage comes into view.

A young man easily five years younger than me walks confidently out and waves at the crowd. At this point in the competition, we don't get our own music for each routine, so he waits for the right moment to start morphing into the mandatory poses.

He shifts a little fast for me, so maybe his nerves are showing. I remind myself to take it easy and slow and use up every second of my allotted time.

He heads to the far side of the stage, where he'll remain while the other competitors take their turn. That's the tiring part, holding position for as long as it takes until all the bodybuilders have posed. It does not pay to be first.

We go up another step.

I'm ready for this.

I can see one side of the crowd, at least the edges where the lights don't blind me. A woman catches my eye. She's somewhat indistinct, but her high ponytail swings when she turns. Is it Camryn? I can't be sure, and I wonder if she's out there watching.

My cock stirs lightly, and I immediately switch gears. No thoughts of that woman. None. For some reason, she's my erectile kryptonite.

The competitor in front of me heads out on stage. I let out a rush of air, trying to relax. It's only my first show. What happens here affects nothing.

I watch the man move through his poses, too fast,

too sloppy. He steps aside without even doing his final pose. I kind of feel bad for him. It's a lot of work to screw up at the end.

My turn. I stride across the stage with a smile and a wave. A shout of "Knock 'em dead, Max!" from the audience tells me Franklin is out there.

I move straight into my first pose, letting it settle before shifting to the next.

My routine is well-practiced, almost muscle memory, and the rhythm of the music is perfectly timed. I turn my back to the audience and pull out my lats, and more cheers go up than I expect from a single friend in attendance.

That's good. I turn and finish out my poses with another wave and a smile, then take my place near the back center, as the right side of the stage is almost full.

Also good. Being in the center is always where you want to be.

The next fifteen minutes are a blur. I focus on light flexing, good posture, solid poses as the attention shifts to the rest of the competitors.

They fill in the other side, near the back to avoid blocking the entrance to the stage.

Then everyone's done, and it's time for the comparison round.

We line up, and I naturally fall near the center due to my placement. A couple of the bodybuilders jostle, trying to get a prime position. Some seem to care a lot about who they're standing next to.

I realize I haven't assessed the others to determine whether or not it's advantageous to be compared to one or the other, but the amount of shifting to avoid being next to me tells me I might be the man to beat.

That's surprising.

We all stand facing front, arms relaxed so our symmetry can be judged, until a man on the microphone starts re-arranging us.

"Twenty move next to seven. Thirteen next to five."

I'm not asked to move, but then, I'm already in the center.

"Everyone step back. Four move forward. Sixteen come forward. Three come forward."

Then I get a surprise.

"Eleven, step forward. Next to four."

I have a callout. It's the best sign that I'm a contender. Franklin's going to piss himself. He didn't get a callout until his fourth show.

The disembodied voice calls out various poses and quarter turns. I move to the instructions and take a quick glance at the men at my right and left. I have no way of competing against them. They are polished, confident, and roll through the poses as if they were born doing it.

Still, I'm here.

At last, we're sent off stage, and I'm free for several hours until the evening show.

When I return to the open room to fetch my gym bag, Franklin is already there. "Max, you crushed it. You were in the last four. You could place!"

"You think so?" I slide on my jacket and zip it up. "How did you do?"

"I got a callout. So, who knows, maybe we'll both

take home something big and shiny." He smacks me on the back. "Looks like Camryn fixed you right up. You were flawless."

"I owe you one for that. How should I pay her?"

Franklin picks up his bag. "She's my sister. She can occasionally do something for me."

I have a feeling Franklin already demands his sister do all his tans for free. But I don't know anything about their arrangement, so I won't cast shade.

"Do you know any of those guys who were called out with me?" I ask. "They looked experienced." My competitive streak is kicking in. Maybe I *do* want to win.

"The one next to you in the yellow is a total asshole." Franklin picks up my gym bag and hands it to me. "I got thrown out of a competition because of that guy."

Franklin's a hothead, but I can't imagine what would get him kicked out of a meet. "What happened?"

"He wouldn't stop hitting on my sister. He was pushy and needed to leave her the fuck alone. So, I punched him."

"Damn, Frank." We head down the hallway.

Franklin pushes his hand through his gelled hair, making it stand straight up. "My sister got her heart stomped about a year ago, to the point I didn't think she'd recover," he says. "And half the fitness junkies in this circuit are absolute shit. I don't want them anywhere near my sister."

"Well, hell. I hope I kick his ass." I pull my bag closer to my side to avoid colliding with a woman in a red bikini hurrying down the corridor.

"Me, too."

We push through the doors and into the sunshine. Franklin twirls his car keys around his finger. "I don't want to think about all the assholes trying to get in my sister's pants. I'd cut off all their fingers if I could. Should we take my truck?"

"Your truck is fine," I say carefully, already imagining him shoving those keys into my eyes upon hearing how his sister got an eyeful of my cock.

If I've just learned anything, it's that Camryn is absolutely off-limits.

She might be gorgeous and funny, and my body is on her side.

But Franklin's a good training partner. With his help, I got a callout on my very first stage appearance. And, despite his flaws, we've been friends for a long time.

I don't need an enemy.

So, I'll forget about her, get a proper tan next time, and everything will be fine.

As long as Camryn doesn't tell her brother about my boner.

6

CAMRYN

I t's been a long day, but I'm finally done and watching the evening show.

And holy pectorals. Max is on stage, and I'm feeling the heat.

Watching him pose to AC/DC's "Highway to Hell" has got me thinking about jumping right on that interstate and taking the ride.

Pun intended.

The seats are full for a competition this small. The auditorium smells of tanning oil. Women sit on either side of me, most likely girlfriends of competitors as they've shrieked their lungs out only once during all the categories, barely clapping for the others.

The red curtains are pulled aside, and the back of the stage is simple, a black banner with sponsor logos. This one isn't much, but it's a means to bigger and better things. Dahlia already won her category. It's a good day.

But Max has got the crowd *going*. He's pure charisma

up there, rolling through the poses with a jaunty sass that is like honey to the bees.

I'm not immune.

Max strikes his final pose and the crowd goes nuts, which is unusual given it's his first time.

I grip my seat handle. I'm glad I helped him. He has potential.

Max gives a wave at the end of his routine and joins the others to wait for callouts.

I let out a long breath of air to steady myself, and the woman next to me nods in understanding. "He's a hot one. Several of them were good."

She's right. There are some clunkers in the lineup, but as the callouts begin, the top contenders are excellent. I have to tear my gaze away from Max.

Of course, he's one of the callouts.

It's clear the others are experienced, and the heavy-weight category is one of the hardest to place in. It can take years for a bodybuilder to bulk up in that category, but Max's genetics are on his side.

Next to him, in yellow trunks, is Brad, who showed interest in me last season until my brother cracked his jaw.

So that relationship was doomed before it started.

I went through a period of rethinking my career choices, seeing as it was putting me way too close to my overbearing brother.

But nothing in the off-season came close to the love of the work I do with the bodybuilders. Since the circuit only threw my brother out for one competition, he'll be around to keep trying for his pro card. Watching. Always watching.

So, getting a bodybuilder boyfriend isn't in the cards.

I shift my attention back to Max. I've already run my hands over most of this man's body. And even though I've had male clients before, somehow, it's different.

Maybe I felt sorry for him with his terrified first-timer's syndrome.

Or maybe it was the way we locked eyes in a packed registration room like no one else was there.

And he blew off Dahlia.

Nobody blows off Dahlia. When she says come, you come.

But not him.

The crowd murmurs as a burly bald announcer dressed in black takes the stage.

"We will announce the winners of the heavyweight competition in a moment," he says. "Afterward, we will have the winners in each class return to the stage for a posedown."

The break won't be long, so I stay in my seat. The bulk of the judging is done during the morning competition. The evening show is mainly the fundraiser part of the day, when attendees pay for tickets to watch all the oiled bodies at work.

But sometimes, if it's close, performing well in the second show can make the difference.

And Max was flawless.

The announcer turns off his mic and chats with the heavyweights on stage. Max shows no sign of nervousness. He talks confidently, his smile broad and easy. He looks nothing like the frightened deer he was this morning.

I'm beginning to think my first impression was way off. I saw him anxious about his tanning problem, and then off the charts when he got his wild boner before the judging.

His easy manner on stage tells me he's much different in ordinary circumstances.

A runner carries a piece of paper up to the announcer. He nods at the men and steps away.

"Ladies and gentlemen, it's time to announce the winners of our heavyweight competition." He pauses for dramatic effect.

A recorded drum roll begins over the speakers. "In third place, we have Brad Peters."

A leggy blonde in a tight red dress and outrageous heels steps forward to place a bronze medal over Brad's head. He gives her a quick nod then strikes his favorite pose. I should feel a pang at the lost opportunity, thanks to my brother, but I don't.

Max stays on the far right, his hands clasped gently in front. The amount of distance he's put between himself and the other callouts suggests he doesn't expect to place. He claps heartily as the second-place medal is given to Jeremy, one of the veterans on the circuit. He was, in fact, expected to win tonight.

Does this mean…

"And our first-place winner tonight might surprise you. It's our rookie, right here from L.A., Max Pickle."

Cheers break out, as well as laughter at the name. My breath hitches. Pickle? Is he the Pickle brother who owns the deli on Lucas Street? I've been there a time or two, and I was vaguely aware the Pickle brothers use the same last name for the franchise. Franklin never mentioned his training partner was an actual Pickle.

Max seems shocked as the gold medal is lifted over his head by Red Dress Girl. He pays her no mind, his eyes seeming to squint to the crowd. Before I can stop myself, I'm standing and screaming and waving my arms. "Way to go, Max!"

I'm shrieking way above the random crowd. I feel faces turn toward me, and I know I'm showing preferential treatment. But I don't care. Max is awesome, and he won. None of the other men are my clients, so it won't cost me too much ill will.

Besides, Max sort of *is* my client.

Isn't he?

I pick out my brother's loud hoots amongst the general noise of the crowd. Having a training partner at this level will be good for him. Franklin didn't place in his category an hour earlier, but he's nearly there. His next competition could be the one.

This is a great day for both of us.

Max strikes his pose, then sweeps his arm into a hearty bow, pleasing the crowd. The noise grows deafening, and even if I shrieked again, I wouldn't be heard.

The announcer nods. "Seems like we have a new favorite here in the Los Angeles bodybuilding circuit. Max Pickle, everyone."

Red Dress Girl takes the gold medal away from Max, since it's time for the posedown. Max doesn't seem the least bit intimidated as the other winners stride out onto the stage. And he shouldn't. He's in the largest category, so he is going to have the most well-developed physique.

I settle back in my chair, enjoying the show. It's usually the spectators' favorite part. All the winners in each class do open posing, trying to impress the judges. The music pulses, and the crowd claps along.

I can't take my eyes off Max. He's obviously never done this before and has not been prepped. He keeps gazing from side-to-side, doing whatever the others do. Somehow, it's even more endearing that he's a little lost, and soon a chant for, "Max! Max! Max!" breaks out.

Eventually the music cuts and the judges' callouts begin. Three numbers are called, and of course Max is one of them. As the heavyweight contender, that would be expected.

The judges request poses in rapid succession.

Max is back in known territory, moving fluidly through the poses. The tingles I felt earlier in the day return, and I know I'm probably not alone. Many of the women are shifting uncomfortably in their chairs as we watch the men display their perfect physiques. Max's overwhelmingly handsome face and charming smile are winning over the crowd.

It's no surprise when Max is named the overall winner for the entire competition. I want to run up to him as the crowd crushes forward. But Franklin is already on stage shaking his hand, and I don't want to clue my brother in to my interest.

Besides, several men in suits are already approaching Max. He's going to have sponsors.

He can't get a pro card from this small of a show, but he will undoubtedly be selected for the invite-only one in two weeks.

Max Pickle is leveling up.

But what makes me smile as I exit the row and head toward the door is one important fact.

If Max is going to keep competing, he's going to need more *tans*.

7
___

MAX

The day after the competition is surreal.

I sit at my desk in the office at L.A. Pickle, the family deli I own, sorting through emails and contracts for sponsorship offers in bodybuilding.

I didn't expect any of this. Not to win. Not to move up so quickly.

I'm simultaneously thrilled and concerned. Franklin seems stoked for me, but I have to wonder if he doesn't resent my immediate success.

And I do have this restaurant to run. My focus was already divided when I was training. Now it will be even more fractured.

A knock at the door drags me from these concerns. I swivel in my chair. "Come in."

The door opens. It's Angelo, an employee who works the sandwich line.

"What's up?" I ask him.

Angelo fingers a blue, pink, and white striped bracelet, pulling it from beneath his plastic glove. He's a pistol and fun to have on staff. "We had an early run on the bread of the month," he says. "Miranda's wondering if she should bake more or if we let it go for today."

I glance at the clock. It's only eleven-thirty. The biggest part of the lunch run will come late on a Sunday. "I think we have time to do another batch."

"I'll tell her."

As he's about to turn away, I ask, "Does she need help? Should I scrub up?"

Angelo gives me a grin. "You know what Miranda's like with her bread. I'd stay far away and let her do her business."

I give him a salute. "Point taken. I leave it in her very competent hands. Thanks for paying attention."

He mimics my salute. "I'll let you know if we need your help in the afternoon. We are short one with Andre out."

My manager is off today. "I'm at your service," I say.

He gives me a grin and heads out.

I spin back to the computer. I shouldn't sit in here thinking about bodybuilding. When I'm at work, I should focus on the deli.

Besides, we close early on Sundays. I'll have plenty of time to get my workout in and confer with Franklin about my next move.

We didn't plan for this possibility. I assumed I would have a whole month before the next small competition in San Bernardino. But now it looks like I won't be attending that one at all. After winning and getting invited to a regional contest, I'm not even eligible for the beginner meet.

I'm doing it again. Thinking about bodybuilding when I should be worried about pickles.

I head out to the kitchen.

Miranda is well into mixing another batch of dough. She works it so hard and fast that the black knot of hair on her head wobbles. She's barely twenty-five but her soul is old. She adds character to the staff, that's for sure.

Her eyes narrow when she sees me. "I'm fine," she says.

I hold out my hands. "The dough is all yours. Can I at least fire-up the proofing oven for you?"

"Already done. I'm a professional, remember?"

"Never doubted it for a minute."

Miranda looks me up and down. "Did you fall asleep in a tanning bed?"

Figures Miranda would be the first one to say something. I exfoliated the hell out of myself last night, but I'm still five shades darker than normal. "Something like that."

"Well, it looks awful. Don't do it again."

I have to laugh. "Noted."

When I turn, Roger, who is busily chopping onions at the cutting block, quickly looks down. He's a shy fellow and seems uncomfortable with Miranda's treatment of me.

I wrap my knuckles on the corner of the chopping block as I walk by. "Thanks for your hard work, Roger."

He barely nods in acknowledgment.

Out in the main dining room, the line is starting to grow to the door. Time to jump in.

Tiana has the cash register well in hand, so I tie on an apron to help Angelo with the sandwiches. I greet an elderly couple and recommend a sandwich and pickle combination.

The line moves, and the three of us fall into a rhythm. I take orders and start the sandwiches, passing the tray along to Angelo for sides. I slide into a flow, an endless sea of sliced bread, deli meats, cheese, and pickles.

I have my head down, wiping up breadcrumbs between customers, when I realize I've asked, "How do you take your pickle?" and haven't received an answer.

I glance up to a vision both familiar and entirely strange.

It's Camryn, looking completely different than she did yesterday in her ponytail and yoga pants.

Her glorious mix of brown and auburn hair is down, curling gently at the end to cup those perfect breasts. She wears a black lace tank top with tiny spaghetti straps I've already begun to envision sliding off her shoulders.

Sparks shoot through my groin, and I can't believe it's already coming to life merely by spotting her in the sandwich shop.

"What are you doing here?" I ask.

She tilts her head. "Is that how you always greet your customers, Max Pickle?"

I have to physically shake myself. "I'm sorry. Did you want a sandwich? I'm happy to make one for you."

Her eyes sparkle as they meet mine. She's teasing me. "Maybe."

My heart pounds like I've just come off a deadlift. "Can I interest you in the bread of the day?"

She leans forward against the glass protecting the sandwich line. "Can you describe it to me in succulent detail?"

My cock stirs even more at the word *succulent* coming from her lips. I feel completely brain-dead. What is it about her that turns me into a drooling twelve-year-old?

Angelo pops over to help me out. "Our bread of the day is called 'Olive You So Much.' It's mostly olives, but also has garlic and artichoke."

"Thank you," she says to Angelo. "Is your boss always this speechless?"

Angelo glances from me to Camryn and back again. "Not usually."

"I'll take a veggie sandwich on that bread," Camryn says. "And your hottest pickle. I assume you have a really...hot...pickle." Her gaze never leaves my face as she says it.

Angelo clears his throat. "Sure. And it's a really big *dill*..." He smirks to himself at his joke and begins making the sandwich.

I tug at the collar of my shirt. Suddenly I'm frying in this apron.

I glance behind Camryn. There's only one other couple in line, and they are holding a laminated menu like they've never seen it before. With no other customers in sight, it seems safe enough to leave the sandwiches to Angelo and Tiana.

I take the basket with the sandwich from Angelo and add the hot pickles myself. "I'll handle this one," I tell him.

"I bet you will," he says.

I walk around the counter, snatching up an empty cup as I go. We head toward the soda fountain. "My treat."

"Thank you," she says, taking the cup to fill it with mango tea. "I wanted to congratulate you on your big win."

"Thanks." I glance around. "Let's take this table here."

She follows me to a secluded spot tucked behind the drink station. We're mostly out of view of the sandwich line. Tiana and Angelo are already whispering and looking our way.

I set her basket on the table and pull out her chair, then settle across from her. "Thank you for stopping by. I think you probably saved my fledgling career."

She unfolds a napkin. "I'm glad we were able to fix your tan. Turns out you were absolutely worth the extra trouble."

"That feels like high praise."

She pulls a bit of bread from the sandwich. "It is." She pops the bite in her mouth. "Oh, this is good."

"My brother Anthony comes up with all the bread recipes. He's great."

Camryn looks around. "I've been here before. But I've forgotten how bright and happy a place it is."

"Thank you."

She takes a bite of the sandwich and sighs. "So good."

"I have a great team."

She wipes her mouth. I could watch this all day.

"So," she says. "It seemed like you had the suits all fired up last night after your win."

I clasp my hands together on the table. "You mean the sponsorships? Yeah, I have a company lawyer looking over the contracts for two of them. Seems they want to be in my corner as I head to the next competition."

She plucks another bite of the bread. "You know, this doesn't happen to just anybody. And it doesn't even always happen to the overall winner. You've got real star power. They see it."

Franklin said the same thing last night. "I'm a little overwhelmed," I say. "I didn't expect it to happen this way."

"Well, it has. So, what's your next move?"

"Decide whether or not to take the sponsorships. And I guess I compete in two weeks."

"You're going to do it?" Her eyes light up.

"Of course I am. It would be insulting not to after everyone was so gracious."

"Who's going to do your tanning?"

Now I get it. She's here on a professional basis. I ignore the curdle of disappointment in my belly.

"I'm not sure. I haven't booked any more Pro Tans for three weeks, because I didn't think I was going to compete again until San Bernardino."

She nods. "They might have an opening or two for

this situation. People often unexpectedly level up and need a last-minute spot."

"Are you suggesting I go back to Pro Tan?"

"I would certainly rather you go there than Ride 'em Shiny."

"I won't use them again."

"And you know to keep your pants on for the last day?" Her face is pure mischief.

God, she's beautiful. And cute. And funny. I feel bold. "Do you have a proposition for me?"

She shrugs. "I'm mainly here as your advisor. I thought you did well, and I want to make sure you don't screw up again. But as long as you go through Pro Tan, you'll be fine."

"So you're not here to drum up business with me?" A guy can dream.

"If you want to sign onto my roster, I'm not going to turn you down." Her eyes drop back to the sandwich, and I wave at it to encourage her to keep eating.

"Your brother says you're the best in the business. That you usually have a waitlist."

She nods as she swallows. "I do. But nobody is going to call me out on bumping you in. Because they want to *stay* on my waitlist."

I sit back in my chair. Even if Camryn *is* here on business, having her do my tans means I get her hands on me again.

But then, of course, there is the small matter of my big boner.

"I can't guarantee it won't happen again," I say.

Her eyebrows draw together in confusion. "Winning? I mean that's the hope, right?"

"No. I mean the *incident*. The one that happened before." I drop my eyes to my crotch and then back up to her gaze.

She sits up very straight in her chair. "Oh. You mean that. Oh. Well. It was fine. I mean, you didn't try to flash me or anything. You weren't being a pervert."

At the word *pervert*, several customers glance over at us. She claps her hand over her mouth. "I should shut up, right?"

I grin from ear-to-ear. So, Camryn can lose her composure after all.

"I would love for you to do my tans. You tell me when, and I'll be there."

Her shoulders relax. "Okay good. I assume you have to work around your schedule here." She gestures to the deli.

"More or less. But I can maneuver as long as I have some advance warning. When would I need to do the next tan?"

Camryn reaches into her shoulder bag and pulls out a notebook. The pages are covered in scribbles.

"You keep your schedule by hand?"

She shrugs. "I have some scheduling software thingy Franklin set up for me, but I find this to be easier. I take a picture of the schedule with my phone, in case I lose the book."

"Smart."

"The competition is in thirteen days. So, Wednesday or Thursday for the first round? I'm pretty booked during the day, but evening might work better for you anyway. After you close here?" Her head is tilted down toward the pages, but her eyes lift to look at me. Those fringed lashes get to me. It's the same expression I saw when she was on her knees applying the tan.

I scoot closer to the table when my cock jumps. *Down, boy.*

"Wednesday is our late night, and I usually stay to the end. Thursday would be better."

She pulls a pencil from a loop on the outside of the book. "Thursday evening it is. Seven? Eight?"

"Where are you located? I might be able to make seven."

"Not far from Buster's Gym."

"That's close to here," I say. "So, seven works. Any special instructions?"

She closes her notebook. "Unlike your final tan, which should be done wearing the trunks so you don't have to slide them on and off, your base tan should be done without the possibility of tan lines. I will be using a spray, and we will go slowly and carefully to make sure we avoid fine lines in between your muscles. Drink lots of water, let those muscles fill out. We don't need you to be super cut for the base. We want the tan to be able to get in all the crevices."

Pro Tan never told me any of these things. I nod. "So wear something loose and plan to be naked."

The word *naked* makes an elderly woman I served earlier turn toward me with a big smile. I lean forward. "That's what you're saying, right? I should skip underwear altogether, so I won't have to wrangle it on afterward?"

I'm not positive, but I think Camryn's cheeks pink up a shade. "Most of my clients find it best to wear only loose shorts and an oversized tank top for the sessions. Plus, slip-on shoes. What's your number so I can remind you of your appointment and send the address?"

Even though she's all business, her eyes lock on mine as we both seem to consider my lack of clothing ahead. My mouth goes dry, but I manage to give her my number.

She nods, setting her pencil down. Then, watching my face, she lifts the pickle from her plate and takes a hearty chomp.

Oh, she's going to regret taking a bite that big.

I wait while she sucks in a breath, her eyes watering. "Oh my gosh! It really is a hot pickle!"

I have nothing to say to that.

8

CAMRYN

I've almost got everything ready for Max's arrival.

The screens are set up for where he'll change.

The tanning tent is prepped so the spray won't hit my walls or settle on my rugs.

The ceiling fan is set on high to keep the room aired out.

But I'm feeling guilty.

I can tell *you* why, right? You're a random spectator and can't tell Max a single thing.

But you wouldn't do that anyway, right?

Good. I knew I could trust you.

So here goes.

Max doesn't need a tan this early.

Don't worry, I'm not trying to bilk him out of money. I'm not even going to charge him for this session.

I want to see him.

The tan's the excuse.

It's what you would do, right? If you had access to the perfect man?

I can't waste any time.

Since meeting him on Sunday, I've been waiting for the brotherly shoe to drop, for Max to tell Franklin I'm doing his tan again. For Franklin to call and do a lot of yelling.

But it hasn't happened.

So, Max clearly hasn't mentioned it.

Maybe he knows somehow not to.

And I definitely haven't mentioned it.

I *certainly* know not to.

I pass the full-length oval mirror set into a frame in the corner.

Am I ready to see Max again?

My hair is pulled back into a ponytail. There's no changing that, as I can't let it get in the way of my work.

I'm wearing a black yoga top and pants with a bit of flair on the bottom. It's best not to have anything loose or flappy, as I could brush against a wet tan.

And bare feet. I work best that way. I did paint my toenails a soft green. I'm not sure why. Green is for go, maybe?

I'm so nervous.

Max is the full package. Gorgeous, funny, fit, *hot*. He owns his own business. I can tell from the way he banters with his employees that he's a good boss.

It took a while for me to figure out whether or not he was single. I searched for him everywhere possible. All social media. New articles. Society columns.

But I couldn't find any pictures of him with a woman.

For a while, I thought maybe he was gay. It's common in bodybuilding.

But I eventually drummed up a girlfriend from a few years back. And once I did a deep dive into the public feeds of his college crowd, there were plenty of girls.

Yes, I'm stalking him.

I don't intend to throw myself at him or anything. But it's good to know what you're up against. I'm not a homewrecker. I don't go full-tilt after somebody else's man.

But he's single. So, all bets are off.

Because I like this guy.

And I think, judging by his reaction during our tanning session, that maybe there's interest on his end, too.

I pause by the mirror for the thousandth time, questioning the spirals of hair near my ears. I agonized with a curling wand for twenty minutes over two simple curls. Was it obvious? Had I done too much?

God, I'm nervous.

I'm so excited to see him. I haven't felt this way in a long time. I hope he's everything I think he is. And if so, I should work fast. His meteoric rise up the bodybuilder ranks means every woman on the circuit is going to make a play for him.

Dahlia sure did.

And yet he popped that boner for *me*.

My phone buzzes. It's my brother.

God, he has terrible timing.

You're working the Open Classic, right?

I tap out an impatient reply: *Expecting a client any second.*

I stare at the door, wondering why he's asking. I *am* working the Open in two weeks, but Max won't be there. He'll be at the invitational.

The phone buzzes.

Who's coming?

My stomach twists. I can't tell him, but I also don't want to be caught in a lie.

They're here. Later.

I set the phone on silent.

The last thing I want is an interruption. Or to answer my brother's question.

A sharp rap on my door startles me out of my skin.

He's here.

Max Pickle is at my door!

Everything inside me wants to sing. I've only seen him twice in my life, but after all my stalking, I feel like I know him.

Still, I have to be professional today. I can't come on too strong. I must do my job and see where it leads.

When I open the door, Max holds up a white L.A. Pickle bag. "I brought you a veggie sandwich on olive bread."

I accept the gift, the aroma making my mouth water.

Or maybe it's Max.

"That is amazingly sweet."

My heart wants to hammer straight out of my skin. I've never believed in that love-at-first-sight business. And honestly, it wasn't love at first sight. I thought he was a big pain in my schedule the first time.

But seeing him today, it's different. I can't remember being this excited to see someone before.

Certainly not Malachi.

"Let me run this to the fridge," I say. "Be right back."

When I return to the living room, Max stands with his hands clasped behind his back, gazing up at the artwork covering the walls. "There's some beautiful stuff in here."

"I like supporting local artists. I practically live at farmers markets."

He turns to gaze at me and I melt a little. He's so arrestingly handsome, his sparkly eyes, half-smile, and that bulked-up body in a thin white tank top and shiny red shorts.

For a moment I think about his lack of underwear, and I know if I possessed the right anatomy, I'd be popping a boner the size of a baseball bat.

I have to get back to business.

"So, here's how it'll go." I gesture to a colorful hand-painted set of screens in the corner. "You'll change back there."

I walk to the center of the room where a stool rests on top of a bright-blue tarp. "Here is where I will do the initial exfoliating and moisturizing. That way your skin will be prepped for the first layer of tan."

I turn to a narrow pop-up tent. "Over here is where I'll spray you. And I'll have you stand under the ceiling fan while you dry."

He nods as he looks around. "It's a great setup. Lived here long?"

"I moved into this neighborhood about eighteen months ago. I get a lot of my clients from Buster's Gym, so it made sense to be closer. I'm centrally located to several competitions."

He nods again. "I'm grateful you took me on as a client. You certainly got me out of a jam. I feel absolutely confident knowing my tan is in your hands."

My hands itch to get onto his body. My professional detachment is out the window, but I have to roll with it. "You ready?"

"As ready as I'll ever be." He heads to the screen in the corner.

I watch the shadow of him undressing, beset with nerves. I'm on my own turf, doing what I do best.

But something about Max Pickle has me completely off balance.

9
___

MAX

I need an anti-Viagra.

Taking off my clothes in Camryn's apartment is fucking hot, even if I'm behind a screen. I can hear her moving around only a few feet away.

I bite the inside of my cheek. I'm not going to have a repeat of last weekend.

Not.

I act like this is the doctor's office and she's about to dig for my prostrate.

That helps.

When I step out, Camryn waits on the canvas tarp. She snaps out a large colorful towel and I have to look away as she bends down to straighten it. That ass is perfect in her fitted yoga pants, and I'll never keep control.

She turns, glances down, and lets out a sudden, "Oh!"

I look too, wondering if I was rising to the occasion.

"Did you bring a modesty pouch for your…" She hesitates. "I have some."

"I think it's too late for modesty?"

She bites her lip in a gloriously sexy way. She takes a bright-white towel from a stack on a side table and hands it to me. "You can cover things I haven't gotten to yet."

I unfurl the towel in a hurry because it's happening again already, the blood-rush to my junk. Damn. "So, what first?"

"I'll look for dry patches of skin to exfoliate."

That isn't sexy at all, so it simmers me down.

She points to the stool at the center of the tarp. "Sit here for this part."

I keep the towel on my lap as she sets a white pail full of bottles and scrubbies next to me.

"Since your hair is short, I'll start with the ears and neck. Then we'll work our way down."

I nod.

Her hands feel along my jaw, neck, and shoulders. Her hands are cool and soft. I take in more of the room. She's bohemian, with hand-hooked rugs and tie-dyed silks on the walls. A large painting portrays two figures entwined. Only after I stare at it for a while do I realize the swirls of colors depict them having sex.

Must. Avert. Eyes.

I think of changing the oil in my car. Scrubbing the grill at the deli. Cutting jalapeños.

That's better.

Camryn switches to a loofa and begins gently rubbing it near the center of my back.

"I'll have to undo what I did before, since it was a patch job," she says. "There's product build-up here."

I drop my head as she moves down, the scratch of the loofa like the perfect ease of a terrible itch.

She moves in front of me. "Chest time. Look up."

I stare at the ceiling as her thumb presses against every muscle, feels inside every crevice. She's like a sculptor making sure every ounce of clay is exactly as it should be.

"I'm going to shift this," she says, and the towel moves. She spreads my knees and the stirring begins again. I'm covered, so I let my imagination go wild, her cool hands moving up my thigh, and in my mind, grasping my heavy cock. She works it before sliding it into her mouth, her hair falling across my knees.

And I went too far. I'm at such full-mast the tent of the towel could be seen from space.

"Other side," she says, shifting to my other leg.

Her elbow almost brushes against it, so I make a show of pinning the towel in place, pushing my raging cock flat against the leg she already checked.

Jesus. What is with my body and this woman?

"So, stand up," she says. "I need to get the back of your thighs."

I breathe easier now that she's behind me. Her hands find something behind my knee and the loofa works again.

The wisps of her hair tickle my bare ass, and the fantasies roll up again. Her lips against my skin, kissing her way around. Those gorgeous eyes lifting to look up at me.

Fuck. I'm full-mast again.

"I'm going to spray you in a second, so you will need to set the towel aside."

Already? I have to get this sucker down.

Come on. I grasp for anything to cool my jets. Spoiled meat. Toe jam. Roadkill.

She stands behind me. "I'm ready for the first coat. We're going to move over to the tent to catch the spray." She walks to a corner of the room where a pop-up tent, similar to the one at Ride 'em Shiny, is set up. She picks up a wand attached to a steel canister.

Crap.

I should admit it.

So, I will.

"It's happening again."

The wand stills. "What is?"

"Same as last time."

"Oh." Her eyebrows arch.

"Should I just…go?"

Camryn taps the wand against her palm, her head tilted. The towel hides me, but with every motion she makes, I can feel my dick jump, whacking against my terry cloth.

I'm a teenage boy, I swear.

"We'll have to prep all over again if you leave," she says.

"I'm glad to pay twice. I have no idea why I'm so out of control around you."

She bites back a smile. "You mean this doesn't happen often?"

I shake my head. "Not since I was sixteen."

"That must have been a very difficult high school experience."

"It wasn't — oh, hell. I don't know." This is fucking ridiculous. I want to tell my cock to *knock it off*, but it seems to be enjoying this conversation and strains to get a better listen.

"What will get you out of it?" she asks.

My vision dances with possibilities. Her mouth. Her hand. Her body. God. Now it's worse. My voice is strangled when I ask, "What do you mean?"

"How did you get rid of it last weekend?"

"You left."

Her mouth drops open for a moment. "Should I leave?"

"You'll just come back in again."

She glances around. "I don't think I'm that hot."

I want to tell her exactly how hot she is, but I know all my blood flow is in the wrong head, so I keep my mouth shut.

"Why don't you take five behind the screen," she suggests. "See if you can pull it together."

I nod. I don't have any better ideas. As much as I want her to be my tanning artist, it seems having her hands on me is way too much.

She sets her wand down. "Let me know when you're ready."

I hold the towel in front of me, but I haven't taken two steps toward the corner when my damn foot catches on the corner of it, and just like that, the towel hits the floor.

And there we are, standing at attention.

"Shit." It's all I can think to say.

But then I add, "Sorry." I reach down for the towel.

I don't even want to look at her, but when I do, she's covering a smile with her hand. I can see it in her eyes.

"It's fine," she says.

"I feel like it's an unsolicited dick pic."

A giggle escapes. "Even if you had worn your trunks, you'd be boinking out of here like a hot dog on the run."

I let out a long breath. Her humor is helping. I'm the one with the uncontrolled body parts.

"I guess it's too late for the modesty pouch?"

"I'm not sure you'd fit. But let me grab one for when you're ready. The spray isn't toxic, but I prefer not to get it directly on your…you know."

She heads to a cabinet and passes me a small stretchy thing that reminds me of the pantyhose Grammy Alma used to hang over her shower rod.

That's calming me down.

I step behind the screen, cursing my damn cock.

What the hell is wrong with you?

It seems to say, "Sorry, but she's fuck-all hot."

I grip the towel in my hands. I have to get over this.

Camryn calls out, "Don't worry about the time. You're the end of my day. Would you like some water?"

Maybe to dunk this cock in.

"No, thank you. So, what happens next?" I ask. Stalling, really.

"We go to the tent. I work quickly so I can apply an even base," she says, and it's as if we aren't discussing my fully erect cock right here in her living room. "You'll face away and hold a lat spread so we can get an even coat."

She rambles on about dry times and peak color.

And I get it.

She's not interested in me as a man.

Or my dick, as a fuck toy.

I'm just a client.

She's a professional.

In fact, I'm probably handling it like a damn amateur.

And there we go, all the way down.

I stretch the bit of fabric over my junk and step out.

"Oh, good," she says, careful to keep her eyes up *here*.

I move to the tent, and soon she's spraying me like I'm nothing more than another mound of muscle to decorate.

My reaction to her obviously isn't reciprocated.

And apparently, her ability to resist me isn't nearly so *hard*.

10

CAMRYN

O h my God, that cock.

Ninety percent of me is on task, evenly spraying tanning solution across Max's naked back.

The rest of me is absolutely dying.

I may be stoic on the outside, but inside I'm on fire.

I want to take pictures, make a life-size print, staple it to my ceiling over my bed so I can see him first thing each morning.

God, I've got it *bad, bad, bad*.

I release the nozzle to kill the spray. "Turn," I tell Max. He has to face me now.

I take care to only look at what I'm spraying, but of course, I have to make my way down.

Of course, he's back in control and covered up by the stretchy bit of nylon.

I'm not sure if I'm relieved or disappointed. I mean, if he can't keep it in his pants, like, literally, then he probably shouldn't be my client. It's a liability, not that I'd put him on the rack for sexual harassment or anything. But because a random hard-on isn't something he should be worrying about right before going on stage.

So, it's good he got it controlled.

We're good.

I finish out the coat.

"I'm going to let you dry in privacy while I eat my sandwich," I tell him, even though I'd rather stare at him the whole time.

I tuck the wand away and hurry ahead to move the stool.

Above the tarp, the oversized arms of the fan, a custom install I did myself, whir lazily, wafting a nice, even breeze on my face.

I needed that.

When I turn, Max still waits in the tent. I give him a quick nod and head off to the kitchen.

By the time I return to my living room, Max is back behind the screen. I busy myself with picking up the tarp and towels, setting aside the things that will need to be washed and putting away the bottles of moisturizer and oil.

I can't possibly tan him for several more days, and I wrack my brain for a way to see him again before then.

I should probably be a modern woman and ask him out. But something about the awkwardness of our encounters, plus our client relationship, make me hesitate.

There's also the not-so-small matter of my brother.

Max steps out from behind the screen. "What should I do with the…"

"Keep it for next time," I say quickly.

He nods and sticks the modesty pouch in a pocket.

This draws my gaze to the shiny red shorts.

All is well down there.

I'm almost disappointed.

"I should see you tomorrow," I blurt before my sense of caution can stop me.

One of those devastating brows arches. "Really?"

Hell. I have to think fast. My words rush out like lemmings falling off a cliff. "I want to see how this color looks on you. I can adjust the shade as we get closer. I had to guess."

He nods slowly. "I could come by tomorrow night. Unless you want to drop by the deli and see what it looks like in natural light."

I want to say both but check myself. We don't need his employees to talk. And if Franklin ever goes there, and someone says something, we're doomed.

"It won't get dark until after eight. Maybe meet at a park?"

He nods. "It's a date. I mean, a plan. I'll bring sandwiches. I don't want you to get sick of veggie, though. Is there something else you would like to try?"

"Surprise me," I say.

"Are you vegetarian?"

"Yes. No. I mean, I generally eat vegetarian, but I'm not opposed to meat." Even the word *meat* makes my cheeks heat up.

Guys, I'm a mess.

Another quick nod. "I'm sure I can whip up something especially for you. So, what do I owe you?"

I try to wave him off, but his face darkens. "I'm not

going to take advantage of you.”

“You’re not. To be honest, you probably shouldn’t have had your first tan for a few more days. But this is a very important meet. You are going to be new and I want to make sure you’re perfect.”

And I desperately wanted to see you again, I add silently.

“I’m sure it was good for you to straighten out my mess from Saturday anyway,” he says.

“That, too.”

“But I will be paying for the tans.” His voice is firm.

“Absolutely. And I’m stupidly expensive. So, you better sell a lot of sandwiches tomorrow.”

He grins at that. “Well worth it. I’ll see you tomorrow, then. The park at the corner two blocks past the deli?”

“Sounds perfect. Don’t worry if you run late.”

I walk him to the door. It could be my imagination, but I think we’re both hesitating.

He’s so close that if I had a stepladder, I could lean in and kiss him.

But I do not have a stepladder. And I should not kiss him.

I hardly know him. This is only the third time we’ve crossed paths.

But as we bid each other yet another farewell, and this time he walks outside the door, I think to myself, maybe not today. Or tomorrow.

But someday soon…

I will be kissing this man.

And I can’t wait.

11

MAX

When I walk into Buster's Gym the next morning, my mind is on Camryn.

Buster himself stands by the check-in desk, greeting everybody. He's sixty, tall, and built, his shiny bald head a fixture at his gym. He doesn't have a list or an electronic scan for his members. He knows us all by name.

"Franklin's warming up," Buster says. "And it sounds like we may be putting someone else's name over the front door before long. Never had a winning bodybuilder here."

"I wouldn't count on that," I say. "Beginner's luck."

Buster shakes his head. "No such thing. It's all preparation and performance."

"I guess we'll find out." I cross the tiny entryway and poke my head into the weight room.

Franklin sits on a bench doing bicep curls. He spots me, and I point behind me. "Let me drop off my stuff."

He nods in acknowledgment and turns back to his weights.

The gym is busy at this time in the morning. I'm letting the deli crew open up, so I can get in a good, long workout. I'm buoyed by the thought of seeing Camryn later today. But I'm also conflicted because neither of us has told Franklin that we've seen each other again. Twice.

It shouldn't be a big deal. She's a service provider, and I'm a customer. After all, Franklin himself put us together.

But still. I know I'm hesitating.

I shove my bag in a locker. When I slam it closed and spin the combination, I decide I'll mention Camryn to him casually, in passing. It won't stand out as anything important. But it'll be off my back.

When I return to the weight room, Franklin's already stacking weights on the bench press bar so we can spot each other. He's lucky to have found an open rack. The room is crowded, and the accordion door stretched across the opening to the annex means a member of the McClure team, all MMA champions, is working out inside. Their family frequently has closed workouts when someone's prepping for a match.

I try to imagine Buster taking down the sign that announces these famous fighters work out here and replacing it with my ordinary mug. Ridiculous. Body-builders don't command the fame that fighters do. They're on pay-per-view, after all. Even our biggest events at the international level are only promoted in snippets shown on sports channels.

"Prepping a warm-up stack," Franklin says. He's about to grab another plate when he pauses and squints his eye at me. "I swear you're darker than yesterday."

He's given me an opening, so I take it. "Camryn's touching me up to make sure everything's even for the final coats. I don't want to make the same mistake I did last time."

I don't expect his reaction whatsoever.

He slams the plate down with a clang.

When he turns to me, his expression is nothing like I've seen before. Pure, unadulterated fury.

"Do you mean to say you went over to her apartment without telling me?"

Shit. He's on me like a vulture on roadkill. There's something more than what he told me, some rogue asshole coming onto her last year. Or the ex who broke her heart.

They can't be all that close. I lived with this dude for two years in college, and I've worked out with him for the last sixteen months. Camryn hasn't gotten more than a passing mention.

But I have to bring him down. He looks like he's going to pop a vein in his forehead.

"Wasn't aware I needed permission. She let me know she should buff out all the extra crap she had to put on me to fix the Ride 'Em Shiny disaster."

"And neither of you thought to tell me about this." His face is mottled red to the roots of his hair, like he's been sprinting in the heat.

Damn. He needs to chill. "It was no big deal. Like twenty minutes of quick fixing stuff up. She's a pro, dude. What's your problem?"

I say this as casually as I can, although inside I'm seething. What the hell does he think is happening between me and Cam?

He holds my eyes for several long beats. I remain relaxed and slightly inquisitive as I return the stare.

After a moment, he picks the plate back up and slides it on the end of the bar. "I like to know these things," he says. "There are some real dicks in our business."

He passes me a plate, and I add it to the other side. "Well, I'm assuming I'm not one of them."

He moves into place behind the bar, and I lie back on the bench.

His face, bright from the confrontation, hovers over mine. I'm not sure he's calmed down yet.

I slide my hands into place, but I don't apply any muscle to the bar. Not yet. "Seriously, Franklin. She saved my ass, and I wanted to throw a little business her way. That's it."

It's not a lie. Even if I did want more, Camryn didn't appear to have any interest in me beyond my worth to her as a client.

Franklin positions himself close to the bar. "You should know she's looking for some promising prospect to sink her claws into. She's tired of the low-level scene and wants to go along for somebody's ride." His voice is low, like every word is a threat.

"Good for her," I say.

"Don't think that anything she does isn't calculated toward getting her where she wants to be in her career."

This is a hell of a thing for him to say about family.

"All that's irrelevant to me," I say. "I'm only trying to make sure I have a decent tan for the next competition. And we better get to work, or I won't get it done before I have to go slap meat on sandwich bread, which is my real life's calling."

My self-deprecation seems to work, because his face relaxes. He nods at me to lift.

I jerk the bar from the rack and bring it to my chest. It's only the warm-up weight, so I easily pump my reps and rack it.

Franklin adds weight to both sides. "She's been through some real shit. I watch out for her."

"It's good she has you around," I say carefully. I've never known Franklin to be anything but a training partner and a mostly absent roommate. Thinking back on other difficult moments, confrontations when things would inevitably go wrong between young, stupid guys all living together, Franklin was often swift to anger.

I'd never gotten on his bad side before.

Not that I am now. Not yet. I glance at the weights and lie down again. "You already added the fifty."

"You should push," he says. "We want you clean and cut for next weekend."

We usually work up to this weight, but I lift it easily and balance the bar.

Ten reps of this are something I definitely feel. I fumble a bit as I rack the weight. But I'm glad we're talking normally again. "I should probably figure out the posedown part. I wasn't ready for it."

"True. Your lack of confidence worked for you as a first-timer, but it won't where you're headed next."

Franklin adds twenty-five more pounds to each side. This creates a new high weight for me.

He's trying to make a point.

I lie back down on the bench.

"I'll call Amy and get more lessons in before the meet."

Franklin moves into position. "That's a plan. You got this opportunity fast. Don't blow it."

I take a deep breath and exhale slowly before arranging my hands. I lift the new weight and hold it there a moment, letting the change settle in, and mentally prepare myself for a tough set.

The first two reps come fairly easy, the third one slower.

By the fourth, I'm dogging it, and by the fifth I'm feeling my left arm start to go.

"Spot," I say.

"Push yourself," Franklin says. "You have to earn what you got."

He's right. My first success came too easy. It could wreck me.

I pump out two more reps, feeling the quiver in my arms.

"Get to ten," he says.

It's not the first time we've pushed each other. That's how we've gotten where we are. But because of the conversation before, it feels different. I hit nine, but I'm not sure I have that tenth one in me.

I bring the weight to my chest and as I start to lift, I can't hold the balance required to keep the weight steady.

I'm about to say *spot*, when I see Franklin's eyes boring into mine. It's a warning, clear as day. *Don't hide anything about my sister or you will regret it.*

I let out a long, guttural groan and force the weight back in the air.

"Ten," I growl.

Franklin guides the weight back into its safety position on the rack.

"Good," he says. "You know I'm behind you one-hundred percent."

Sure he is. As long as I leave his sister alone.

I stand to shake out my arms, and we switch positions. I can see why Camryn didn't tell her brother we met again. I remember his big boast that day at the meet when he talked about the other men who came after her. And how he'd been thrown out of a competition for throwing a punch at one.

My gut tells me there's more to the story, so for now I'm going to give Franklin the benefit of the doubt. We've been friends for a long time, and he wouldn't be acting this way if he didn't have his reasons.

I pull the extra weights off the bar to take Franklin down to his warm-up weight.

The two of us make a good team. I won't jeopardize that.

But like hell will I let him get in the way if I think I have a shot with his sister.

12

CAMRYN

Waiting for Max in the neighborhood park is like one of those happy dreams where you know something wonderful is about to happen, and you never want to wake up.

I'm on one of the swings, the metal chains in my hands, and I've worked my way up to the backside of the arc, looking down at the dirt.

Then, *whoosh*, I glide forward, past the ground and up toward the sky. The air cools my face, lifting my hair to trail behind me. The entire row of swings is empty, so I don't feel too guilty snagging one for myself.

Four children congregate on a pyramid-shaped contraption made of ropes. They climb and laugh and hang like monkeys as I drop back toward the ground and up the other side.

It's glorious.

The sun begins its slide toward the horizon as I reach another apex, my toes stretching toward the trees.

Mothers murmur together on a bench near the path. I could be five years old and happily playing while my mother sat among the others.

This old childhood fantasy of mine rushes back to me with sharp familiarity.

In truth, my mother was never clustered with others. She fought depression all her life and spent most of her time in front of the television, mindlessly watching show after show. I don't know if she tried to get help, or if nothing worked for her. I have never asked. We didn't acknowledge the problem in my house.

My dad worked, and I didn't see him a lot. He always had somewhere else to be, something else to do. I had the sense he didn't quite approve of his kids. Maybe Mom was fine before we came along.

Franklin and I often wandered to a park much like this one. All those times I raced for the swings for this feeling of flying without a care, he'd always been there.

Other kids got brave and learned to jump during the height of the swing to thud into the grass beyond the scraped-out dirt.

But I was cautious. Even though my brother was there, my parents were not. I'd seen more than one kid crash and hurt themselves, running to their mothers for solace.

That wasn't an option for me, so I played it safe.

A shriek from the pyramid draws everyone's attention, and two of the mothers stand up to look.

One of the kids is hanging upside down from her knees and can't reach up for the ropes.

A mother shifts her baby to her hip and heads over to give the little girl a push so she can lift her dangling torso back to safety.

"Try it on the lower ones until your tummy's strong enough for the higher ones," the mother says, then heads back to the knot of women.

She's totally chill. The mothers in my day would have shouted, "You got into it, get yourself out of it!"

I wouldn't have minded. I wanted my mother to say something, anything. Just be there.

I shift my attention to the sky. A few striated clouds break the blue. I got here early, wanting to think about where I might sit and how I might look when Max approaches.

I wear jeans and an off-the-shoulder top. My hair is down, albeit tangled after my swinging. That's okay. I have a feeling Max doesn't go for perfect.

The air whooshes over my skin, and I close my eyes to revel in the sensation of flying.

My childhood was not ideal. But good enough. Most people had it worse. We had a home. Food. We were safe. I speak to my parents every few months, short stilted conversations that assuage my guilt. We don't go out of our way to see each other, even though we all live right here in L.A.

You can't miss what you've never had, and the distance now is scarcely different from the separateness we all had growing up.

It was fine. I'm fine.

Another child shouts, and I open my eyes.

Max is there, smiling at me in a broad, open way

that makes my heart turn over. My toes almost touch his head, but he stands out of range.

"You know, I fell off one of these as a kid and broke my arm," he says. "My brother Jason pushed me too hard and I flew right out."

"Living dangerously."

"Don't we all."

My hair streams behind me is I rush toward him. He holds out his hand, and the toe of my sandal grazes his fingertips.

"You have a good eye," I call as I rush away.

He approaches another swing, and I think he will join me. But instead, he leaps up, grabbing the cross-beam of the frame. He smoothly lifts his body until his belly is flush against the bar.

I forget to keep my arc as I watch him fluidly lift his legs over until he sits at the top, high above my head.

I'm afraid to kick the ground to stop as I might jar the frame, so I slow down gradually until I'm still, peering up at him.

"You like to live dangerously," I say.

"I've been told I'm a show-off."

I stand up and rub my grimy hands against my jeans. My anxiety is high, seeing him up there. I picture every sort of disaster. "Well, come down here so I can look at that tan."

My heart doesn't stop hammering until he swings his way down and drops onto the ground beside me.

The mothers on their bench clap for him, and he bows.

"You were made for show business," I say.

"And I guess I've taken the bodybuilding route. Maybe I will be like Arnold Schwarzenegger and become famous for saying something pithy like *I'll be back*."

I can't stop the laugh from bubbling out. "I think every bodybuilder's goal is to be Arnold Schwarzenegger."

Max holds out his arms and turns in the circle. "What do you think? How am I shaping up tan-wise?"

I can feel the stares of the mothers as I cock a hip and cross my arms across my chest. "Stand still so I can see."

He stops, arms outstretched. The sun shines its golden light on him. He wears jeans and a green L.A. Pickle T-shirt that reads, "Call me a pickle." It stretches across those pecs and shoulders that I remember all too well from his tanning sessions.

He's fantastic. Absolutely perfect. My throat feels tight.

"Arms look good," I say. "I can't see much else."

His grin is full of mischief. "Should I strip down so you can see more?"

The thought of it sends a zing through me.

"Maybe the park wasn't the best idea," I say.

He shrugs. "We could take a walk, find a more secluded spot."

We stroll along the central concrete path. As we leave the playscape area, the mothers call the children in. It's dinner time.

"Hey, weren't you supposed to bring me a sandwich?" I tease.

"In the car, in a cooler," he says. "I wasn't sure you'd want to eat it right away."

"You're right. I don't." I like the thought of having something else we're going to do together. That our time will stretch into the evening.

We pass through a line of trees, and a dirt path peels off to a small metal toolshed for the maintenance crew.

"Over here," I say. "I could take a quick look and see how that tan developed on your chest and back." The very idea of him even partially stripping in this public park makes sparks fly through my body.

He nods. When we're hidden away behind the toolshed, he grabs the back of his collar and pulls his shirt over his head.

Even though I've seen him this way before, my knees knock together as his skin is revealed.

I feel like I've memorized him, smoothing moisturizer over each muscle and crease. I manage to step closer and say, "So far, so good."

I walk around the side of him, then the back, and I cannot stop myself, but I touch his skin, warm and smooth.

"Find something?"

I pull my hand away. "I thought so, but it was a shadow."

He is perfect. Strong. Ripped. I see the differences from last night, and from last weekend. He's laid off the carbs, leaving his muscles flatter than Saturday. And today he's had plenty of water, filling in the creases. His veins are less pronounced.

I know his body too well.

"I'm pleased," I say.

"I don't think taking my pants off in the kid park would be a good idea." He pulls his shirt back over his head.

"If your chest and back look good, I'm sure everything else does, too."

"I did notice one thing." His lips press together.

"A problem?"

"A small one." He hesitates. "I think the modesty pouch might've rubbed one of my thighs, because I have a white patch."

I nod. "That can happen when someone is…" I struggle for the words. Well endowed? Overly large? At half-mast?

But he stops me. "I see. I get it. So, I guess you patch that little thing at the last minute? Or is it nothing major and the judges wouldn't see it anyway?"

"I'm happy to be completely thorough," I say.

Soooo happy to get next to that business.

"I could fix it tonight if you wanted to come over."

I hear myself saying the words, and I want to give myself a good hard smack. *Stop it, Camryn. He's going to know you're coming on to him.*

But he laughs. "I'm sure it will be fine. There's a week to go."

Damn. So close. "Absolutely. Your pants are going to rub it anyway. Most things can't be perfected until competition day."

"So, you'll be there? On competition day?"

I hesitate. Dahlia will be there, too, but she hasn't

booked me. Plus, I have a different competition to attend.

"I have six appointments at the amateur open that day, but I might be able to get over to the invitational."

"I could come to you," he says. "Early that morning before you leave. Would that work?"

I nod. That's smarter. It will make sure I get him done. "I can do that."

We take up walking along the path again.

"See, I knew this was all professional," he says. "I tried to explain that to Franklin."

I halt. "Franklin knows you came over for a tan?"

"I couldn't exactly hide my skin. He saw the darker shade immediately."

Oh, God. "What did he say?"

"I'm not perfectly sure, but I think he might have tried to kill me via bench press."

My mouth drops open. "Seriously?"

But Max gives me another one of his signature grins. "It was fine. He added a lot of weight, but I handled it. And I think we came to an understanding I would be your client, and he didn't have to worry about it."

I stare at the ground as we resume walking. "He's very overprotective."

"Got that loud and clear," Max says. "Don't worry. I can handle Franklin."

"How long have you known him?"

"We roomed together in college."

"That far back?"

Max shoves his hands into his pockets. "We've been

training together for almost a year and a half. I guess you two aren't very close? He sure acts like you are by the way he responds to any threat to you."

A woman walking a poodle crosses in front of us and I let her pass before I respond. "Franklin likes to insert himself in my life when he feels I'm making a mistake." I glance over to Max and meet his dark gaze. "Our parents were pretty absent, so we grew tight."

"But then?"

"Franklin liked the idea he was my protector. But when he went to college and got a life of his own, I took more chances. I picked the wrong crowd. The wrong boyfriend. He interfered big time last year when I tried to date a bodybuilder."

"I heard about that. Socked his jaw?"

"Yeah. And I hadn't even dated that one yet." I don't want to get into my relationship history. I barely know Max. And I don't want to put him off.

Max leads us toward the path that will circle us back to the playscape. "He seemed to feel he ought to know I'd been to your apartment. That you were doing my tans."

"I don't care what he thinks," I say. "He can't control who's on my client list."

"I assume you have lots of male bodybuilders."

"I mostly do women. But I do have some men. And Franklin knows that. I don't know why you're any different."

"Me neither. He acted like I was going to drag you off by the hair to my cave."

I'm not sure I object to that idea, but I simply shrug. "I think he enjoys using me as an opportunity to overreact. Getting hyped up like that gives him a charge."

"Must be tough to do your job, then."

We pass the maintenance shed again, and I'm already nostalgic about what happened there earlier. "Franklin is the one who suggested I try this job. I was doing low-end brow waxes and tanning bed work before this. I never know why Franklin selects certain people to keep away from me." I glance up at him. "Unless there's something about you I ought to know."

Max gestures to his shirt. "I'm your basic low-level sandwich maker."

"Who owns the restaurant."

We approach the swings. "One more round?" he asks.

"Only if you promise not to get on top of the frame."

"Made you nervous?"

"I'm protecting your hard head. Race you. Don't steal the tall one." I take off in a dead sprint. Max lets out an uproarious laugh and makes chase. We fly past the empty playscape and rush for the swings.

I grab the chain of the higher one, right as Max snatches it, too.

"I told you it was mine!" I pull the swing toward me, but Max comes with it.

And suddenly we're close. Really close.

It's not my hands on his skin, like I've done before.

But face-to-face.

He's down in the dugout base of the swing, which lessens our height difference. I feel the powerful need to stand on my tiptoes and kiss him.

"What will you give me for it?" he asks.

My answer comes before I can catch myself. "A kiss."

His expression never wavers. "So, if I give you a kiss, I get the swing?"

I laugh. "Oh, no. If I give *you* a kiss, you let *me* have the swing."

The sun has sunk low, and the shadows falling across the park are deep. The tiny ball of gold behind Max gives him an ethereal glow, like an Olympian god who has come down to find a human bride. Simply looking at him makes me shiver.

But I stand my ground. I want this kiss. I want him.

He leans forward, and for the barest moment, our lips brush together. Like the sudden flare of a match struck against the edge of the box, the need of him flashes through me, bright and hot.

But he pulls away and lets go of the chain. "You swing, I'll push."

I can scarcely breathe at what's happened, but I settle down on the thick rubber seat.

Max grasps the two metal triangles at the base of the chains and draws me back like an arrow in a bow.

I lift my feet, sinking into the nearness of him at my back.

When he's brought the seat as far as it can go, he releases me.

I sail into the sky. It's exhilarating, the wind on my

face, this man at my back. I reach the peak and retreat down, hurtling toward his body. He reaches out and firmly presses his hands low on my waist to return me to the clouds.

I have never felt so high, so exhilarated, so full of anticipation.

He pushes me three, four, five more times before I turn my head and say, "I'm starving."

He clasps the base of the chain and carefully draws my swing to a stop.

My back is pressed against his chest, and it is temptingly close to an embrace.

We wait there for the span of a few breaths, and I start to believe he feels the same way I do.

I want to rush toward what I know comes next. Both of us naked, tangled together, kissing, sucking, feasting on each other.

But it's too soon. We've only barely met.

I step down from the swing and turn to face him.

I want to tell him what I'm feeling, but I'm not sure what's happening with him. Maybe he has someone already, some lovely thing tucked away so well I couldn't find her in my search. Maybe he'll go see her after this and do all the things I'm already longing for.

My jealousy for this unknown woman burns hard. But Max is only a client. He only came because I asked to see his tan.

And yet, he did give me that kiss.

"Ready for a sandwich?" he asks. "I see an empty picnic table calling our name."

"Of course," I say. "Thank you for bringing it."

"Anything for my tanning expert."

I follow him to his car, trying to force down my feelings.

That's what I am. His service provider.

For now, it will have to be enough.

13

MAX

During workouts over the next few days, Franklin and I avoid the topic of his sister.

He doesn't ask if I'm doing more tans with her.

And I don't volunteer any information.

Particularly the part where I always seem to *rise* to the occasion.

And we're doing more tans. Over sandwiches at a picnic table in the park, Camryn and I worked out the ideal schedule leading up to next Saturday's competition.

She was a total pro, talking about optimum timing and moisturizing regimens like I was any other client on her list.

Despite her demand of a kiss earlier, she was all business.

I'll bide my time.

As I move through the days until I can see her again, I try out her recommended loofah in the shower, remembering when she used it on me in her apartment.

Just the image of her gets me rock hard. I have no hope I'll control my cock on the next tan any better than I did before.

Some things you have to let go.

I'll see her three times this week. Tan one on Tuesday for the new base, tan two on Thursday to get it *deeper*.

You caught that, right?

I thought so.

We Pickles like our puns.

Then there's the final competition tan on Saturday morning at the crack of dawn. I'll be dressed for that one. I know not to take off my trunks after the Ride 'em Shiny disaster.

Not that leaving them on helped me resist the effect Camryn has on me.

By Monday night, I'm home alone and feeling over-whelmed at the mere thought of her. Those pale shoulders in that ruffled shirt she wore to the park. Her hair spilling down her back, then billowing out in the wind as she rode the swing. It had taken all my self control to kiss her lightly, and not consume her.

But right now, alone on my bed after a long day, I let the fantasies run loose. The offending member is in my hand, and I dive into all the thoughts of her I've collected since we met.

In this one, we're back in her apartment, the colorful art all around. And it's Camryn who's stripping down. I watch every bit of her body be revealed, lustrous, and soft. I rub her with lotion, my hands everywhere. I shift her hair away to press my lips to a sensitive spot on the back of her neck.

I stroke harder as I imagine her naked walk to the tent, admiring the perfect round ass I've only seen in yoga pants and jeans. She turns to look at me, her hair falling in a wave, one pert breast peeking out.

"Front or back?" she asks.

"Front."

She lifts her arms, twisting her hair on top of her head. Her breasts are uplifted, and she is completely naked for me to admire. I groan out loud, imagining every inch of her on display, her knowing smile, those long lashes.

My cock is so hot and hard. I imagine turning on the spray and watching her nipples pucker in the cold. She lifts her chin, eyes closed, letting out a sigh as I spray her. And that's it, the fantasy creates a real-life reaction as I let loose.

I fall back on my cold pillow. Shit. I've got it bad. And while I might've gotten crazy with my thoughts here alone in my apartment, I'll need an iron will to keep control when I see her tomorrow.

And this fantasy I just indulged in?

I have to forget about it.

The next morning at the deli, I'm so distracted with thoughts of seeing Camryn that I fill the mayo squeeze bottles with mustard.

Tiana takes them away with a toss of her long braids

Angelo shakes his head. "What's got you in such a fog, boss?"

"Nothing."

Tiana empties the mustard into the proper bottles and gathers the mayo bottles to wash. "It's that woman," she says. "I can see it in his eyes."

If I'm that obvious to my staff, there's no way in hell I'll keep my obsession from Camryn herself.

I spend the day practicing my focus. Timesheets. Invoices. Deliveries.

Only when I shoulder my bag before closing time does Angelo pause in wiping down the counter to say what's probably on everybody's mind. "So, is that girl the reason you're working fewer hours lately?"

I hesitate. They've noticed.

The cut in hours is due to the workouts, but I'd rather confess about Camryn than the bodybuilding at this point. "I might be seeing her tonight."

Tiana shakes her head, her arms crossed as I head for the door. "We're losing the boss man to a woman."

"Never," I say over my shoulder. "The deli is my first love."

"We do have the best pickles," Angelo says with a smirk. "Maybe you should take her the hot ones again."

I head out to the sidewalk without remarking on that.

When I arrive at Camryn's door, I stand there a moment, collecting myself.

I brought my modesty pouch. It probably will not keep things modest. But I can say I tried.

I have to remember I'm her client. Even though she dared me with a kiss, I can't assume too much.

But if I can move this along, I will consider tonight a victory.

Because the fact is, I want to kiss Camryn Schultz again.

Thoroughly this time. No quick peck.

I just have to make sure my pecker is under wraps.

When Camryn opens the door, there's no hint this is anything different from our last tanning session.

She wears yoga pants and a fitted top, today in electric blue.

Her hair is back in a ponytail. But those lashes. They kill me.

"Welcome, Max." She rubs her hands together, as if she just put lotion on. "Today will go a lot like the last time. You can change behind the screens." She bumps the door closed with her elbow.

"Thanks."

I step behind the screen, trying to gather myself. Despite my insistence in leaving last night's fantasy behind me, it roars back. Camryn, naked, tanning tent.

Somebody douse me in ice water.

I kick off my shoes. Beyond the screen, I can hear Camryn moving things around.

"Has it been a busy day for you?" I ask.

"Not too bad. Our lovely friend Dahlia was here earlier. She competes at your invitational Saturday, too."

"Did she ask you to go?" I would love it if Camryn could show up at the competition.

"She insisted. But the women's program is much

later than yours. So, I still want to see you first thing that morning."

My pulse jumps. "But you will be there?"

"Sounds like it. For an hour, anyway. How is your training going?"

I slide my jeans to the floor and stuff them in the bag. "I meet with Amy tomorrow to go over the pose-down. I think I looked pretty lost last time."

"It was cute," she says.

She was there?

"So, you saw?" I jerk my shirt over my head and ball it up inside the bag.

"Of course. I usually go to the evening show, since all my work is done. I like to see my clients compete."

Of course. She was there for her other clients.

"What time will you be there Saturday?" I ask.

"Around twelve-thirty. I'll use my lunch break from the other show."

"Would you like to have a sandwich together?" I squeeze my eyes shut behind the screen, hoping I haven't asked for too much.

"Hmm. I might be able to fit that in. You and Dahlia are my only clients there. She won't take the whole hour."

Yes! I feel like a teen scoring his first real date.

"Veggie on olive bread? With hot pickles?" I peel off my socks and shove them in the bag.

"Sounds like a date. I'm sure you'll be carbing up. Should I bring you some chocolate?"

She wants to bring something for me? I drop my boxers to the floor. Half-mast. Dammit. I give my dick a stern look as I say, "You don't have to do that."

"I'd like to. There's one in particular that helps. And it's delicious."

"All right, then. Thank you."

I pull out the modesty pouch and slide it over my mind-of-its-own dick. The pouch is very stretchy, but as soon as I try to pull it over my damn erection, it pops off like a slingshot.

Shit!

I snatch it from the air before it sails over the screen. What is with my body around this woman?

So, what do I do?

Any ideas?

What's the worst thing you can come up with?

Toilet bowl water?

Oh…port o' potty.

Nice. Good one.

I take deep breaths. For good measure, I pretend Franklin is beyond the screen, and he will immediately notice the state of my bodily functions.

This gets me.

Down he goes.

Modesty pouch, achieved.

I wrap the towel around my waist and step out from the screen. "What first?"

"Over to the stool. Let's make sure there are no dry spots. Have you been using the moisturizer?"

I nod and sit down, the towel draped over my thighs.

Her fingers float along my shoulders, arms, and elbows. "You're doing a good job. This looks so much better than last week. Your tan is going to absolutely glow."

"I get them from the best," I say.

"It will be a definite improvement over Ride 'em Shiny."

Something cool spreads across the back of my neck as her fingers move across my skin.

"I'm going to focus more up here today," she says. "I'll do a base on your face today, then we'll skip it on the next one. I'll hit it again for the final. I don't like too much buildup on the face."

I nod. "Some of the competitors do look odd."

"If you win this one, there will be a photo shoot. You don't want to look raccoon-ish or uneven."

A photo shoot. I guess Franklin's never gotten this far, so he wouldn't know what to tell me. "What else should I know? Do you have other clients at this level?"

"I have clients who travel to China. Brazil. Europe."

"Wow. You ever go with them?"

She comes around to the front and lifts my chin. "Not so far. It sounds glamorous, but unless you have big sponsors, or a bunch of them, you might be traveling on a shoestring, piling into hotel rooms with other competitors. There's no budget to bring your own personal tanner. We're everywhere, so you can hire one on-site."

"Not as good as you."

She holds my eyes for a moment. "I'm sure I'm an amateur compared to many. But I do well enough here."

I relax back on the stool. I'm in good hands. Her touch is light and easy. As long as I keep my thoughts under wraps, this will be no problem.

She runs the back of her hand across my cheek. "As much as I like this scruff, most bodybuilders lose their facial hair as they move up."

My knuckles graze my stubble. It's a look I've had a while. "Really?"

"You don't have to, but go look up any major bodybuilding competition that's gotten press. You'll see very little facial hair."

"I believe you."

"I'd like to shave you. Is that all right?"

"Sure. I can regrow it later."

"Exactly. When you come in Saturday morning, make sure you shave. I'll do whatever moisturizing and cleaning up I need to do before we apply the last tan."

"Got it."

She moves to one of her many cabinets and rummages around. I watch the easy grace with which she moves, the way she examines a bottle and sets it on a fresh towel.

Then she removes a long blade and scrapes it across a sharpening block.

Whoa.

She approaches with the razor and a bowl.

"You do it the old-fashioned way."

She smiles. "Same as any barber worth his salt. It's the best shave."

"Do guys get worried when you bring out a blade like that?"

She tilts her head and gives me an impish smile. "Max Pickle, are you nervous? Do you think I might slip and slice this beautiful throat of yours?"

"No, ma'am."

"Don't make me an enemy." She winks.

"Wouldn't dream of it. Not with that in your hand."

She moves in close, her legs straddling one of mine.

I take in all her scents. Something lightly floral. Something else citrusy. She smells delicious.

She spreads cream on my face, then the only sound in the room is the gentle scrape of the blade across my cheek.

She moves quickly with precise motions and absolute concentration.

I watch her face as she works. She's inches from me, the closest we've probably ever been, except for that one brief kiss.

I'm desperate to touch her. Put my hands on her waist, her hips, to learn the curves of her.

But I have to content myself with her nearness. She switches to the other side. For a moment, our eyes meet, her lips tantalizingly close. She hesitates. "You probably know you're brutally handsome, right?"

I should probably play this off, make a joke, but instead I say, "My sincerest hope is that you think so."

She doesn't move, gently breathing in and out. Our gazes hold.

Then her gaze flicks down to my lips.

Is she thinking about kissing me?

It takes two-thousand percent of my control not to lean in.

"You've got something right here." She uses her thumb to rub my upper lip. But then her touch remains.

There are moments from your life that imprint on

your memory. Your mom laughing. Racing your brother before jumping in a pool. Your father's hand on your shoulder.

This is one of those moments. Camryn is so close her breath caresses my cheek. Her thumb lingers on my mouth. I've never felt so much anticipation before. Like everything I've ever wanted has come into reach.

"I do," she says finally. "I think you're magnificent."

I'm not going to let that go unreciprocated. "You are the most beautiful creature I've ever laid eyes on." And I mean it.

Our gaze holds a moment more, but something's changed. I feel it bubbling up inside me. She must, too, because a second later, we're both shaking with laughter.

Camryn carefully holds the blade away as she bends over, one arm over her belly.

"Good Lord," she says. "It's like we're filming some sappy romance."

I press my fingers against my eyes to stem the tears of laughter. "It's true. You say these things in all sincerity, but when they come out of your mouth, they sound ridiculous."

We laugh a little longer, and then I can't resist anymore, and rest my hand lightly on her waist. "I do mean it, though. I am completely infatuated with you."

Camryn's face turns serious. "I need to finish this shave. Let me think about this a minute."

I move my hand back to my own leg. Will she fire me as a client? Avoid me completely?

She works more swiftly than before, scraping the blade across my cheek with quick, even strokes. Then she draws away. "Here's a warm towel. Press it to your face."

I take it and lift it to my cheeks.

She heads off into the kitchen. Water runs. A few things clang.

I feel like my fate is being decided.

Her footsteps return, and I lower the towel.

"I feel the same way," she says. "But we're kind of stuck."

"Your brother?"

She sits on the floor in front of me, cross-legged. "It's more than that. Yes, my brother would flip his shit. But I can handle him. There's a lot at stake here. If we blow up spectacularly, and you're always on the circuit, my heart might not be able to take having to see you."

"You're thinking about our breakup before we even start?"

She drops her gaze to the floor. "I just…"

I wonder if she's thinking about the old love affair. Franklin mentioned it. That he didn't think she would recover.

"You want to tell me about it?"

Her eyes lift to meet mine, and damn, it's those lashes again. She looks vulnerable, like a child.

"You don't have to," I say quickly. "Only if it would help."

"Not yet," she says. "Let's see where this goes. I'm not necessarily afraid." She laughs shakily. "Well, obviously I am. I just said so. But I feel very mixed up around you. I sometimes feel very bold, like when I told you to kiss me."

"That was nice."

"But then there's now. Facing the reality of it."

"We can take this as slow as you want."

Now her quirky smile reappears. "Right. Because I don't see you naked three times a week."

"You saying you're feeling tempted?"

A smile flirts with the corners of her mouth. "I freely admit I'm tempted as hell."

"Then let's build on that temptation carefully. Like a tan. In layers."

"Until it goes *deep*." The minx has her head tilted, and she doesn't look vulnerable at all.

"You're the one who told me how much you liked my hot pickle."

This makes her laugh. "I hope you brought one for me. I saw a paper bag."

I smack my forehead. "I was so stressed out walking in here, I forgot to give it to you!'

"Why would you be stressed out coming to see me?"

"Maybe because every time I'm near you, my anatomy misbehaves."

Camryn stands, stepping away from me. "Let's get you sprayed. I have a feeling if we talk about it too much, it will become a self-fulfilling prophecy."

She's right.

"Into the tent, you scalawag. Time to hose you down."

I stand up and set the towels on the stool.

Everything seems to be in order, and the pouch is in place.

Whew.

We can go slow. Not address the attraction too fast.

It will be fine.

But when I turn around to glance at Camryn, I'm pretty sure—actually, I'm certain—she's checking out my naked ass.

14

CAMRYN

The next day, I find excuses to text Max. I tell him I forgot to mention that I felt the white patch was perfectly fixable.

I send him a reminder of our appointment on Thursday.

I suggest he replace his loofah every couple of weeks.

I try not to stare at my phone, waiting for replies.

At first, his responses are normal, what you would expect from a client. *Thank you, got it, will do.*

But when I text him, *look forward to seeing you tomorrow night,* his tone changes.

He writes:

Throughout the day, whether I'm instructing the staff, helping out on the sandwich line, or greeting customers, you are constantly on my mind. I often look at the door, wondering if you will miracu-

lously appear there, sunshine in your hair, a happy smile on your lips.

I set down the phone. Whoa.

I'm not sure how to respond. It's like he saw through my ruse of client texts and gave me what I wanted.

And he *is* what I want.

I think.

It's a quiet workday for me, since it's midweek before the next set of competitions. So I message my friend Sofia, who I've known since my eyebrow waxing days, to see if she's available to hang out.

We settle on a seedy bar on South First. Sofia is already there when I arrive, her glossy black hair falling in waves down her back.

She chats with the bartender, who looks like he wants to gobble her up.

I can tell from this distance that she's not interested, even though he seems like her type. Tall, lanky, easily amused.

Sofia is perpetually single. Her family is large and friendly, and I have often spent a happy Sunday in the chaos, *chili rellenos* being stuffed at the table, and children running amok. But she feels oppressed by it all. She likes quiet. Men always want to get all up in her space, so she dumps them by date three.

I slide into the seat beside her. "Hey friend," I say, a mischievous bolt striking through me. "Where's your husband? Or did you leave this one, too?"

The bartender makes a face and steps back. "Let me

know if you need anything." He takes off down the bar like we're on fire.

Sofia laughs. "You're the best anti-wingman."

"But that one seemed like your type."

She runs a finger along the rim of the glass. "Too pushy. How's the tanning business today?"

"Light. But I have a hectic Saturday with two competitions."

"Any hot guys you can toss my way?" She always asks, but I'm clear I'm never going to set her up with any of my clients. She would break their hearts, and my business model.

"No. But one seems interested in me."

"Oh? Does dear brother Franklin know about this?"

I wave at the bartender to try to get a drink, but he ignores us. Great. They always shoot the messenger. "He's his training partner."

Sofia smacks her hand on the bar. "Get out of town! And he hasn't already castrated this dude for looking at you?"

"I don't think Franklin has figured out this one wants to be more than a client."

Sofia smacks the bar again. "Camryn! Are you banging some hot guy and haven't told me?"

Several customers at the bar turn our way. Sofia likes to be heard. I'm used to it.

"I'm not banging him. I'm just saying he's interested. But because of the Franklin situation, I'm nervous about it."

"That brother of yours needs to stay out of your business."

"I know. But I can't change how he is."

"He clocked that guy last year for talking to you."

"I know." A second bartender, a woman this time, appears from the back and walks along the bar. I signal for her attention. Maybe I'll get a drink after all.

"So, tell me all about him," Sofia says.

The new bartender approaches, and I order a hard cider before launching into my explanation of Max.

"He's a heavyweight. Pure muscle. Gorgeous. Kind."

"Oh my God! Does he have a brother?"

"Two. He's not unknown around here."

Sofia narrows her eyes. "You're not dating a politician, are you? Because I don't think I can handle it if you're dating a politician."

"Why did you go for politics? We're in L.A! He could be an actor."

Sofia shakes her head. "No. You don't go for boys like that."

"All right, fine. He owns a deli. L.A. Pickle."

"Oh! Right. The Pickle brothers. What's the name of this one?"

"Max. He's forever bringing me sandwiches when he comes for tans."

"That's sweet. I might prefer it if he brought diamonds, though."

I elbow her. "We're not even dating."

"But you're thinking about it."

The bartender sets my drink down, and I wrap both hands around the glass. "So, what should I do? Keep this relationship on the down-low? Lie to my brother? Or avoid this man and the drama?"

Sofia takes a sip, pondering. "You like this one."

"I think so."

"And he seems to be onboard with not giving your brother any savory details?"

"He didn't tell him anything at all until Franklin asked him about his tan."

Sofia twirls her glass. "They're training partners. That's one hell of a secret to keep."

"We're doing it so far."

"I guess you've seen him naked if you're tanning him, right?"

"Several times."

Sofia shakes her head. "Girl, you know that's not even fair."

"What's not fair?"

"You got your hands all over his hard body. He has to prance around naked for you."

"It can't be helped. It's part of my job."

She nods. "It's still weird, though. Can you pawn him off on some other tanning artist if you're going to date him?"

"And let her have *her* hands all over his naked body?"

"You're right. Forget I said that. But I wonder about all that nakedness affecting whether or not you have good chemistry. It's hard to avoid feeling squishy about a hot naked dude in your living room. You basically control him. You tell him when to get naked, right? When he can cover up?"

"That's how it works."

"And he probably knows that if he doesn't obey you, a bad tan can affect his score and his career."

Well, hell. I hadn't thought about it that way.

Sofia sips her drink. "Until you two figure out what's what, you should stay professional. Classy. Now, if you want to bang him, then tell him. And get your clothes off, too."

"Okay, okay."

"When do you see him again?"

"Tomorrow night. We have one more base tan, then he'll do his final round on Saturday before he competes."

"Is there some rule about not having sex on competition day?"

"You watch too many old Barbara Streisand movies."

"No! It's a thing."

"It is not a thing. Besides, we're not having sex! He's my client."

My phone buzzes with a message. I glance down. It's Max. My cheeks heat up.

"It's him, isn't it?"

"Just confirming appointments."

"You give that phone to me."

I try to snatch it, but she's too fast.

She holds it in front of her face and reads aloud. "I've got three flavors of pickles here and trying to decide which one you might like best tomorrow night. The sweet one? Let the sugar lie on your tongue?" Sofia looks up at me. "Girl, this is not a professional client conversation."

"Give it back."

She holds the phone away. "No. This is too good.

Here's what he says next. 'Or should it be spicy, something that dances in your mouth?'" She gives me a squinty eye. "That's some crazy shit, girl." She looks at the phone again. "Holy crap. He says, 'Or should it be one straight-up hot pickle?'"

She passes the phone back to me. "If someone was writing me messages like that, I would be all over it. You figure it out. You hear me?"

I look down at the message. Out of context, I can see how it looks. Like we're already a thing. It's suggestive, no matter how you slice it. But in the context of all the things we've said to each other, it fits. Max and I have developed a funny way of expressing our strange situation that belongs solely to us.

And I like it.

15

MAX

I run late Thursday evening getting to Camryn's. A million complications came up at the deli, and at the last minute Camryn texts me to bring my competition trunks.

So I have to swing by my house and pick them up.

I'm confused on that score. I thought she told me we needed an even base until the last day. But she's the professional.

When I arrive at Camryn's apartment, she's dressed differently. She has the usual yoga pants on, this time in a cool sea green. But instead of a fitted yoga top, she wears a loose T-shirt, tied in a knot at the thighs like a big balloon of cotton.

I'm not sure what it means. I sent her several tentative messages feeling out our relationship beyond the tanning. She's only responded in emojis, so I'm as clueless now as I was before.

Still, I'm here for a tan, not to ogle her.

"Hey, Max," she says. "Did you bring the trunks?"

"I had to run home for them. Sorry I'm late."

"That's okay. You're the last of the day, so it doesn't matter if we run behind."

I consider a suggestive remark about how we have all the time in the world, but something about her demeanor keeps me quiet. Has she changed her mind? Did she decide it wasn't worth the trouble of poking her brother's ire?

I head to the corner to change. "Should I go straight to the trunks?"

"Yes, please. That way I can see where your tan is landing."

I step behind the screen. It's a big deal that I'm getting dressed today. Or at least wearing something other than the modesty pouch. Maybe she needs to figure out if she has to fix that white patch or not. I shouldn't be upset that I won't be standing around with my dick hanging out.

But something seems off.

I undress and slide on the trunks. No need for a towel. This is exactly how I will go on stage in front of thousands of people in two days.

A shot of nerves bolts through me. I don't have anything at stake here other than competitive pride, but I am nervous. Franklin will be at the amateur show, so I won't have my best bud with me.

I haven't confessed to anyone that I'm competing. So I don't have anyone else to come along.

Amy will be there for a pep talk before I go on stage. But mainly I'll be dealing with my nerves on my own. At least I don't have to worry about my tan. And other than this photo shoot Camryn talked about, I should know the drill.

Camryn gives me a quick nod when I come out. "Excellent. Come over to the stool and let's make sure everything is in good shape. I expect with a week's worth of quality moisturizing, you're going to be fine."

I take a seat. Even her voice sounds different, like I'm a stranger. A client.

She takes a quick walk around me, only touching lightly in a few places. Lotion goes on one spot near the middle of my back.

"That's probably hard for me to reach," I say.

"You're doing great," she says. "Makes my job easy."

In no time flat, she's leading me over to the tanning tent.

"Did you want to check the pale patch?" I ask, kicking my knee out so she can see the inside of my thigh.

"I think since the color rubs off so easily there, we will have to patch on the last day. I might send something with you in case you need to touch up at the end. I won't be able to see you right before you go on."

She picks up the spray wand and steps forward, then stops, her lips all scrunched. "Can you roll that waistband down a little? And maybe lift them in the back to make sure we cross that tan line?"

"Sure."

I fight with the tight trunks for a moment, trying to get the waistband to budge. It doesn't want to move down. They are fitted to my skin.

I hold out my hands in defeat. "I don't think it's gonna move. So, I guess that means it's not an issue."

Camryn frowns. "I was afraid of that. This is a lot easier with the physique competitors with their loose trunks."

"I don't mind doing the spray without the trunks," I say. "The look is the important thing." I give her a big grin to ease her mind. "I'm not shy."

But her face is as serious as it was when I arrived.

"Let me give it a shot." She sets the wand on the canister and tugs on my trunks. She succeeds in getting the back part up an inch, but the top won't roll down no matter how hard she tugs.

She sighs with frustration. "I'm going to turn around. You pull the trunks down and back up again. I need to see if they ever change position or if they're steady in their spot."

Turn around? When she's seen every inch of me before? I'm not sure what's happening, but our old camaraderie is completely gone.

Still, I do what she says. I slide the trunks down to my ankles, then pull them back up.

"All good," I say.

She turns around. "Shoot. It's lower than it was the first time. I can see the indentions in your skin from the elastic line." She taps her bare foot in annoyance. "Okay. The trunks have to go. It probably has to do with your water percentage. Until you're wearing them the way they'll sit the whole day, like on Saturday morning, I can't risk a tan line."

This is what she said before. I'm not sure what

changed her mind. I grab the waistband, and I'm about to pull them down when she says, "Where's your modesty pouch?"

Okay. Something is up. "It's in my bag."

"You might want to put it on behind the screen."

"Okay."

I'm halfway across the room before I decide that no, I'm going to hit this head-on. "Camryn, what's going on? Why all the concern? We were joking about it last time. Did someone say something to you?" I couldn't imagine who. I don't tell a soul that I'm here or what goes on during my tanning sessions.

Camryn opens her mouth, then closes it again. "Maybe I was acting inappropriately before."

She won't meet my eyes. I walk up to her. "Camryn, I don't think anything of the sort. But if you're more comfortable with me being covered up, absolutely I will do it. The last thing I want to do is make you anxious."

That gets her attention. "I'm just, I don't know. I got some advice. And I don't know what to do."

I want to draw her into my arms, but I know it's not the right thing at this moment. So I simply stand there. "When we're here together," I say, "it's just you and me. We make the rules. We're two adults in a professional relationship that partially depends on me getting naked. Even when I have a boner the size of New Jersey."

That gets her. She looks down at my trunks. "You don't have one now."

"I'm about to if you keep looking at him."

She rubs the heel of her hand against her forehead. "Okay. I'm fine. I'm sorry. This whole thing is complicated. I don't want to screw up, or take advantage of you, or whatever."

This time I reach out and take her hand. "We're fine. Coming here and getting naked for you is the highlight of my week."

Her laugh is the best thing I've heard in days. "Well, get out of those damn trunks, then."

"Should I still get the modesty pouch?"

"We do need to cover your assets," she says. "Trust me, it's not pretty covered in tanning oil, especially when it starts to wear off in weird bits like spray tan leprosy."

"And…all boners contained," I say with a laugh. "One modesty pouch, coming right up."

I step behind the screen to change, in deference to this hard conversation we've had.

I don't know what advice she's been given, what made her feel guilty. It can't be her brother. He would've punched my jaw over it.

But I think I understand the root of the problem. She wants us to stay in a professional relationship. She just drew the line.

So, as I tuck my junk in a pouch to protect it from her spray, I also tuck away my disappointment.

She's loud and clear. Now is not the time. I remain grateful I can rely on her to help me with my career. Maybe more will come.

16

CAMRYN

My alarm clock buzzes way too early on Saturday morning.

I force myself to sit up immediately, or I'll be tempted to fall back asleep.

Max is arriving in twenty minutes. And I have to prep him for his competition. Plus, Lora, another female competitor, right after.

Then six appointments at the amateur open. A dash over to the invitational to do Dahlia.

And of course, eat a sandwich with Max.

Except…we arranged that date before our awkward tanning on Thursday.

I sure messed that up.

Were we still on for lunch?

I slide on a pair of charcoal yoga pants and the navy top I laid out last night. Dark colors not easily stained by the oils I will be applying all day.

When my hair is tamed and smoothed into a ponytail, I apply a light smudge of eyeliner and my magical mascara.

While I brush my teeth, I berate myself for holding Max at arm's length. Dating someone should be simple, right?

But it can't be when your brother tries to murder him with a bench press, and all your interactions involve him being naked.

No, this is no ordinary relationship whatsoever.

I start some coffee, adding extra cups in case Max and Lora want some. They'll both have to hold back on liquids today, so probably not, but I want to offer.

It's only five minutes until his appointment, so I swiftly pull out the canister with his color and set out the tarp and stool. I arrange my creams plus all the base makeup for Lora.

It's going to start crazy and go long.

I'm not sure what Max's chances are at the invitational. I'm not caught up on the competitive level of the heavyweights. But if he shows the same charisma he did two weeks ago he has a shot at placing no matter how developed everyone is. Stage presence matters.

A light rap on the door startles me to the next level of awake. *Come on, Camryn. Time to get moving.*

It's dark outside, so Max is lit only by the tiny yellow lamp over the door.

"Good morning," he mumbles.

"You're not a morning person either?"

"Not even close." He rubs his chin. "Sometimes I wonder if I'm better off staying up all night."

"I made some coffee if you'd like a few sips. I know you can't have much."

"That would be awesome. Maybe a quarter cup?"

I hurry to the kitchen to fetch it. It feels nice doing something small for him, something normal between a couple, even if I probably killed that idea two days ago.

I pour his in a mug and fill a travel container for myself. I'm going to need plenty of caffeine until I hit my stride around nine.

When I come out, he's already down to his posing trunks and sitting on the stool.

"You know the drill," I say.

He accepts the mug and brings it to his lips. "Ahhh. Smells so good." He takes a small sip. "You can make coffee for me any morning."

Then he seems to catch himself. "If I have an appointment, of course."

I've put him off. I need to land somewhere in between the outrageous flirting we were doing in the early sessions, and the extreme version where I try to play it safe.

"What's on your schedule this morning?" I ask.

"After this, I meet Franklin for a mega breakfast. Then we will part ways, and I'll go back home and pack everything I need for the day. My prejudging's two hours later than his."

"I'm doing a tan on Franklin during that gap."

Max grimaces. "You going to say anything about me?"

"No way. But I look forward to seeing you at lunch."

He takes another sip of coffee and lifts his gaze to

meet mine. "That's going to be the highlight of my day."

Okay, I haven't totally blown it. I punch his shoulder. "You might win the whole thing. The next level gets you in range for a pro card."

He shakes his head. "I can't imagine in a million years that will happen. I don't even know what I would do with the pro card. That's a big traveling circuit, isn't it?"

I set my coffee mug on the counter and pick up a tube of moisturizer. Time to get started. "It can be. At that point, you choose which competitions you want to apply for, and they accept you or not. Sometimes they reach out to you with an invitation. But you can always turn it down."

"I've got a lot to learn."

"Plenty of time to figure it out."

He tips the cup and downs the rest of his coffee. "That was delicious. It'll get me through the next few hours."

"I'm sorry you have to dehydrate yourself. But you look good." I press my finger along his muscles. His veins have already begun to visibly pop out, which is exactly what you want on competition day.

"I'm a little flat. But I haven't eaten or pumped. That will come."

"It's good to be flat for the tan," I say. "So when you stretch out, everything will be a nice even color."

I walk around him, moisturizing everything lightly and evenly. I find no rough patches. Our extra attention has paid off.

"Let's step in the tent. I'll spray you, and then we'll come over here and I'll finish out your face."

"Sounds good."

I follow him over to the tent. The spray takes only a few minutes, and as he dries beneath the fan I arrange the creams.

"I might touch you up when I see you for lunch, if that's okay. On the house."

"I'd love that," he says. "But I'm happy to pay."

"We'll see." I dab dots of color along his cheekbones and spread them with a sponge. It's a high reach for me, and as soon as he's dry, I drag the stool over to make it easier.

"What all will you eat for breakfast?" I ask. The bodybuilders love to talk about the food they consume on competition day. It's a feast after months of famine.

"So much French toast. So many pancakes. All the hash browns. I might even pick up a cheeseburger on the way." He closes his eyes and rubs his belly.

I laugh. "You make it sound better than sex."

His eyes pop open. "No way." His voice rumbles as he says it, and I can feel it all the way to my core.

"I can't wait to hear how you do."

I take a step back to see if I have gotten everything perfectly even, and he reaches out to grasp my wrist.

"I know you want to be at the final show at the open, to see your clients. But if you can make it over to mine, it would mean a lot."

Wow. He's really asking.

"I don't have to stay for the whole open. No one expects it. It's a courtesy."

"So, you'll come?" His face is so full of hope, I could never turn him down.

"I'll come."

He squeezes my hand. "Thank you. So how are we doing? Am I acceptable?"

"Stand up and let's take a final look."

I walk around him, checking out every inch. Ankles. Thighs. Back. Shoulders. Neck. Face. Tan. Dry. Perfect.

"You're stunning," I say. "You're going to bring this competition to its knees."

His Adam's apple bobs as he swallows. I don't know if it's because he's thirsty, or if it's because of the way I've examined him.

His voice is scratchy as he says, "Text me when you arrive and are finished with Dahlia. I'll have lunch for us."

"I will."

We stand there another moment, emotion playing across his face. And I can't bear it. He probably thinks I don't care about him anymore after Thursday.

I have to find a middle ground.

What would you do?

Let him go?

Or make him stay?

There's a lot at stake.

But the sparkle in those dark eyes of his makes the decision for me.

"Can I kiss you for luck?" I ask.

He doesn't answer but draws me against him fiercely. When his lips meet mine, it's no gentle peck. It's a torrent of passion and need. I want to drown in it, lose myself, let the world fall away.

His lips are insistent. His arms crush me against him, and I can feel every muscle hard against mine.

I want to fall into the bliss of it, hold on forever. Taste him. Do all the things I've thought about.

But there's a knock at the door.

"Another early client," I whisper.

He nods and reluctantly lets me go.

"Lunch, then," he says.

"Lunch."

I touch my lips as he heads behind the screen to put on his clothes. By the time I open the door for Lora, I have composed myself.

When Max comes out, he waves at both of us and wishes Lora luck. Then he's out into the dim light of sunrise.

"Whoa, he's something," Lora says.

I can only nod.

Because he really is something.

17

MAX

The invitational is a completely different experience from the beginner contest. There are no tents in the parking lot, hawking their wares to the masses of competitors.

The numbers are controlled, and none of the rooms are crowded.

It's strange being alone, and I start to wonder if I shouldn't hire a trainer to be with me on these days. Everyone stands around in pairs, completing their weigh-in, chatting up the registration people.

I sit against the wall in the massive room, idly pumping a small barbell with one hand while eating rice cakes.

If I thought the last competition had fit, bulked-up bodies, it's nothing compared to this.

As competitors ditch their sweats for oil and pump, I'm blown away by how professional they all look. And big. Really big.

I'm not alone for long. Amy arrives in a shiny red

tracksuit, joking around with a karate chop to tell me to kill it on stage. We run through my routine, make a plan for a potential posedown, plus go over other optional comparison rounds the judges might request on stage.

She sits with me a while, and we watch the light-weights and middleweights prep for the stage. "Life would be a lot easier if you'd drop ten pounds and go light heavyweight," she says. "There are some real monsters when you move up."

"I've never been strategic. I am what I am."

She laughs. "Like Popeye. Fair enough. You never did strike me as a career pro." She passes me a protein bar. "You're going on soon. Eat one of these."

When she takes off to see one of her other clients, I think about what she said. Not a career pro. If she sees that, the judges probably will, too.

The announcer shouts for the heavyweights to get on deck. I cram two more rice cakes down, take a single swig of water, and run through a set of push-ups.

It's go-time.

When we line up, I count twelve of us, and to be honest, I'm nowhere near the top of the field.

Not everyone is huge. Maybe half of us are roughly the same size.

But at the top end of the spectrum, the men are unbelievable. Veins popping. Muscles on top of muscles. This is an entirely different level.

I'm not disappointed that I'm going to lose today. Bodybuilding isn't my bag, really. I like doing it. But I do have my deli and a whole life outside of it.

Maybe I shouldn't have asked Camryn to come to the evening show tonight. I'm going to get skunked.

As the routines begin, there are no rookie mistakes like I saw two weeks ago. Everyone hits the poses and holds them well. Charming smiles.

I spot some subtle nuances in the way they move, trying to set themselves apart. Amy has shown me ways to hide flaws. A waist that's thicker than you'd like. Underdeveloped calves. She tells me I'm lucky to be so balanced. Some competitors get grossly overdeveloped in one area over another, and that costs them points.

When it's my turn to step out, I work fluidly through the routine. Even though this is technically a more prestigious competition, I sense there are fewer people in the audience. Maybe it's the newbies starting out who have the most support from friends and family. At this point in many careers, maybe it's gotten old.

The dedication required makes it easy to lose friends who don't understand this way of life. My brothers already tease the hell out of me about not drinking anymore. I didn't even eat cake at my nephew's first birthday. Sugar is a beast, and even one slip-up can send you spiraling into a carb crisis that's impossible to resist.

I finish up and take my spot in the back, near the far left of the stage. Probably the worst position I could be in.

But I wait, staying semi-flexed as the other men do their routines.

When we all move into a line for comparisons, I figure the callouts will tell me what I need to know about how I'm doing.

But the judges don't send people to the back. They keep rearranging us, asking for pose after pose. Side triceps. Side chest. Front lat spread.

I'm never placed next to the monstrous men, so I figure I'm not in the running against them.

When we leave the stage, I have the sense of, *well, that was fun.* There are competitions I can do, open contests where they allow former winners to compete with the ones starting out.

But who knows? Maybe I'm done. I can support Franklin's efforts without exerting my own.

Been there, had a good time.

I'm super glad I didn't sign with any sponsors. They might have required me to do more competitions than I'd like.

Dodged a bullet.

When I get back to the hall where we all sit and wait, I spot Dahlia.

She sees me at about the same time, and even though she'll probably be flirtier than I want to deal with, she's a friendly face.

"It's the man candy from two weeks ago," she purrs. "Did you already go on, darling?"

Man, this woman is tall. She meets me eye-to-eye in her heels. She's switched out her shiny gold bikini for red satin.

"Yeah, I think I probably maxed out my ability to impress the judges, but it was fun," I say. "Have you already seen Camryn?"

"Heading her way. Maybe I'll talk to you later?"

"Sure. Good luck."

She gives me a wink with spidery false eyelashes and heads down another hall. I'm tempted to follow at a distance, just to get a glimpse of Camryn.

But I don't. I can wait my turn. I head back to my space with my weights, my duffel bag, and my warm-ups stacked on top.

I slide on my sweats and pick up a couple of rice cakes, then set them back down again, unwilling to eat them in my already dehydrated state. They'll go down like sidewalk chalk.

I'll hold out for Camryn and chocolate.

Time seems to stand still. The physique classes approach the registration desk to get their pins. I envy them in their long board shorts. That's loose enough to hide a Camryn-level sin, unlike my tiny trunks.

I check my phone. It's been forty minutes since I ran into Dahlia. I feel jealous of the time, worried I won't get to see her after all.

But then Camryn enters the room, a tiny figure against the backdrop of the muscled crowd.

I jump to my feet and wave as she hurries forward.

"I'm sorry it took so long. Dahlia had a lot of issues for us to manage. Cleavage shadow doesn't draw itself."

I'm not sure I should, but I lean forward and place a soft kiss on her lips. I haven't forgotten our morning encounter and hope this can be our new normal.

She responds lightly, squeezing my arm as she pulls away. "How did it go this morning?"

"I'm outclassed. I have a feeling this is going to be the end of my rise to the top."

"You sure? Because I talked to some people who

watched the heavyweights, and they said you had the best stage presence, even if a couple of them were more developed."

I shrug. "I think the muscles are going to matter a lot."

"I'll be able to tell you more after watching the evening show. Remember big isn't always better if there isn't symmetry."

We sit back down in my spot. I feel completely different with Camryn kneeling next to me. On top of the world.

I pull a small insulated cooler from inside my bag. "I packed the bread separate from the inside of your sand-wich so it wouldn't get soggy."

"Brilliant." She accepts the cooler. "Did I get a hot pickle?"

"Of course you did. I wouldn't dare deprive you of that."

Her smile is like dawn breaking. My day is completely turned around. The inferiority I felt on the stage falls away. Bodybuilding brought me Camryn. It's done more than I could have asked for.

She opens the pouch and quickly assembles her sandwich. "I'm starving," she says before taking a healthy chomp.

"I've already eaten more than I want to today, but I know I will have to cram more in."

"No lunch for you then?"

"Maybe in a bit."

Her eyebrows lift. "Oh! I have chocolate for you."

She unzips a side pocket on the complicated belt that holds all her brushes and tools.

After a bit of tugging, she extracts a slender bar and passes it to me. "Dark chocolate, almonds, cranberry, and bits of peach. Divine."

"Sounds like it." I tear off the end and take a bite. The chocolate melts against my tongue like sin.

"So good," I say.

She sits up taller. "I knew you'd love it."

We face each other, grinning foolishly. I feel completely and utterly happy.

She swallows another bite and says, "Dahlia said you ran into her. That you would only talk about me."

"It's true. I've been looking forward to this all day."

"This morning was something, wasn't it?" Her eyes practically spark.

"I most certainly look forward to the next opportunity to kiss you like I mean it."

She pokes the last bite of her sandwich in her mouth and chews slowly. When she swallows, she says, "I know a very quiet place here. I have another ten or fifteen minutes. You want to go?"

"Hell, yes."

We exit into a long hall. We pass fewer and fewer competitors until it is almost quiet.

"In here," she says.

We enter a large room filled wall-to-wall with stacked chairs. Camryn takes my hand and leads me to a far corner, well away from the door. "About as private as you can get in the middle of a competition."

"Ms. Schultz, should I question your intentions?"

Her hand reaches behind my neck to pull me closer. Her kiss is soft, inquisitive, as if she's asking me if it's okay.

I wrap my arms around her to draw her close. I return the kiss as lightly and gently as she gave it.

Her arms encircle my neck. She tastes of pickles, deli meat, and mustard. It's like home to me, growing up sitting on a stool in Grammy Alma's deli, then my father's, and now my own.

Her fingers slide into my hair, and I feel every part of her, breasts crushing against my ribs, even the ends of the brushes filling in her belt. My hands slide down her back, over the belt, and cup her luscious round ass.

She shifts closer, her mouth seeking mine with more fervor. Our tongues mingle, and I breathe in the scent of her, that combination of light floral and tanning solution that is uniquely her.

She breaks away for a moment, gasping. "I thought about you all day."

I press my forehead to hers. "Same."

"It was so hard to tan my brother. I wanted to tell him to get the hell out of my life and leave me alone."

"Same for me at breakfast. It took everything I had not to say, 'By the way, you can stop trying to control your sister.'"

She runs her thumb along my chin and jaw. "We'll have to tell him eventually though, right?"

"I think we can worry about that later."

I dive in again, desperate to have her mouth on mine. The kiss is frenzied, passionate, deep. Secretive. Dark. Thrilling.

I need more of her, so I move my hands beneath her thighs and lift so she straddles my hips.

The close contact has its usual effect, and I grind my erection against her body.

"It feels as good as it looks," she whispers.

"Don't tempt me," I say.

"That's exactly what I want to do."

"Do you, now?" I press into her even harder.

She sucks in a breath. "We're in dangerous territory."

"Are we?"

"I'm desperate to do a whole lot more with you, and here we are in a room full of chairs."

I clutch at her, moving our bodies together in a hard, grinding rhythm. Her eyes are half-closed, those heavenly lashes flirting with her cheeks.

Her phone buzzes once, twice, and then a third time.

"All my alarms," she says. "I have to get back to the classic. I have so many clients who need me today."

"But you'll be here tonight?" I ask.

"Yes. I'll be the one wriggling uncomfortably in my seat."

"Make sure you don't sit where I can see you," I warn her. "Or the evening show may be a lot more X-rated than intended."

She laughs as she kisses my cheek, then runs her tongue along my jaw to my ear.

I let out a groan. "Do that again, and these chairs will get a show."

She laughs. "A preview of coming attractions."

I set her legs to the floor. "I think I better stay here with my nonjudgmental company until things are more under control."

She gives my arm a quick squeeze and hurries out the door. Only when the door is closed behind her do I press my hands against the wall, willing myself to get control again.

Whatever's going on between us, it's starting to flare hot and fast.

18

CAMRYN

I should be exhausted as I empty the remaining brushes from my belt and pack up the tanning supplies in the trunk of my car. It's been a long day, starting with Max before dawn and splitting my hours between two competitions.

But I'm headed to the evening show to see Max compete, and my body jitters like I just drank an entire pot of coffee.

I race over to the second arena and enter the auditorium right as the lightweights leave the stage. Good. I can settle in and take a breather before Max's class arrives.

The competitors may be fiercer at this level of competition, but the fans are the same. They wave giant signs and screech when their favorites come out.

The physique class walks on stage, and I watch carefully, wondering what keeps my brother from moving up.

Franklin has good symmetry, and when I tanned him this morning, he had good tone and vein reveal. But I think it's something more than pure musculature. Franklin doesn't have that presence on stage. He's forgettable.

Not that I would tell him. He's got enough cause to be annoyed with me without my critique. Surely Amy has tried to help him. She must be a good posing coach, because the work she's done with Max has been phenomenal.

My phone buzzes against my hip. I don't want to be rude and look at it in the middle of the competition, so I wait until the competitors have left the stage to take a peek.

It's Franklin, of all people, wondering where I am. I didn't tell him I wasn't staying for the evening show at the open where he was competing today.

I type out a quick *tied up with clients* and shove the phone in my pocket again.

The first heavyweight strides out. He's outrageously developed, shoulders so broad he probably doesn't fit through doors, and his lat spread looks like wings unfurling.

A lot of cheers go up for him, so he's probably used to winning. He has great presence. He's someone to beat.

The next three don't impress me quite as much. One is well-developed, the other two less so, more Max's size. But they don't have much going for them other than their tanned, oiled muscles.

Max comes out to a smattering of applause, and I can't help but shriek his name and scream, to make sure the judges know he is supported here. I wonder if he hasn't told anyone that he does this, or if his friends aren't supportive. I'll have to ask.

I realize we don't know a lot about each other outside of our jobs. I want to change that.

Max strikes his first pose with confidence and grace. His megawatt smile reaches out to the audience, and soon quite a few are clapping along to the music as he moves through his routine.

By the time he has finished, I don't need to shriek for him, he's gathered tons of new fans during his brief time on stage.

That's good. Really good. The energy he gives off will move him up, help him close the gap between him and the competitors with bigger physiques.

I settle back in my chair, preferring to only have eyes for Max. But I promised him I would help him figure out what might be different between him and the others at this level.

So I drag my gaze from him and watch the other men do their routines.

The judges request only a short comparison round, suggesting they have already decided the winner. When all twelve men hit the Most Muscular pose, the roar of the crowd makes my ears ring.

That's fun. I hope Max is enjoying himself up there.

Unfortunately, I don't think he's going to win. As much as I love his stage presence above the others, the first one who came out is equally as charismatic, and at least a third larger. He's got the gold medal, hands down.

The men shift to the back of the stage as the announcer fills in time while scores are tallied.

The crowd is on fire, and they begin clapping and stomping in unison, encouraging the bodybuilders on stage to resume posing.

Max is one of the first to comply, and the others have to quickly jump forward to join in.

This move could help him if the judges are still considering placements. The old-school scores are all about muscle development, but increasingly, the judges consider the marketability of a bodybuilder and how they help bring in spectators.

Finally, a runner takes the card up to the announcer, and the crowd quiets down.

"In third place, for the bronze medal…" The announcer pauses while the requisite hot girl in heels can approach with the medal. "Goes to number seven, Max Pickle."

I jump from my seat. Holy cow, he's placed. At this level, you don't have to win the gold to move up. He will be eligible for next week's national qualifier. Dang. My ears ring with my own shrieking for his win as he strikes his pose.

After a moment, I realize I'm the only one left screaming for Max, and I drop into my chair.

A woman two seats down reaches out to bump my arm. "Girl, I'd be hollering too if he was my man." The woman on the other side of her nods.

True.

But he's not mine. Not yet.

Max steps back. The silver medal is awarded to one of the well-developed men with a decent stage act.

And as expected, the crowd favorite wins the gold medal.

The three medalists step forward for one more pose, and I smile when Max does Most Muscular. He's already figured out he needs to work the crowd based on what they love.

He walks off the stage, leaving the winner to be joined by the gold medalists of the other categories for their final posedown and grand champion.

I don't want to stay for this. I want to get to Max. Since he didn't win, he won't have the photo shoot. He's free for the night.

I bump my way out of the row before the winners get on stage and burst through the back doors.

My rainbow Converse slap along the shining floors down the length of the rotunda to the door leading backstage. I flash my vendor pass at the security guard and rush to the back room where the competitors line up.

Max's things are still in their spot by the wall. I stop in the middle of the room, where a few competitors are hanging out. Where is he?

I turn and see him wander through the door, shaking the hands of the other heavyweights. I careen into him and wrap my arms around his neck.

"You placed! You placed!"

He grasps my waist and spins me in a circle. "I did! Who'd have thought it!"

His body is slick with oil, but I don't care. I'm so excited for him, and I don't want to let him go.

We walk arm in arm back to his bag.

"I think we should celebrate!" I say.

"Me too. As soon as I can get all this gunk off me."

Max Pickle naked in the shower. That's a vision.

He squeezes my hand. "I think something decadent might be in order since I can technically eat carbs on competition day. Some Italian? A steakhouse?"

"Anything you want."

He pulls on his jacket. "I should go easy on the carbs. I don't even know what's next."

"Well, you qualified for the next level, which happens in one week. That one is a national qualifier."

He shrugs. "What does that mean?"

"It means you're working toward being a professional bodybuilder. Sponsors. Traveling. The whole thing!"

He pulls on his pants, his eyes down. "It's a lot to take in. I have a deli to run."

"You know what. Don't worry about the future. Let's celebrate today," I say.

"Now that I can do." He shoulders his bag, and we walk hand-in-hand out to the parking lot.

"You have your car here?" Max asks.

"Yeah. Did you want to meet at a restaurant or something?"

My phone buzzes, but I ignore it. Max is more important.

He punches his remote to unlock a sleek blue sports car. "We could meet at my place. It's a bit of a haul from here, but not too far from you."

Before I can answer, Max's phone buzzes.

Then mine again. Then his.

"What the hell's going on?" Max digs his phone out of his pocket.

I glance down at mine.

When we look up at each other, we both say the same word simultaneously.

"Franklin."

"What's he saying to you?" Max asks.

I sigh. "He wonders why I wasn't there for his evening show. Apparently, he placed."

"That's what he told me!" Max says. "It's what he's always wanted."

"He might qualify for the same show you're going to next week. That open he was at today has higher standing than the one you did two weeks ago, and he already has a history."

"Even better," Max says. "He and I can go together. Today was a bummer without my best bud. We did this together."

Then his eyes meet mine. "Oh. Right."

"Exactly," I say.

"He's asking me to celebrate with him tonight," Max says. "I can put him off."

I reach out and squeeze his arm. "He didn't ask me to celebrate," I say. "I think you should go with him. This is big for him. He's been waiting three years for it."

Max steps closer to me. "But it feels like I've been waiting three years to be alone with you."

A thrill zips through me as he pulls my body close to his. The night is cool, the parking lot quiet since the final event is still going on inside the arena.

"Are you going to compete next week, though?" I ask.

"Probably," he says. "It'll be fun to level up with Franklin."

I shift the collar of his jacket. "I'm going to see you plenty this week. In fact, I should see you tomorrow, to prep for the new tan."

His grin is infectious, and his white teeth flash from the streetlamp. "Are you saying you're going to have those lovely talented hands all over me?"

"That, I can guarantee."

He leans in to kiss me, and my heart soars. There's no rush here. We're at the best part right now, everything full of promise. His career will go where he wants, or he'll let it go.

But we're already on a journey that isn't going to end regardless of where his bodybuilding future falls.

And I love having something to look forward to.

The next day, I have many things to think about as I wait for Max to arrive for his tanning session.

His searing kisses from the weekend have kept me up at night. How his hands roved my body. His blatant desire.

But I'm not sure what I'm ready for.

I've been worried about our tanning sessions. He's always naked. He hasn't been able to hide his attraction to me, even as I played coy with him. It's like Sofia said, the balance of power is all off.

Except I have an idea on how to make things more equitable between us. Show him, without a doubt, where we're headed.

My heart hammers so hard when he knocks on my door that I'm not sure which is louder.

When I open it, Max takes a moment to look at me. "Has it only been a day since I've seen you?"

"Just one." I close the door. "How was the celebration with my brother?"

"Surprisingly fun. We went bowling and ate giant cheeseburgers, buns and all."

"My brother can be fun when he wants to be."

Max takes my hand as we head into the room. "He's been my friend for eight years. I admit it feels weird to keep something so big from him."

"Do you think you'll tell him soon?"

"I think that's a decision we have to make together." He reaches out and trails his finger from my shoulder to the inside of my elbow. My body thrums with the low, steady hum of anticipation.

"So, is this where I get naked?" he asks.

"You're still here in a professional capacity."

"I'm here to do your bidding."

My heart hammers. So, do I do this risky thing or not?

My voice wavers a bit as I say, "Then get behind the screen and take your damn clothes off."

I watch him retreat to the corner of the room.

When he's out of sight, I decide, yes. I'm going to do it.

Skin for skin. Well, mostly.

And I slowly drop away my own clothes.

19

MAX

I've shoved my clothes into my bag and am digging around for the modesty pouch when Camryn calls from the other side of the screen.

"Remember, we had that problem with the modesty pouch pulling the color off on you. If you're okay with that, we can skip it today. I'll hold it aside as I work, letting it dry before I do each side."

My cock jumps at her words. I've been able to handle myself during the tans lately, but this time, if she touches me, there's no chance.

Plus, there's the matter of that incredibly hot make-out session at the arena. Even with the madness of the competitions and my future as a bodybuilder zooming at me at warp speed, I think about it constantly. Her, constantly.

I remember the feel of her under my hands, those glorious breasts and round ass. And now I'm too late. Full-mast.

I try to shift my focus.

But the more I try to think of something else, I swear, the harder my cock gets.

It's time to live it. It's not like Camryn doesn't know how hot I am for her.

I'm going to walk out there with the biggest erection of my life. Even the towel will be standing at attention.

But I do snatch one up from the table beside the screen.

I wrap it around my waist and step out.

Then I see her.

And I'm so shocked I drop the towel to the floor.

She's practically naked. The whole of her skin glows pale and luminous in the light where she works by the stool.

Fuuuuck.

My blood rushes to my cock.

The top of her round breasts gleam. Her nipples are small and pink. As I gawk at them, they tighten into buds.

There an indention on either side of her stomach muscles, and her belly button is an innie, not an outie.

I can already picture my tongue dipping inside it.

She wears the tiniest, barest swimsuit bottom, dark blue with black flowers. Beneath it, her legs are slender, her knees adorable. Her toenails are painted pink.

I want to worship her.

"Are you going to stare all day or are we going to get you tan?"

I can barely speak. "Do you…?"

"Do this for all my clients? Of course not. But we're starting something here, and it has felt very unequal.

You've been bared to me the whole time. So here. I'm as naked as you." She holds out her arms, and I swear to God I'm nearly brought to my knees.

"You're a fucking goddess," I manage to say.

She gives me a wry smile. "So, do you think we can do this?"

I've no idea what she's talking about. "Do...what?" My mind races with possibilities. Fuck like rabbits? Lick every inch of each other? Married, children, retirement in the South of France? I can see our whole future laid out.

She gestures to the stool. "The tan. I thought maybe I would work on you a little, then you would do me. I'll moisturize you, then you will put your hands on my body. Equal footing."

Fuuuuck.

I clear my throat to make sure I can form words. "I like this plan. As long as you can stand the elephant in the room." I gesture to my turgid, blood-engorged cock.

She nods. "Seen it before. You're happy to see me. I get it. Now on the stool."

I pick up the towel and sit down, not able to take my eyes off her. I watch her reach down for a loofah, and I'm desperate for my turn.

She walks around my body, checking the spots she knows may need work.

"Looking good. Let's check your thighs," she says.

I slide the towel away, and there's my cock, standing straight up.

She stares down. It jumps in response. "He is an exuberant part of you, isn't he?"

"He can't resist you."

"May I take a look at these inner thighs?"

"You can do anything you want with me."

Camryn kneels between my knees, and for a moment I almost pass out. My life flashes before my eyes.

She widens my legs, her ponytail brushing my skin as she examines the tan.

"I'm going to have to tend to this part by hand and then hold you aside while it dries." She looks up at me with those lashes, and I don't even know how I keep control. But somehow I do.

"Sounds good."

She rolls her tray closer and picks up the tanning lotion. I am absolutely rapt with every motion she makes. She shakes the bottle, and her breasts jiggle. My head goes light again.

She squeezes a bit of color on a finger. "So, here we go."

She presses my leg away with her elbow and cups my balls and shifts my dick to one side. I swear I'm about to lose it right there. Her hand is cool against my rather throbbing cock. I'm absolutely dying.

She glances up at me. "He's really engorged. If I let go, he'll take on the color and wreck the smoothness."

"Do what you have to do."

Her fingers wrap around my cock while the heel of her hand holds my balls aside. I'm on fire. I will spontaneously combust any moment.

I know we are way past the client relationship. She's

playing with me, and I am one-hundred percent onboard.

I couldn't even have made a fantasy as good as this.

She spreads the cream along my thigh and wipes her finger on the towel.

"Now we wait."

Her gaze drifts along my body. It falls on my cock, and she tilts her head, not even trying to hide that she's looking.

I am absolutely dead. "I'm desperate to touch you," I say.

She nods. "Your turn is next. You can wait for it."

We sit a while longer. She checks the skin, determines it to be dry enough, and lays a tissue against where she has added color.

"Now for the other side."

God. I'll never make it.

She repeats the process. My hands itch to cup one of those breasts. I don't even know if it's appropriate. But here she is, mostly naked, and telling me I'll be able to touch her soon.

Please let it be those glorious breasts.

The agony is intense.

After what feels like six years, she lays another tissue against my thigh.

"While that sets, I'll show you one of my trouble spots."

She passes the loofah to me and lifts her hair. "Right here on my neck."

I press my fingers to her skin at last. It's cool to my

fevered touch, and I'm so overwhelmed to be near her naked body, I tremble.

"It all feels perfect to me," I say.

She places her hand over mine and shifts it so my fingers graze this one spot that might be the slightest bit drier than the rest.

She tips the moisturizing bottle to my finger and squeezes out the barest bit. "Rub it into my skin."

The tiny drop slides across her neck. I want to follow it with my mouth. But I do as she asks, letting the moisture seep into her pores.

Her head turns to face me. "I always get to choose what I do to you. I'll let you choose what you want to touch next on me."

"Stand up," I tell her. "So I can decide."

She does as I ask, standing before me, I take in her face, the tendrils of hair coming off her temples. Her shoulders, narrow and delicate.

And those breasts.

I can't resist.

"I don't think you tan those," I say.

"More moisture never hurts." She picks up a different lotion and places a bit on my palm. "Rub them together first, then do as you wish."

She waits, a half-smile on her face. I rub my palms to spread the lotion. My groin is tight and swollen, almost painful. But it's glorious, the anticipation so high for her, desperate for release.

I lift my hands and reach out for those two perfect breasts. She leans in.

My palms cup them, sliding across the radiant skin. Her nipples tighten, and my thumbs cross over them.

She sucks in a breath.

The light moisturizer gives them a glorious glow as I cover every inch. It's cool at first, but as it sinks in, her skin becomes pliant and warm.

I never want to stop touching her.

Her legs waver, and I shift one hand to her hips to pull her closer. Then, I continue to knead her breasts, far beyond what is necessary to apply the lotion.

But she stands there, her eyes closed, her breath shallow and even.

The urge is fierce to take her nipple in my mouth. I want it with the desperation of a man leaving the desert and heading toward water.

But that's not part of the plan here. She's evening the score, allowing me to touch her as she has touched me so many times.

I will obey the rules.

Her eyes flutter open. "Your thighs should be dry."

Reluctantly, I release her breasts. "What now?"

"We're ready for the spray," she says.

"We?"

"It's only fair," she says. "I'll have you spray me first, so you don't accidentally damage yours doing mine."

The idea that my fantasy is about to come true causes a bit of pre-come to slip from the tip of my cock.

"You trust me not to destroy your perfect skin?"

"I'll give you the lightest color. It won't hurt anything, even if you're sloppy."

She removes the tissues, and I follow her to the tanning tent. The swimsuit bottom is a thong, and I get a glorious view of her perfect round ass as she pulls a small tank out of the cabinet. "The palest pale," she says, and I take in everything as she bends over. God, I am hot for her.

She hands me the wand. "The trick is to move swiftly and evenly. Neck and down."

She pulls the ponytail from her hair, and for a moment, it falls in a glorious cascade down her body. I have to set my jaw to maintain any semblance of control. She's every fantasy I've ever had, right in front of me.

Her breasts lift as she raises her arms and rearranges her hair into a tight bun, wrapped with the same elastic.

"I'm ready," she says. "Let's see what you've got."

She holds her arms out from her sides. I imprint this image of her in my mind. Almost naked, glorious, mine.

I turn on the spray.

It moves evenly across her, coating her in the glossy wet shimmer. When I get to her beautiful toes, I turn it off.

"Now the back," she says.

She turns around, and this one is even harder, because she can't see me staring at her.

I take her in for a full minute before she turns her head and says, "Everything okay?"

I swallow hard and say, "Sorry."

I spray the back of her, and she bends over as I reach her ass, allowing her cheeks to spread. My life passes before my eyes.

I spray down both slender calves and shut it off.

"Now you need to dry," I say.

She steps out of the tent and over to the fan, lifting her arms and tilting back her head.

I want to be a painter, or a sculptor, something to capture this incredible beauty in front of me.

But all I can do is set down the spray wand and stare, feasting on the vision of her.

After several minutes, she touches a finger to her inner arm. "All good. Ready for yours?"

I step into the tent while she switches out for a darker spray.

When she moves in front of me, she says, "We have to do something about that. It's more than I bargained for."

I glance down. My cock is rather outrageously out there.

"It's that bad to spray it?"

"It won't hurt you, but it's not a good look when it peels."

I let out a long breath. "I'm way beyond the pale here."

"I don't guess you're going to be able to bring it down?"

"Not with a naked goddess standing in front of me."

"Would it help if I put on some clothes?"

"Not at this point."

"What would help?"

I want to say exactly what would help, but I'm not sure we're there yet. The last thing I want to do is scare her off. I'm ready to work over every inch of her, lick it, taste it, then plunge inside her body. Picturing it makes my head spin.

Whoa, boy. Take it down a notch.

"I'm open to suggestions."

She stares at it again, tapping her finger on her cheek. I can barely take it.

"I'm going to take care of it."

My throat is so tight I can barely ask, "How?"

"You seem pretty far gone." She steps forward, her naked, glowing body almost grazing mine. "I think it might be easy."

She pauses. "This isn't about being my client. This is about where we're headed on a personal level."

"I'm down with whatever you want to do."

Her arms reach up to clasp my shoulders. Then slowly, carefully, she presses her body against mine. My cock is trapped between us.

I'm in heaven. Or hell. It's a thin line because I want her so badly, but I don't want to move too fast.

She's silky smooth after the lotion and the tanning spray. God. I'm so sunk.

"Good thing my color's light," she says.

"Why?"

"It's about to rub on you." She slides down, every soft curve of her body slipping along mine, until her breasts surround my cock. She reaches down to hold my balls. "Nothing I haven't touched before."

She looks up at me, damn, those lashes, and I clutch the sides of the tent.

She makes her way up again, gliding along my abs.

Then back down, my cock appearing again between those breasts.

She rolls my balls in her hand, then moves up and down, sliding along the length of my dick.

Her tits. My cock. Her naked body. Those eyes.

She keeps moving, up and down, quickening her pace. Our bodies are slick and smooth, like silken sheets gliding against each other.

Fuck. It's too much.

I unleash, spurting across those glorious breasts. When I've stopped groaning, she looks down with a smile. "I think we got it taken care of."

She steps back and for a moment I think I've died. She absolutely glows, the tan giving her a luminous quality, and my come is on her body.

"Grab a towel," she says. "I'll clean up, and then we'll give you the perfect tan. Problem solved."

I practically stagger for the stack of towels nearby. I'm completely toast. A goner.

She was absolutely right about one thing.

I'm one-hundred percent under her control.

20

CAMRYN

The morning after my naked tan with Max Pickle, I lie in bed, wondering what the hell I have done.

I went into the evening trying to even the score. I guess I should've known it was going to get dirty.

Honestly, it could've gotten a hell of a lot dirtier.

But I can still feel his body rubbing up and down mine.

I felt so powerful. So in control.

I don't know where to go from here. We're headed into a physical relationship. That makes sense after all those naked sessions.

But what about the rest? Dating. Talking. Getting to know each other.

We have the most abnormal relationship, ever. What have we done together? Six tanning sessions. Two competitions. One walk in the park.

And of course, I guess I did go visit him at the deli that day.

Maybe I should do that again. Strike up an ordinary conversation.

With both of us dressed.

I pull my phone off the side table. But instead of writing Max, I write Sofia.

Did what you said.

Her response is swift.

You banged him??????

No. Took off my clothes.

You tanned him naked????

I did a lot more than that, but I'm not willing to commit it to a text.

Yes. Now I feel like I should have gotten dinner first.

So go get dinner!

Now?

Go get lunch!

She's right. I can do that.

Decision made, I get out of bed and hop in the shower. Maybe I'll put on a different look today. He's used to seeing me work.

What is something I would never wear in a tanning session?

The day is bright and glorious, so I choose a pale-blue sundress and wedge sandals.

I curl my hair into spirals, which is rare for me since it's so long and takes forever. It falls in a glorious cascade of brown and red. A tiny silver circlet holds back a few pieces and gives a romantic feel.

It matches those messages he gave me the day I met Sofia.

I put on more makeup, not a lot, pink gloss on my

lips and a bit of blush in addition to my mega-mascara that I'm pretty sure makes him crazy.

I wait until the lunch rush is over, and head into what I assume is a quiet time on a weekday. When I enter the deli, the two employees I recognize from the first time lean on the counter.

"It's her," singsongs the one at the register, tall with a cascade of black braids falling over her shoulders.

The man, a good foot shorter and wearing a backward baseball cap, says, "Max is in the back. You want me to take you there?"

"You know who I am?" I ask.

"Of course we do," the cashier says. "You're the reason he's in a fog all day."

Really? I smooth my skirt with nervous hands. "I don't want to disturb him if he's busy."

Baseball Cap Boy shakes his head. "He's never going to be too busy for you."

This is all a revelation. Has he spoken about me? How do they know?

I hope they'll say more, but the man comes around the counter and leads me through the swinging door to the kitchen.

Another man is chopping onions, and farther back, a stern-looking woman loads a loaf of bread into a slicer. Neither of them pays any attention to me.

The man knocks on a door near the back wall. "Boss man? You have a visitor."

"Come in." Max's voice is low and deep and suddenly my stomach flutters with butterflies. This is his turf, not mine.

The man opens the door. "There you go."

"Thanks."

Max sits in a desk chair facing a computer. His back is to the door.

When he turns and sees me, his entire expression changes. "Camryn! What a pleasant surprise." He hops up from his chair and closes the door.

"I wasn't busy today. Is this an okay time?"

"Of course. God, you look beautiful." He lifts a long curl from my shoulder. "I've never seen you like this."

"I realized this morning that our encounters have been limited. I thought maybe we could do something unrelated to tans."

His eyes light up. "So, it's official? I can ask you out on a normal date?"

"You mean one where we're not naked?"

He laughs. "This is almost as good. Sit down." He drags another chair close to his. "Should we go somewhere tonight? Dinner? Drinks? What would you like?"

"You're making my point," I say. "You don't know anything about what I like."

He leans in close. "I look forward to finding out every single thing you like."

Heat rises in my body. "I think dinner would be good. Are you free?"

"I'm working out with your brother after we close. It would be a late dinner."

"I don't know how you're doing it. The workouts, running a restaurant. The competitions. The tanning sessions alone are a huge chunk of time."

"I have a great manager. And thankfully, I don't

need a lot of sleep." He reaches out and takes my hand. "I can't tell you how happy I am to see you."

Our gazes meet, and I have a feeling he's thinking about last night. A flush heats my cheeks.

"So, you're thinking about it too," he says.

"I don't know what came over me," I say.

"It was fucking hot," he says. "I want to know when I get to return the favor."

"Soon?" I say.

He glances around. "You know what? They don't need me this afternoon. All my best staff is here. I'm just a figurehead."

"Really?"

"Yeah. Let's make a day of it."

We head through the kitchen to the sandwich line, and Max pulls me behind the counter. The two employees from before are gone, replaced with a young blond woman.

"Where'd Tiana and Angelo go?" Max asks.

"Tiana is on break talking to her man in the alley," the woman says. "Angelo went to fetch more cheese."

Max nods. He seems less comfortable with this worker than the others.

I try to break the tension. "So, I get to see the behind the scenes."

Max smiles. "Nothing fancy here. Let's put something together. A picnic?"

"Sure." I glance along the line at the various breads and sandwich fillings and sides. "Can you eat any of this?"

"Well technically, it's a competition week so I can have carbs. But I'll keep it light. No bread. No pastas."

"But all the pickles you want, right?" I slide on the plastic glove and pick up one of the oversized dills. I wave it in his face.

"Pickles, I can do." He snags another glove and piles pickles into a container.

The woman at the cash register frowns. She's college-aged, lots of attitude. She does not approve of my arrival behind the counter.

"So, Mr. Pickle, who is this?" She flips a long lock of blond hair behind her shoulder and glares at me like I'm poaching on her man.

"This is Camryn. We're heading out for a picnic."

The girl's expression darkens. "In the middle of the workday? I'm the only one on the line until the others get back."

Oh, this employee is not like the others. She seems to think she has some claim on Max. I glance between the two of them. I'm curious how Max will handle this challenge. No doubt more than one employee has tried to get their clutches on him.

"You are very good at what you do, and you will handle it marvelously," Max says.

This mollifies her, but she crosses her arms in front of her green pickle shirt. "Where are you going for this so-called picnic?"

I want to tell her it's none of her damn business, but Max answers as he pops a lid on the pickle container. "Not sure yet. The neighborhood park is small. You're young. What are some great spots to have a picnic around here?"

Her eyes brighten at the "you're young" comment, and she lifts an eyebrow at me while Max extricates another container from the stack.

Readers, I have to admit I'd like to smack her.

Max glances up. "Did you have any ideas?"

"We're in the middle of L.A.," she says. "But I'd head to the beach."

Max turns to me. "That sounds nice. You game for sand and waves?"

"Absolutely."

The girl sighs and drops her chin onto her hands as she braces her elbows on the counter.

Max fills a small container with a white spread. "The beach is a great idea. Thank you, Karen."

I stifle a laugh. Of course her name is Karen.

The man who took me to the back returns, and the tension lifts.

"I'm Angelo," he says. "I figured I better introduce myself since my boss, here, forgets his manners around pretty girls."

This gets a *harrumph* from Karen, but Angelo ignores her as he merrily helps us pack a sandwich for me, and a collection of meat and cheese for Max.

Max drags down an L.A. Pickle cooler from a high shelf to pack everything in. "Andre will close," he tells Karen and Angelo. "And let Miranda know we're testing the anniversary bread tomorrow."

Karen gives a halfhearted salute as she watches us walk out the door.

"Don't do anything I wouldn't do," Angelo calls, and Karen elbows him.

When we're outside, I thread my hand through the crook of his arm. "You know, I think your Karen in there has a bit of a crush on you. If her eyes had death darts, I'd be twitching on the ground."

"Really? I hadn't noticed." He grins down at me, and the matter of his ardent employee disappears.

We take Max's blue sports car to one of the public beaches. It's a good forty-five-minute drive, but my day is free, and Max's is open until his evening workout with my brother.

We're not five steps onto the beach before I reach down to unhook my sandals. "You're going to have shoes full of sand," I warn Max.

He glances down at his shiny work shoes. "Good point."

He scts the cooler down to remove his shoes and socks. His feet are darkly tan against the white sand. My work. They look good.

It's cool here on the beach, the ocean breeze blowing across my skin. He tucks the blanket he pulled from the trunk of his car beneath the strap of the cooler, neatly shifting everything to one hand, leaving one free for me.

The beach is dotted with visitors, seagulls swooping over the water with great squawks. But it's a quiet area, since most everyone's at work or in school mid-afternoon on a weekday.

We head close to the waterline, leaving footprints in the damp sand. Max squeezes my hand and when he smiles at me, my heart is full.

21

MAX

Walking at the water's edge with Camryn is like a dream.

She's braided her long hair aside one shoulder, and with her sunglasses and long dress blowing in the breeze, she could be a model for a vacation ad.

We wander along the beach until we find a secluded stretch, too far from the parking lots for the average beachcomber.

I spread out the blanket and anchor it with my shoes and the cooler. I'm glad I got out of the deli today. We need some easy couple time. Something ordinary after the intense moments we've had since we met.

Camryn goes straight for the pickles. "I believe you packed all the different kinds into one container," she says, plucking the lid off the top. "That most certainly violates the law of pickles."

"No such thing as pickle laws," I say. "Unless I make them. I am a Pickle after all."

She settles cross-legged across from me, the container in her hand. "That can't really be your last name, right?"

I tug a water bottle from the bag. "We were all born as Packwoods. It was Dad's genius idea for us all to function as Pickles. But my driver's license says Packwood."

Camryn scrunches up her nose. "But when you won the prize, they called you Max Pickle."

"Lots of bodybuilders use stage names. Take your friend Behemoth."

"True." She lifts a pickle from the plastic tub. "Your pickle definitely has stage presence."

She catches me mid-swig, so I sputter water into a coughing fit.

Camryn bangs her palm on my back. "Water have a *bone* in it?"

Now it's worse, me cough-laughing. She pounds on me until the coughing subsides and I can take a normal sip of water.

She's really something.

"So, tell me everything there is to know about Camryn Shultz."

She crosses her ankles, legs stretched out on the blanket. "You should know a few things since it's the same as my brother. Grew up in L.A. Two parents, still married, still living here."

"I get the sense Franklin doesn't talk to them."

She frowns. "Neither of us, much. Franklin and I mostly raised ourselves."

"I'm sorry."

She shrugs. "What about you?"

"Dad is great. Very involved with all three of his sons. My mom died when I was a senior in high school. Made graduation tough."

"I'm so sorry."

"Me, too. She was a great lady. Kept my dad out of trouble."

"Is he often in trouble?'

"Not as much as us. But he opened a franchise for each of his sons in the cities we chose. He wanted us to have it easier than he did. His dad died when he was young."

"And you met Franklin at UCLA."

"Yeah. We had a mutual friend and when a spot opened up in the house he was renting, I got invited."

"I would have been graduating high school that year, I think."

"I didn't even know he had a sister, but then, we didn't talk about stuff like that."

She holds the tub of pickles up to examine them. "And you decided to stay. Open your deli here."

"It's a great scene. I like the beaches. The weather."

"It's expensive."

"So is New York."

She nods. "Is it pickle time?" She peers up at me with those lashes, and I'm struck by her absolute beauty for the zillionth time.

"You can have my pickle any time you want."

She plucks a wrinkled green one from the tub and chomps on it. Instantly, her eyes go wide with alarm.

"Oh! Oh! This is more than hot. This is…" She sets down the pickle container and snatches my bottle of water. Only after she's chugged several mouthfuls does she ask, "What was that one?"

"Anthony's latest brainstorm. It's the Pickle of the Month."

"What's it called?"

"Bad Temper," I say with a laugh. "It's bathed in habanero juice."

Camryn waves her hand in front of her mouth. "And what's the hot pickle normally flavored with?"

"Jalapeño. It's milder because we chill the peppers first. We've made one hotter than Bad Temper before."

"How?" Her face is bright from the heat.

"Ghost peppers. I can't even be near those or I break out in a sweat."

"That sounds like something that could kill you."

I take the partially eaten pickle from her. "There's a trick to eating these." I rummage in the cooler until I find the dilled cream cheese I packed. I drag the spicy pickle through the cream cheese. "Dairy products cool the burn. Try it this way."

I hold out the pickle topped with white cream for her to take a bite.

"You sure it's safe?"

"I swear on the Pickle name."

She leans forward and bites the end of the pickle with the cream cheese.

"How's that?" I dip it into the cream cheese a second time.

She swallows her bite. "That worked." She watches me take a bite. "But it needs a new name when it's dipped."

"Mmm hmm." I swallow. It burns so good. "What's that?"

Her face takes on that mischievous look I've come to love. "The Pickle's Cream." Her gaze drops below my belt.

When her eyes return to my face, I'm reminded of that hot, hot moment when I released all over her naked body.

"I'll make a note of that."

"It can be our inside joke." She scoots closer to me and leans her head on my shoulder.

Time stills, other than the roll of waves on the shore and the occasional call of a gull. I drink her in, this quietness, this peace. I need to stop more. Live a little rather than run from place to place. Bodybuilding has done a number on me. I'm all work and muscle. No play.

I turn to press my lips into her hair. She smells like sunshine and jasmine. I could sit here in the sun and breathe her in for the rest of my life.

"Will you come over tonight after your workout?" she asks.

"I was hoping you'd ask." I find her fingers on the blanket and wrap them in mine.

"There might be the usual level of nakedness," she says. She tilts her face up, inches from mine. "Maybe a different purpose."

I've never been more anxious for the sun to go down.

Franklin is seriously pumped as we start our workout later that evening.

He lies on the bench press as I stand over him, ready to spot.

"It's finally happening," he says. "You and me dominating the L.A. circuit."

"I think it's great we get to be at the same meet again. It was a bummer without you there last Saturday."

Franklin adjusts his grip on the bar. "Amy said she stopped by. That you were sitting all alone against the wall."

My mind flashes for a moment to the stacked chairs witnessing my torrid moment with Camryn. And for a brief second, it skips to the evening ahead, after I leave the gym. Not going to be mentioning that, for sure.

"Amy was a great help there at the end. And look, she's got two winners on her roster."

"Hell yeah, she does. Franklin and Max, the dream team." He lifts the bar and begins his set with more vigor than usual.

He pumps his reps, then racks the bar for me to add more plates to the ends.

I fetch a pair of ten-pounders. "So how did you go straight to this bigger meet when I had to do this invitational in between?"

Franklin shakes out his arms. "Some meets level you up faster than others."

"Camryn said that we could qualify for Nationals at this one."

Franklin drops his arms. "So, she's still doing your tans."

I shouldn't have brought her up. Time to scramble. "Thanks to you. And I got the bummer slot at the crack of dawn on Saturday. She said she was going to do yours at a more reasonable hour."

Franklin watches me for a moment as if assessing my words for truth. Finally, he says, "Apparently she was too busy to watch my evening show. Fucking sucks. I finally get somewhere, and my own flesh and blood wasn't there to see it."

Right. Because she was with me.

I redirect. "We should round up a cheering section for Saturday."

Franklin aligns his hands on the bar. "Now that's an idea. But you gotta confess to somebody. You told anybody yet?"

"Nope."

Franklin pounds out another set of reps on the bench, his focus on the bar now that he's approaching his max weight.

He stumbles a bit with the rack, and I guide it back into the slot.

He shakes his arms and sits up. "It's about time we rallied the troops."

Franklin hops to his feet, stepping up on the bench press cushion. "Hear ye, hear ye," he calls out. "I would like to announce that my overdeveloped friend here, as well as myself, have both placed at the top of our most recent bodybuilding competitions."

A grunting cheer erupts from the weightlifters, and Franklin makes an exaggerated bow.

"Both of us will be competing this Saturday at an invitation-only meet to qualify for Nationals. If you would like to attend, hit us up, and we'll see about getting you passes to the evening show."

When he hops down, Buster pushes away from the door frame where he's been watching and heads over. "Sounds like we have a pair of winners on deck. I'll put a sign-up sheet on the front desk, and I'll personally spot the cost of the first twenty passes."

Franklin claps him on the back. "That sounds perfectly grand, Buster. Feel free to put our names on all your marketing materials." He gestures to an imaginary sign. "Franklin Schultz. Max Pickle."

Oh, hell no. "Mine is totally not necessary," I say.

Franklin waves me off. "We'll be happy to recruit for you, if you want to even out the bodybuilders among the MMA fighters the McClure clan has brought."

Buster crosses his arms over his blue Buster's Gym tank. "It's inspiring to see how things evolve. Boxing back in the day. Then MMA. Now bodybuilding. Always something new."

Franklin leaps back onto the bench press cushion to get everyone's attention again. "Buster's got a sign-up at the desk. Get your passes to watch us DOM-IN-ATE." He tightens his arms into the Most Muscular pose and another whoop fills the room.

This is a good idea. I can keep my support within the athletic community and avoid having to talk about it outside of this crowd. There's no need for it to spill out to my personal life. My employees don't need to know. With Franklin and Camryn and the Buster's Gym crew, honestly, I have all the support I need.

22

CAMRYN

Max is coming.

Max is COMING!

I've spent the last two hours dashing around my apartment, making sure everything is how I want it.

Then myself.

I've showered and applied lighter makeup, something I can sleep in (with MAX!) Shaved all the things. Moisturized all the things. Well, most of them. I chose a different sundress, pale-yellow.

No bra.

Cute white underwear with yellow flowers.

I left my hair in curls, now all brushed and loose.

The bed is turned down. Fresh sheets. Candles burn on both nightstands.

FOR MAX!

A text buzzes through.

How are you?

I try to settle myself as I reply.

I'm good. How was the workout with my brother?

Too long.
Where are you?
In the parking lot of your apartment complex.
I jump up.
He's here.
A feverish heat blasts through me. It's time.
Coming to the door.

I pad across the apartment in my bare feet. When I open the door, he's there, freshly showered, hair damp, wearing jeans and a short-sleeved collared shirt.

"You don't look like you just had a killer workout," I say.

"I stopped by my house first."

I step back to let him in and close the door.

"So, this is my living room when it's not all set up for tanning." I gesture to the room.

He glances around. "It converts nicely." His gaze falls back on me, my eyes, dropping to my neck, then the swell of my breasts in the sundress.

"Can I get you something to drink?" I ask, barely able to get the words out.

"I hydrated after my workout."

"Right. No alcohol during competition season."

He sets his keys on the cabinet by the door. "I wasn't done kissing you at the beach."

"Is that your plan? To finish the job?"

"I absolutely intend to finish the job."

Then he's on me, his arms wrapped around my waist, his mouth crushing my lips.

I gasp, the power and heat coming off of him over-whelming.

His fingers tangle in my hair, wrapping around his fist and pulling my head down. "I don't think I can wait any longer for you."

I nod. I feel the same. The gentleness he shows during our sessions is gone. We're back to the fierceness, the heat, and pent-up need.

He lifts me by the thighs to straddle his body. His hands slide beneath my skirt, grinding me against him. He's rock-hard, and I can picture every inch of him. I want to see it again. Feel it. Do more. Everything.

His mouth has complete control of mine, his tongue exploring me. He tastes of mint gum and smells like aftershave.

He's greedy, his mouth unrelenting. His hands rove up my back. He finds the zipper to my dress and pulls it down.

"I've only seen you once," he says. "I need to see you again."

I lock my feet around his waist as he pulls one spaghetti strap over my arm, then the other. His mouth moves to my neck, then collarbone as he leaves a trail of hot kisses along my skin.

He peels the dress away from my breasts, and I arch to him as his mouth claims a nipple.

He walks us to the side of the room where a pile of cushions decorates one corner. He lays me down on them and drags the dress off my body.

"You're more beautiful than I remember," he says, and tosses the dress across the room. "And I am going to feast on it."

His hands cup my breasts as his mouth captures one,

then the other. He continues exploring, feathering kisses along the side of my waist, across my belly button, and dipping his tongue inside.

I arch my hips to him as his fingers grasp the edge of my lace panties and peel them down.

His mouth follows their descent, skipping along my hipbone, and down my thigh, to the inside of my knee.

When the panties are lying next to my dress, he begins to work his way back up.

I clutch one of the pillows, feeling the wetness between my thighs.

His mouth finds its way to that heat, and his fingers spread me wide.

When his tongue slides inside, I arch to him again, letting out a long groan of need.

One of his hands goes beneath me, lifting my body to his mouth.

He plunges there, working me, a thumb quickly circling my nub.

I can barely catch my breath, it's so fast, so hard, so intense.

His tongue laps at me, matching the rhythmic movements of my body, feeding them, pushing them higher.

He squeezes me, sliding his tongue more deeply inside. When his mouth sucks my nub, the lightning that has been sparking through my body focuses its energy where he works me.

The pulse of the orgasm begins, slowly, heavy, then suddenly bursts out.

I shriek, my entire body a crashing wave.

He holds me in place, not letting me go, drawing the orgasm out until I feel like I might collapse.

At last, he slows it down, and I sink into the cushions.

He spreads wet kisses along my thighs to my knee and down my shin. He nips at my calf, making me laugh.

"That tickles," I say.

"You're still with us?"

"I might've died. But I am resurrected."

He shifts forward over my body, propping his head over me. He's still fully dressed.

"I like this change," he says. "You naked. Me fully clothed."

I reach up and rub my hand along the back of his hair. "I do, too."

He kisses my neck and works his way back down to a breast. "I will never get tired of the view."

"You always get naked behind the screen," I say. "Maybe I'd like to undress you myself for once.

"Feel free."

He kneels on the floor next to the pile of pillows. I sit in front of him and grasp the bottom of his shirt to pull it over that incredibly developed chest.

I've touched him a thousand ways, with solutions, tanning creams, and loofahs.

But now I can touch him how I want, with a caress, followed with the soft press of my lips on all the places I've admired for weeks.

I reach for his belt, sliding the leather through the loops, revealing the button to his fly.

He stands up, and I kneel, lowering the zipper, pulling the waistband away and pushing the jeans down.

His boxers are black and silky, and there is no missing the erection filling out the front.

I've touched it before, shifting it aside while tanning, and once, pressing it between my breasts.

But I want so much more.

I wrap my hand around it, sheathed in the black silk, and stroke up and down.

Max lets out a long groan.

I lift the elastic waistband away from his skin and peel it down, allowing his cock to come free.

It's finally mine to hold onto, admire, and taste.

I push the boxers down and cup his balls the way I did at the naked tanning session.

And at long last, I get to slide that glorious cock into my mouth.

His hands tangle in my hair, gripping my head. I take him in, my tongue licking his length. He smells of soap and tastes of pure, clean skin. I grip the base with both hands while my mouth slides up and down the tip.

He presses my face more tightly against his body, his hips moving with my motions.

"Camryn," he breathes.

I slow down a notch, not wanting to move too fast. I ease up the pressure and slide my tongue along to the end.

When I pull away, he stands up, kicking off his shoes and shoving the jeans and boxers out of his way.

"Should we try a bed this time?" I ask.

He picks me up from the floor and cradles me in his

arms. "Show me the way."

"Through the beads and down the hall."

When we arrive in the bedroom, he lays me down on the bed like I'm something precious.

"I have longed for this day," he whispers against my neck as he positions his body over mine. "I have a condom."

"Unless there's a reason for it, I'd rather rely on my pills."

"Done." His mouth captures a breast again as fingers slip inside my body.

I can scarcely catch my breath as he moves me back into that airy space of oblivion, ready for him.

He shifts, nudging his cock against the entrance as his fingers continue to circle my nub.

When he thrusts inside, I arch to him and cry out. I feel split wide, a thousand flashes of fire darting through my body like a sparkler has been lit.

He kisses my ear, my cheek, my mouth, consuming me with his lips.

His body moves over me gently, easily, until I press against his back to quicken the pace.

His arms come around my waist to pull me up to him, away from the bed, and he thrusts into me with all the pent-up need we've both suppressed since that first day in the dressing room at the arena.

All those moments flash through my mind. His body. My hands on him. Lotion. Spray. His erections. Toying with each other.

All leading to this.

He pulls me closer until we've shifted, and I'm sitting

in his lap, my legs driving our speed, his hands clasping my waist and giving me lift, then I crash down on his cock, shuddering with pleasure.

I never want it to end, and move and move and move, up and down, clutching, burying my face in his neck.

"Camryn, Camryn, Camryn," he whispers against my ear.

The tightness begins, clenching around him with a fiery grip. I slam down, once, twice and then I know it's coming, and a careening cry starts low in my throat.

The pulsing has already begun when suddenly everything clenches down even harder. The orgasm billows out like an ocean wave. I am consumed, rocking against him, sweating, exhausted, exhilarated, so high.

He clutches my back and pounds upward until I feel his belly tighten, and the warmth spreads into me.

I remember it spurting on my body, and a second wave of orgasm in my body spasms around his cock.

He clutches me tight, pulsing inside me, refusing to let go.

We're both breathing hard, clutching each other like we're drowning.

He falls back on the bed, bringing me with him. We roll until I'm curled up against his chest, one leg thrown over his thighs.

He pushes the hair away from my face and gazes at me.

There are no words.

"I am never going to get enough of you," he says.

I know exactly how he feels.

23

MAX

When I wake up the next morning in Camryn's bed, she's asleep.

The dull gray light outside the windows tells me dawn has barely broken. I'm used to getting up early.

I'm not in a rush, though. I don't have to work out before I head to the deli, since I took care of that last night with Franklin.

Franklin.

If he could see the two of us right now, he'd bust an artery.

I think it should fall to me to tell him, when we do. I'd rather him take out his anger on me, not Camryn.

Camryn.

She's really something.

A long loose tendril of her hair falls across the pillow. I aimlessly twirl it in my finger.

The scenario has definitely flipped.

Before I was concerned about losing my training buddy.

No longer.

Now it's her.

I wonder how much trouble Franklin can make for his sister in the bodybuilding circuit. He interfered last season, clocking a competitor who wanted to date her.

And then there's this mysterious past relationship.

Camryn seems to have come through those incidents fine, as popular as ever with her services.

So hopefully Franklin doesn't exercise any influence there. Or, if he does, he knows not to use it against his own flesh and blood.

Me, on the other hand, he might destroy.

Would that be such a bad thing? Camryn comes first. I'd trade any time on the stage for these hours with her.

I prop myself up on my elbow to watch her sleep. She must sense me staring at her, because she shifts beneath the sheets until she faces me.

"I'm sure you're used to getting up early," she says sleepily.

I smooth more hair away from her face. It's everywhere, glorious in reds and browns.

"Every day," I say.

"I'm not a morning person." She buries her head back in the pillow.

"How about I go make us some coffee?"

Her head pops up. "Can you drink any?"

"A little. The next competition isn't until Saturday."

She reaches out and pokes my arm muscles. "How long does it take to dehydrate?"

"A few days. I won't overindulge."

"Crazy life, isn't it?"

"It brought me to you."

Her smile is everything. "Go fetch my coffee, peasant."

I tweak her nose and slide out of the sheets.

Her kitchen is small and tidy. I spot the coffee pot easily enough and find the bag of ground beans in the cabinet above. Soon, the smell of percolating fills the room.

I pause by her refrigerator. It's covered in magnets, notes, and old ticket stubs.

She likes pop music. She's seen Taylor Swift and Katy Perry. Or maybe she has some connection for tickets. Both appear to be comp passes. I wouldn't doubt that someone like Camryn knows all the right people.

I want to learn everything about her.

I pause on a photo of her and Franklin. It's from a few years ago, as I remember this haircut of Franklin's from our college days. It's one of their birthdays, although it isn't clear whose as they're both by the cake.

I wonder again what makes Franklin so overbearing with her. It's a question I hope I can broach with her soon. We'll need a game plan for how to break it to him that we've become a couple.

Several other images show Camryn and another woman with long black hair. They hold champagne glasses in a shadowy bar. In another, they laugh as they eat tacos in someone's backyard. Clearly a good friend.

"That's Sofia," Camryn says with a yawn. She rubs the heel of her hand into her eye. "She knows about you. I had drinks with her a week or so ago."

Camryn has slipped on a thin pajama tank top and adorable pink shorts. But the outline of those nipples I feasted on last night are visible.

Her gaze takes me in, stark naked. As usual.

"Someone's awake this morning," she says.

I glance down. The morning wood is rising and shining. "It's my perpetual state around you."

"Let me get some coffee in me, and maybe we can do something with that."

Now he's standing at full attention.

Her hair is glorious chaos, red and brown strands tangled around her face and down her back.

As she pours herself a cup and sips it black, I run my fingers through the long strands to tame them.

"That's nice," she says.

When the bulk of her hair is more or less straightened out, I divide it into three sections and begin to braid.

As the plait lengthens, Camryn turns to look at the piece on her shoulder. "Nice work. Where did you pick up that skill?"

"I had an entrepreneurial phase in about fourth grade. I made friendship bracelets and sold them on the playground."

"A business owner from way back."

"I think I would've gone in the hole on supplies if Mom hadn't kept me in thread."

"What was she like?"

My throat tightens involuntarily, as it always does. "Perfect. The kind who made cookies after school. Who asked questions and made you answer. She wanted to know everything."

"Do you talk about what happened to her?"

"Ovarian cancer. It was quick."

Camryn turns and I pinch the end of her braid.

"I'm so sorry."

"Me too. She was a great lady."

"And your brothers?"

"My youngest brother Anthony is taking over the main Pickle deli in Manhattan, as well as the overall franchise. Dad put us up to a competition last year. Anthony won."

Camryn's grin is mischievous. "And not you? You weren't feeling competitive?"

"I was already tied up in these workouts. And no, controlling the franchise was something I felt Anthony would do best. I came in dead last, anyway."

"The underachiever. Somehow I don't believe that."

"It was competitive. We all thought I would skunk my brother Jason, but he came from behind."

She sips her coffee, and then sets the mug on the counter.

"Well, you did an excellent job on the braid. I assume you wanted my hair out of the way?" She deftly opens a drawer behind her and pulls out a twist tie. She wraps it around the base of the braid and pinches to lock it in tight.

"Now what about this?" Her eyes dropped meaning-fully to my crotch.

She doesn't have to ask me twice. I grasp the bottom of her tank top and yank it overhead.

I feast on her mouth, tasting the hazelnut coffee, and a hint of toothpaste she must've used before coming out.

I quickly work my way down her body. The sun streams through the kitchen window, and lights her up like she is dawn itself.

Both breasts fit neatly in my palms, and I lift one to capture a nipple in my mouth.

She arches her back and hangs onto the counter. Her braid falls back and dips into the sink.

My mouth works its way down the center between her ribs to her belly button.

Then the shorts have to go, so I slide them down her legs until they pool at her ankles. My tanned hands are dark against her pale body. I lift her by the waist to sit on the counter beside the sink and spread her knees.

She's open for me, and my mouth starts at her knee and works its way up. When my tongue dips into her folds, she arches again, gripping the edge of the counter.

I pull her knees to my shoulders and take a deep dive, feeling her shudder beneath my hands.

I grip her glorious ass and pull her tightly to me.

Her body moves with me as I work her long and hard, my tongue sliding from one end to the other.

I press my thumb into the soft indention of her ass, testing her out, feeling my way.

She gasps, but shifts toward the pressure, so I delve gently inside.

"I've never," she says, but when I press a touch harder, she sucks in a breath and changes her reply to "Yes."

I keep it light and easy there while working deeply with my mouth.

This new exciting combination for her sends her over the edge quickly, and soon she's pulsing against my lips.

One leg kicks straight into the air as she comes on my mouth. "Oh my God, oh my God, Max."

I hold her tight, stretching it out, keeping her going as long as I can. When she relaxes back against the counter, I lift her back to the floor.

Before she can say anything, I whip her around to face the sink and knock her ankles further apart, my hand wrapping around the long braid until my fist is against her skull.

"Holy shit," she says, holding on to the counter for dear life.

I take that as a good sign, so I slide into the slickness of her, my cock filling her until our bodies are flush against each other.

She sucks in another breath. "Oh my God, Max. Oh my God."

I used her own slickness on my thumb and press into that tiny hole again, now that it's so readily in front of me.

Camryn scrambles to clutch something, her mug, then the faucet, and finally finds purchase with one hand on the edge of the sink, and the other grasping the window ledge.

Dawn breaks brighter and more golden as I hold her hip with one hand, working her little pucker with the other. The light tips the peaks of her breasts as they heave forward and back.

The kitchen looks out on a bit of open grass, probably a dog park for the complex. Thankfully, it's deserted at the moment, because Camryn's heaving breasts would be front and center of the window otherwise.

A bird flits to the window and tilts its head at us for a moment as if wondering what the hell we're doing. Then it flies away again.

Camryn laughs. "We scared it off."

I press my thumb more deeply inside her, and she gasps again. "That is so darkly good."

She straightens her arms to shove back against me harder, and I pick up the pace. It's a glorious, excruciatingly pleasurable experience, filling her from behind in this golden kitchen at dawn.

I never want it to end, to keep going on and on until we're both lost in oblivion and the world envelops us.

But the pressure starts to build. I let go of her hip and reach around to find that warm, well-worked clit again.

She sucks in another breath, losing her grip on the window ledge.

"It's so much," she says. "I can't stop."

When her body begins another shuddering pulse, I relinquish my control and empty into her. She collapses forward, her head on the counter, her body quivering in my arms. Her voice is raspy as she says, "Max, Max, Max."

When we have both gone still, I wrap my arms around her. My head fits perfectly between her shoulder blades, and we stay there a moment, locked together against her kitchen counter.

The smell of fresh coffee wafts over us. More birds tweet at each other beyond the window. The world is waking up.

It feels like more than a new day. It's a whole new world.

For a long time, my deli was why I got up every day.

And then for a while, it was the workouts, the muscle mass, the challenge.

But now, it's her.

24

CAMRYN

I spend much of the day reminiscing over my night—
and morning—with Max Pickle.

I'm even sentimental about the coffee he made me,
unwilling to wash the mug or rinse out the coffee pot
until late afternoon.

Every time a bird flies by my kitchen window, my
heart hammers.

What has he done to me?

But by afternoon, I have to pull myself together, and
fast. Max isn't the only one competing this weekend. So
is my brother.

Thankfully, Franklin is easier to tan than Max. He
does the physique competitions, so he wears lengthy
board shorts and requires much less hands-on work.

Because that would be weird.

As I set up for my brother's tan, I make sure I have
my head straight. Don't gush about Max. If Franklin
asks about him, shrug off the question quickly as if Max
is nothing more than another client I have to deal with.

Don't forget I wasn't supposed to be at the evening show with Max, so don't mention it.

Definitely don't bring up his magnificent cock.

My brother's knocking on the door when I suddenly remember all the L.A. Pickle containers in my fridge.

I take a deep breath, remind myself not to let Franklin anywhere near my kitchen, and open the door.

"Sis," he says with a thrust of his chin. "Are you stoked for me? I'm finally moving up in the world."

I step back to let him in. "I am. I really am. Let's make sure you look perfect."

Franklin kicks off his slip-on shoes and pulls his T-shirt over his head.

"You're going with the red shorts again for this competition?" He's wearing them now.

"They're my good luck shorts," he says.

"Red requires a deeper color."

"I trust you to fix me up."

I look him over for any dry spots that will absorb too much tanner and pass him a bottle. "Moisturize the tops of your shoulders and your elbows. I'll be right back."

Franklin squirts lotion into his hand as I head to the kitchen. My nerves are jangling. I'm not ready for him to know about me and Max, and I can't have him figuring it out.

I open the fridge and quickly shove anything marked with the deli's logo to the very back and hide it behind a watermelon.

"What're you doing?" Franklin calls.

"Grabbing some cold water. You want some?"

"No. Trying to keep my muscles defined."

"Right."

I quickly dump some water in a glass to explain my disappearance.

I pause at the doorway as he rubs moisturizer in his elbows. "You might want to get your hands and feet, too. I feel like they were blotchy last time."

He nods. "Did that tall chick make it?"

"No. Dahlia didn't advance. But one of my female clients at your meet also moved up. Camille."

"Are you gonna be there Saturday?"

Of course I'll be there. With Max!

But I keep my face neutral. "There's no beginner meet that day, so I can devote myself to the qualifier. I've got both you and Camille to manage."

"Don't forget Max," he says.

"Oh, right. Max."

Damn, I'm good.

"It should be an easy day for you," he says. "Just us three."

I cross over to the tanning tent to switch out the color. "It will be a nice break. I guess you and Max will get to hang out the whole time."

"Yeah. I get the sense he was all alone last time. I'm sure he'll be glad to have company."

My memory flashes to our hot and heavy make-out session in the room with the chairs.

"I bet he will."

"Good thing we're back at the same level."

"Seems like he was a good influence on you."

Franklin drops the bottle to the floor. "Hardly. I'm the one who got *him* started."

Apparently, Franklin's planning to take credit for everything.

"Time to spray," I say. "Maybe Max needs some bodybuilding friends."

"He's got a hell of a surprise coming tonight. I think we'll have the whole gym coming to see us compete."

I turn to him. "Really?"

"Buster's putting us on the banner over the gym door."

"Instead of the MMA fighters? You're replacing the McClures?"

Franklin rocks back on his heels. "We sure are. Buster's even paying for tickets for everyone to go. That sort of makes the gym a sponsor. Damn." He rubs his hands together. "I should get a logo for my bag. Or a shirt or something."

I have to hold back from rolling my eyes. Franklin's always had a chip on his shoulder that he's never had a sponsor. He thinks it's the mark of having "made it."

"Good for you. I'm ready for you if you want to step over here."

Franklin heads into the tent and turns to face me. "What do you think of Max? You must be getting to know him with all the tans he's had to do."

My throat constricts. *Keep it cool, Camryn.* "He's polite. I can see why you were friends in college."

Franklin laughs. "Too bad he's stuck running that crappy deli."

My ire rises, but I stuff it down. "I've eaten there. It seemed all right."

"It's no five-star restaurant."

"Here comes the spray," I tell him, mostly to make him shut his mouth.

I run the spray over him quickly and evenly. I'm not feeling particularly charitable about him, but I do my usual good job.

"Turn around."

When I finish, he steps out to dry under the fan, and I make sure I'm calm before I approach him again.

"I guess I'll probably mostly hang out with Camille," I say. I'm realizing it might not be a good idea for Max to be around me while Franklin is there.

My brother might see right through us. There are a million tiny things we could do to give ourselves away. Glances. Easy touches.

Franklin picks up on these things easily. He's always on the prowl to make sure men aren't looking at me too long or standing too close. Max will do both of those things.

"That's cool," he says. "Maybe we can grab lunch together between the prejudging and the evening show."

Right. Because we always do that.

But I simply say, "Sure."

I drag the stool out to the middle of the tarp. "Let me do your face real quick, so you have a base coat."

He's mostly quiet while I apply a light layer of tan to his face, ears, and neck.

But when I step away, I can tell he's been holding something inside for a while.

"If you were seeing Max, you'd tell me, right?" His dark eyes pierce mine.

Wow. He's hitting it head-on.

"You know I've sworn off bodybuilders." And that's not a lie.

But sometimes even when you swear something, it happens anyway.

"I guess you heard Malachi dropped out of the circuit entirely."

My belly drops at the mention of the evil ex's name. "No, I wasn't aware." I blocked Malachi on every social media, and I either unfriended or unfollowed anybody close to him so news wouldn't accidentally trickle my way.

Still, I scan the rosters of the open meets, so I won't be caught unaware if he shows up. I hadn't seen him this year, but that didn't mean he wasn't competing somewhere.

And despite not wanting to know his whereabouts, I have to ask. "Does anybody know why?"

Franklin laughs. "Probably got fat."

"How do you know he dropped out? He doesn't usually compete at these lower-level competitions we do."

Franklin stands up and heads to his shoes. "I have my ways. I keep an eye on that jerk. He's not signed up for anything in the L.A. area this year."

"Just as well."

"If he ever comes near you again…"

I hold up a hand. "Enough. It's been over a year. I'm over it."

Which isn't true.

Or is it?

I haven't thought of Malachi since I met Max.

"Well, I'll bust his ass, or anybody's ass who lays a hand on you. There isn't a bodybuilder on this planet worth your time."

"Sure. Okay." I've learned not to bother arguing with him on this.

As Franklin leaves and closes the door, I sit down on the stool myself.

We're going to have to tread carefully.

But I don't think we should confess. If Franklin thinks Max needs to go down, he might have the ratty connections that could wreck his rising career.

25

———

MAX

Franklin insists we go to Buster's Gym early that night.

I'm not in the mood for a lot of shenanigans. I fielded calls from Anthony, Dad, and Jason, all getting on my case that the fiftieth anniversary of Grammy Alma's deli is approaching, and the entire Pickle franchise is hosting an insane amount of events, specials, and other time-consuming plans for the occasion.

I'm grateful for a competent manager and hardworking staff, because I'm stuck in my office most of the day fielding calls from family. Jason even manages to joke that I'm looking as negligent as he did a year ago.

Like that could happen.

I know he and Nova are the deli hotshots, ready to open a second Austin Pickle franchise. And Anthony is the heart and soul of the chain, dreaming up all the recipe creations and keeping the dishes clever and fresh. But I do have other things on my mind.

A clandestine relationship.

A burgeoning bodybuilding career.

A double-double life.

But I don't confess anything. Now is not the time.

When I lock up the front door of the deli, Franklin's beat-up green truck idles outside.

Great.

I'm bone tired after the late night with Camryn. Dehydrated since I can't drink as much as I ordinarily would with the competition on Saturday.

The lack of carbs is going to my head.

And now the best friend whose sister I'm banging is outside my deli as if he knows I'm thinking about ditching a workout.

Franklin slithers out the driver's side window and pops his head over the hood of the truck. "Max, my man! It's time for our hero's welcome. Hop in."

I have no idea what he's talking about, and I don't want to do this. But this is exactly the scenario training partners are for. They make you work out when you don't want to.

So I snatch my bag from the trunk of my car and hop in the passenger seat of his truck. It's a big week for Franklin. He's finally getting where he wants to be. I don't want to bring him down.

"What's up?" I ask.

"You're going to have to wait and see."

He blasts down the street toward Buster's Gym.

He's darker than he was last night. "You see Camryn today?" Saying her name sends a zip through me. I might be exhausted, but it was worth every minute.

"Yeah. She felt I needed to bring on the color for the red shorts. She always tries to make me go with blue."

"No way. The red's good. A power color." It feels right to take his side on this small thing, to throw him off.

Even if she's right.

He punches my arm. "Exactly. That's what I told her. Bitches don't always know best."

I have to grit my teeth, but I'm not going to tip him off.

"What's all the hoopla about?" I ask.

"Not going to give anything away." Franklin laughs and bangs his hand on the steering wheel. "Damn things are good."

He looks like the cat that ate the canary as we pull up to the front of Buster's Gym. "Now lookie there," he says, leaning forward over the steering wheel to peer out the front windshield.

I follow his gaze. A new sign flaps over the door.

Work out with bodybuilding champions Franklin Schultz and Max Pickle.

Oh, damn. Just what I need. Bodybuilding publicity. "What the hell is that?"

"What you mean what the hell? It's awesome. We're celebrities." He opens his door and jumps out, jerking his bag from behind the seat. "Come on."

I heave a sigh and follow him. Inside, the foyer is crammed with the regulars and two guys with cameras.

Buster stands by the front desk. "And here they are, everyone, our rising bodybuilding stars."

Everyone claps and cheers. A few flashes pop off.

Great. Hopefully this is some small specialty rag and the picture will only appear on a random bodybuilding blog. I do my part, smiling and waving, wishing I was wearing anything other than an L.A. Pickle shirt.

The rumble dies, and I think we're done. But no, there's another roar, and another surge of people approach from the weight room.

Now there's a ton more cameras, an absolute strobe effect going off.

What now?

The crowd parts, and none other than MMA fighter Colt McClure and his brother-in-law Hudson approach the desk.

Colt is wildly tall, his curling blond hair lit up close to the lights. He's in a full suit, and I feel even more stupidly dressed in my green T-shirt. Hudson is shorter and considerably leaner, but he looks like he could drop you in a single punch. He, thankfully, is in fighter workout gear.

They're formidable.

A woman steps forward, and her press ID reads *Los Angeles Times*.

Oh, great.

"What a winning tradition you have here at Buster's Gym," the woman says. She holds out her hand and Franklin shakes it first. "Nice to meet both of you. We plan to run a feature on the gym. Would you mind doing some pictures before you change into workout gear?"

More cameras flash. The woman leads the McClures, Buster, Franklin, and me out to the front to take pictures under the new sign. Franklin strikes the first bodybuilding pose, and the photographers ask us to both show them some muscle. I'm not keen on doing this in jeans and my Pickle shirt, but I do as they ask.

As soon as the story hits the websites, our social media person will pick up on the tags.

And my family is going to be all over this.

I'm cold busted.

Finally, we're allowed to change to workout gear and ushered into the private annex where the MMA fighters work out.

I've been in it before. Gym members are allowed back here when there are no private workouts.

The massive octagon where the McClure clan spars, and where frequent amateur matches are held, dominates one side of the room. Around it, a few bleachers are set up for the workouts. The entire room can be converted into a small arena when needed.

Inside the cage, two women punch and kick. When we enter, they stop to look. A slender woman with a long ponytail ducks through the opening above the stairs.

It's Jo, Colt McClure's wife. She's a popular MMA trainer and the reason there are so many women at the gym. I've spotted more than one of her fighters on workouts. They are fierce.

"Is the paparazzi coming this way?" Jo asks.

"Any second," Colt calls up, already removing his tie and jacket. He doesn't seem to enjoy them.

Jo shakes her head. "I'm out of here, if you don't mind. I've had more than my share of photographers in my life."

Colt laughs. "I'll sneak you out the back."

While they take off, Hudson approaches to shake my hand. We're about the same height, although I'm probably bulkier. Even as a fighter, he's retained a boyish quality. "I've seen you around," he says.

"I've seen you on TV."

He grins. "You follow MMA?"

"Definitely the fighters from this gym," I say.

Franklin charges right up and extends his hand. "I'm Franklin Schultz. Pleased to be back here with the other star athletes."

I wince. Franklin is something else.

But Hudson takes it in stride. "Nice to have you. It'll be fun seeing how you guys do your thing compared to ours."

"We can't mess up our beautiful faces." Franklin waves his hand across his ugly mug. "It's all about the judging."

Hudson laughs and shakes his head.

The photographers set up numerous shots of us doing push-ups and performing the bodybuilding poses. They have Buster stand behind us, arms crossed, as if he's overseeing the champions himself.

I want to argue that this is an awful lot of fuss for a couple of guys who only won some small meets, but this is Franklin's moment. He can have it.

I keep my reservations about my future in the sport to myself.

Eventually the reporter and photographers head out, and we're left with the family and Buster.

"We may not have everything you need back here,"

Buster says. "But I can have some things moved in if you need it."

I glance around. The area is set up for fighters. A kettlebell station. A line of punching bags. And of course, the cage.

But there's an entire set of free weights in the back corner. Mats. Stretch bands and sandbags. "I think we've got everything but maybe a lat pull," I say. "We're fine going back out to the main room for that."

Franklin cuts me off. "A lat pull would be great," he says. "And make sure the stacks go in increments of twenty-five and ten."

Buster nods. "I'll take care of it. You guys have fun." He claps me on the back and heads through the accordion door back to the regular weight room.

Franklin seems positively giddy. "Well, we're here. What do we do?"

"Our workout," I say. "We have a competition on Saturday."

Colt pops through the back door. He's chucked his suit for fight shorts and a tank top. "Photos over?"

"All clear," I say. "Do they follow you around?" Colt's been off the circuit for quite a few years. He and his wife have at least two kids, but before all that, they were quite the newsworthy couple. The L.A. papers were all over them in my college years.

"It's Hudson's time to shine," Colt says. "But because it's all in the family, from my dad right on down through me, Jo, and Hudson, they never leave us alone."

"And here we brought them back to your door," I say.

"It's all right." Colt leans in. "But I wouldn't mind a bit of a scandal to put them off our scent."

I laugh. If only he knew.

Hudson gestures to the weight set. "I'm about to throw down some reps, you want to come?"

Franklin jumps at it. "I do. Let's see what you've got."

I plunk down on a bench to pull on my weightlifting gloves. "It's quite a setup you've got back here."

Colt sits beside me. "Didn't used to be. Was a big empty hole. My dad made Buster add this on when he expected me to start killing it on the circuit. I was a sore disappointment for a long time."

This is news to me. "Really? Why so?"

Colt laughs. "Big, fat loser. He brought me back here to get back to my roots. Or rather, *his* roots. Buster's good, though. He's got a solid head on his shoulders. If you need advice, he's a good man to talk to."

I fiddle with the gloves. Advice might be exactly what I need.

"So, did I hear you own a restaurant or something?" Colt asks.

I nod. "Family business. I'm expected to do a lot with it, so this bodybuilding thing is getting in the way."

"But they support you, right?"

Might as well confess. "They don't know about it." I glance back at the accordion door. "But after tonight, that's going to change."

Colt rears back on the bench. "Oh, hell. Nobody told us you were keeping this on the down low. We could have called off the press hounds."

I shrug. "That was for my buddy Franklin. I can't hide the whole thing much longer. I'm getting out of the obscure levels and into the part where people start paying attention. It was bound to get out."

Colt nods. "It can be a bit of a bumpy ride. So, you gonna call them up before they hear from somebody else?"

"You think I should?"

"Definitely. If your old man is anything like mine, the last thing you want is him roaring like a wildebeest over the telephone."

"I think you've got that one pegged exactly right. Maybe I'll go do that before they wire their stories in."

"We'll be here."

I head out the back door, giving Franklin a thumbs up as he spots Hudson. "Making a quick call," I say.

Time to fess up to my family.

My two careers are about to clash.

26

CAMRYN

I don't expect the text from Max that night after his workout with my brother.

Bone tired but want to see you.

My late night is catching up with me, too, but the idea of him coming over sparks a rush of exhilaration.

We can take it light and easy.

Despite what he said, when I open my door, Max isn't the weary man I expect. His eyes are bright, and he's in workout gear.

"I didn't want to take the time to stop at home."

"That's fine."

I close the door and lean against it. "Has something happened?"

He rubs his head, dropping his bag to the floor. "Franklin ambushed me at Buster's Gym with a whole press junket. The *L.A. Times* is doing a feature on Buster's Gym and all the champions who have come out of it."

I push away from the door. "But isn't that great?"

"It would be, except I haven't told anyone about the bodybuilding."

I lead him over to the pillows in the corner. I straighten the tiny pink shorts I wore this morning and arrange my tank as we settle in. Obviously, we're here to do some talking.

"So, no one at work? Your brothers?"

He shakes his head, leaning over to unlace his crosstrainers. "It's a hobby."

"Big hobby."

He grins. "The first competition I signed up for was basically a dare by your brother."

"He's like that." When Max pulls off his shoes, I hook them together and set them aside. "So, are you going to tell them?"

"I called one of my brothers and sent a quick message to my dad. Our PR department will pick up on it tomorrow when it hits the paper anyway. It's out."

"Is that such a bad thing?"

His thumb rubs against the symbol imprinted near the hem of his black shorts. "They'll rib me about it incessantly, but it's fine. It's just a lot. Coming clean on my second vocation. And then there's you."

He pulls me onto his lap. "We'll have to tell your brother eventually."

I might as well fess up, too. "Franklin drilled me about it today during his tan. I had to straight-up lie."

Max sighs. "I don't want to disrupt anything before this next competition. But maybe when Franklin and I get knocked out of the running, it will be time to bring it up."

I lay my head against his chest and nod. "I think that's a good idea. Otherwise he will blame us for messing with his mojo."

"Sounds about right." He runs his thumb up and down the inside of my elbow, and the sparks begin to stir in my body.

"So, you think I could borrow your shower?"

I shift in his lap to face him. Now that I'm close, I do see the tiredness in the corners of his eyes. But they are bright with eagerness. And we're young. Resilient. "On one condition."

He squeezes my waist. "What's that?"

"That you share it with me."

"That's a condition I was hoping for." His grin is slow and lazy and promises all sorts of devilish things.

I roll out of his lap. "I'll get the water started."

I pull two towels from the closet and set them on the counter by the sink. My bathroom is nothing fancy, your typical apartment-style with a narrow counter, plus a toilet and ceramic tub against the wall.

But I do have a cool wall socket lamp. It's an over-sized nightlight that emits a vivid blue, and when it warms up, a set of butterflies on filigree wires dance and shift with the heat of the light.

It creates the effect of a meadow at twilight, so I snap off the overhead and flip it on.

"That's a cool light." Max's voice rumbles through the small space. I can feel the vibrations in my toes.

He leaves his bag outside the door. "I think someone needs to get naked."

I turn to him in the wavering blue light. So far, he's always undressed me.

He leans against the frame of the door, arms crossed as he waits.

I guess I'm going to do this thing. I'm not wearing much, a tank top and pajama shorts.

I grab the hem of the shirt and slowly pull it up. The fabric catches on my breasts, then tugs free.

My hair is long and loose and falls everywhere as I pull the shirt over my head.

When I can see again, Max's watching with a half-smile. "Perfection."

I drop the shirt to the floor. I take my time inching the bottoms over my hips. I watch his shorts begin to tent out. With every jump of his cock, I slide my shorts down a little more. Only when he seems to be fully erect, do I let them fall to my ankles.

"Nice." He rubs a palm across his cheek. "I don't have near the reveal you do."

"I think I've already gotten to know you pretty well." I step forward. "I can do the honors."

I grasp the bottom of his shirt and pull it over his head. And it's true. I know every plane of his body, every indention and muscle. I can tell when he's hydrated. When he hasn't had carbs for a few days.

I run my hands over his chest, up that thick, corded neck, and down both bulging shoulders to the muscles of his upper arms.

If we want to get technical, I once loved someone who's gone far past Max's level of body development. Another bodybuilder on his way up. Malachi didn't rise fast, but he did rise through all the levels Max is at now and kept going.

Without me.

He banged every woman, and, as I later found out, every man, he needed to get every advantage, every opportunity. Free supplements. Invitations to meets. One of the last images I was sent by a jealous female body-builder was of Malachi with his mouth in the crotch of another man.

I have to shake this off. I know as my feelings grow for Max, I'll have to fight my fear more and more.

But it *is* different this time.

Max's gentlemanly manners, open kindness, and devastating physique is a combination Malachi could never have boasted. He had a cruel streak and cared most about winning.

Max doesn't have a cruel bone in his body.

I slip my hand into the waistband of the fitted shorts. I slide them down an inch, revealing the charcoal gray of fitted boxers. I decide to speed up the process and bring both down at the same time.

Standing barefoot in front of him, I barely reach his chest. "Ready to get wet?" I ask.

"I'm hoping you already are."

He has that right.

I shift the shower curtain aside and step into the tub. The room is dim and blue, and the spray cascades down my body like a waterfall in a hidden lagoon.

Max steps in behind me and immediately envelops me in an embrace. His hands go everywhere, following the contours of my body, cupping my breasts.

"I thought I was exhausted," he says. "But right now, I am painfully awake."

He dips his head in the water, then shakes, droplets flying. I laugh and cover my face. "You're like a dog!"

"Exactly." He grabs my hips and pulls me back against his hard cock.

I suck in a breath. I am so ready for him.

He turns me around to face him. "The height differential isn't doing us any favors."

I laugh. "It's true."

He kneels in front of me, pressing his head against my ribs.

I sink my fingers into his wet hair, curling in the spray. His kisses move down my belly, and he lifts one of my thighs to his shoulder.

Fingers slip inside me.

I suck in a breath and clutch his shoulders, water streaming across my shoulders and down my body to where his hands work me, his mouth drifting lower.

I clutch his head, holding on for dear life, but my standing leg wants to give out.

I lean down. "Take me."

He sits on the bottom of the tub. He guides my knees around his waist and settles me down on his cock.

The water flows over both of us, my hair slick. His hands grasp my thighs, and he lifts me until I'm at the tip, then brings me down again.

I think it's going to be hot and heavy and fast, but it somehow isn't.

He looks up at me, his wet lashes framing those beautiful eyes. "You're a goddess," he whispers.

He makes me feel like one. The blue light dances in the shadows. My hair cascades between us. Ripples of pleasure pulse through my body as we move together.

The bathroom fills with steam, and it's a grotto, the water, the man, and me floating over him.

That first aching tendril of emotion slips through me. I knew it was there, waiting to be nurtured.

But there's no denying it. I'm falling for this man. Our affair may be secret, illicit, known only to us. But in this space, we melt together in the semi-dark, his hands caressing my body. His expressive face tells me everything about what he's feeling, and I know it is so much more.

I hold onto his strong arms and move my own body over his. I'm swamped with emotion and pleasure and passion for him.

His hands tighten on my back, and I move faster, up and down, our eyes locked together.

The tension mounts, winding like a clock.

Before I've prepared for it, before I know it's there, the orgasm springs, rippling out like a stone dropped in a pond. I gasp out loud, and Max holds me tight.

He pulses inside me, warm, gentle, like life itself. I can see it all. Mornings and days and nights. Good times. Hard times. Stretching out beyond this moment into our future.

My tears mix with the water raining down. How did this happen? How did I find this man? How did he become mine?

There's nothing like this feeling. It obliterates

anything I felt with Malachi. Anything that came before. It's pure, untouchable, as bright as starlight.

We exhale together, and he keeps me close. His face is buried in my breasts and he clutches me like there is nothing left in the world but us.

MAX

I know exactly when my employees find out about the bodybuilding article.

I'm in the kitchen with my manager Andre, discussing all the extra work required for the fiftieth anniversary and who to give extra shifts to cover it.

Andre is quiet and listens carefully. He's mid-fifties, soft-spoken, and dependable. His tall, lanky figure is a fixture at my deli, and has been for years.

But I glance through the door to the restaurant and spot Tiana and Karen whispering over their phones behind the register.

I pause in talking to Andre as they wave Angelo over.

The restaurant is quiet, only a few customers sitting at tables. Ordinarily, I would assume that someone found a funny meme and wants to share.

But the way they keep looking through the open door to the kitchen, and how their eyes skitter away from me when they catch me observing them, tells me they have discovered my secret.

Time for a staff meeting.

But I guess I better break it to Andre first. "Let's head to my office," I say.

Andre checks his watch. "Don't you need to be heading out? You said you'd only be here till mid-afternoon today."

"I think my plans may have just changed."

Andre closes the door behind him. "What's up, Max?"

I drop into my rolling chair. "I was interviewed by the newspaper last night."

"That's great," Andre says. "Is it about the fiftieth anniversary?"

"Not exactly. I suppose most everybody's noticed I've taken on a fitness hobby in the last year and a half."

"Hard to miss."

I'm sure. "I was convinced by my training partner to do a bodybuilding competition, and I won."

Andre stands straighter. "You won? That's awesome!"

I nod. "Yeah, it was fun. But then I advanced to the next level and I placed there. So, I'm headed to a competition this weekend that's a biggish deal."

"Are you going to be like Arnold Schwarzenegger?" Andre asks.

I force my smile. Everyone always thinks of Arnold. "No. I'm not going for that level. In fact, I'm quite sure I'll be knocked out at this round. I was already outclassed last time. It was a miracle that I placed in the top three."

"Should we all show up for your big event? We could make a team outing of it."

"No, no." I imagine all my employees gawking at me in tiny bodybuilding trunks and cringe. Thankfully I was able to stay in normal workout clothes for the photos they took last night.

"Really?" Andre frowns. "I think it would be fun."

"I wanted to mention it to everyone, since I'm going to be in the newspaper. I didn't want everyone to feel like they'd been left out of something that's fairly public knowledge."

Andre nods. "Got it. I still think we should all show up."

I shake my head. "I'm quite certain it isn't necessary. We don't—well, the outfits are a little…"

Andre nods vigorously. "Got it."

I do have to put him off. Andre is the type of manager who will rally the staff to support me. But it's more than tiny trunks at stake. Several staff members have seen me with Camryn, and I can't risk them talking about her in front of Franklin.

My phone buzzes. My brother's ugly mug fills the screen.

Andre steps back. "Would you like me to go tell everybody? Or did you want to make a big deal about it yourself?"

"Actually, you tell them. Downplay it. I'm going to deal with this call from my brother. We have a ton to do for Grammy's celebration."

Andre heads out, and I pick up the phone. "What's up, bro."

Jason's face is ridiculously close to the camera. "It's bruh now. You're stuck in the 90s."

"I was in kindergarten in the 90s."

Jason scrunches his face. "You're still old."

"I could squish you like a bug." I press my thumb to the screen.

"You're about to get your chance."

"At the fiftieth?"

"Nope. We got an all-points bulletin this morning about the bodybuilding empire involving our own dear brother. We know all about your big competition in three days, so Nova and I thought we'd come down and hang with the family and go watch you get your butt kicked on stage."

"Wait? When are you arriving?"

He waves his phone around and now I can see he's at LAX.

"You're here?"

"You catch on slow." Jason laughs again.

"You want me to pick you up?"

"Nope. Already rented a car. A big one. We're waiting on Dad and Anthony to arrive."

Oh, man. "The whole crew is coming?"

"Not Grammy. Or the cousins. They said they didn't want to see you in your underwear on stage."

"Thank God."

"Hey, look who I found!"

The phone blurs for a second, then the face of my brother Anthony appears. "We made signs." He unrolls a long sign that says *Nobody beats a Pickle like Max.*

Oh. My. God.

"Please tell me there are only one of those," I say.

"Good point, bruh," Jason says. "We'll see if we can get more made by Saturday. "Thanks for the tip.""

"Tip of the pickle," Anthony says with a laugh.

Jason turns the phone to his face. "Our baby brother made a sexual innuendo. He's all growed up."

Anthony punches Jason's arm, and the phone blurs again.

Jason's face returns. "We're heading to Dad's gate to snag him. You want to go for dinner?"

"I have to work out. I can't eat carbs until Friday."

"No prob. We'll pick a steak place that's open late. If you have any ideas, text us, otherwise Dad will do his thing and call around."

I can see I'm outvoted. There goes an evening with Camryn. Would she want to come?

Before I think it through, I say, "I might bring somebody."

I instantly regret it. Anthony grabs the phone back. "Max's got a girlfriend!" he sings-songs.

Jason grabs the phone back. "Real ho or bro ho?"

God, we're all teenagers again. "Real. And I need to ask her if she even wants to come. You might be too much. In fact, I know you are."

"What? Us?" Jason makes another crazy face. "Besides, we brought reinforcements. Nova's here." He angles the phone and Nova gives a wave. She's walking several steps behind the brothers, no doubt to distance herself from their antics.

"Hey, Nova!" I call.

"I'm trying to keep them in line." She shakes her head. "And failing."

"It's been tried before, my love," Jason says. He slows down so they can both be in the frame, like a cheesy selfie. "Nobody tames the BEASTS!"

Nova rolls her eyes. "Help!" she says.

"He's no help," Jason says. "He's the worst of us all."

The phone blurs again. "Oh, I see Dad. Catch you later." He waves and the call ends.

Holy shit. The entire Pickle clan is descending on California to watch me on stage.

And Buster is paying for gym members to come as well.

If I wanted to keep quiet about my hobby, that ship has sailed.

I shove the phone in my pocket and head out to the kitchen.

Andre has all the staff surrounding him. "And there he is, our champion bodybuilder."

A great cheer erupts, and I play the part, clasping my hands over my head in the champion pose.

"We need a display case," Angelo says. "Right by the register. We could show off your medals or trophies or whatever it is you get."

"I'm not sure that's necessary," I say.

"Of course it is," Tiana argues. "We've got ourselves a winner. We want everyone to know it. Besides, we can point to your killer picture, and nobody is going to argue over expired coupons."

I laugh. "We'll see. I have to head out. The other Pickles have descended for the competition. Make sure everything looks good. You know how Dad is. He's going to show up unannounced to inspect. We need everything well-stocked and as fresh as we've got."

"We'll take care of it," Andre says. "Go have fun."

I jingle my keys in my pocket as I head out to my car. I'm grateful for my team. Because my life just got a thousand times more complicated.

28

CAMRYN

Life turns down a notch for the next couple of days. Max's family comes to town, and although he asks if I want to meet them, I decide that's not the greatest idea. If his brothers, who from all accounts appear to be quite the rambunctious pranksters, figure out I'm the girl he mentioned, they could easily expose it to my brother at the meet. And we're not ready for that explosion yet.

Stupid Franklin. Stupid mess.

I do my work, tanning and prepping clients for the big weekend. We decide Max can wait until the night before the competition for his last tan.

I miss him, and our evenings together play over and over in my mind. But I am glad to catch up on my sleep.

Today I'm meeting Amy, Max and Franklin's posing coach. She asked to get together for a late lunch so we can discuss a business opportunity for us both.

I warn her I'm completely booked with a full waiting list, but she says I'll want to hear what she has to say.

She's picking up the tab, so I'm fine with a quick lunch. Besides, it's fun to talk about Max with someone who knows him. Other than Dahlia, of course, who still mentions licking that man candy whenever she comes over for a touch up. It's hard as hell to keep the secret.

When I arrive at the bistro, Amy sits at a table along the back wall. Her blond ponytail swings as she waves at me. We don't know each other terribly well, so there's no hugs or familiarity as I sit down.

"So glad you came," she says.

We order pasta and I ask her, "So what's going on?"

"Franklin told me you're interested in traveling. I know you have a lot of great clients here, but the opportunity I'm looking at would mostly fall after the amateur season. And if it goes well enough, you might want to leave your beginners behind."

I stir my straw in my glass of water. "Tell me more."

"So, there's a company that contracts on-site assistance for the bodybuilders once they start traveling. They want there to be some continuity, plus provide English speakers so the competitors can communicate what they need. We're not assigned bodybuilders, and the roster might change some from location to location, but there are enough of them who do the entire circuit that they could become regulars."

"So what level are we talking about?" My heart is already thumping at the idea of traveling.

"We would handle most of the international meets in Europe, two in Australia, and one in South Africa. Over here, with everyone already speaking English, there's less opportunity. But in these other countries, the bigger companies hire people to travel and provide services. People like us."

It's the next step up. I'm being offered it. "Are you going to do it?"

"I already signed a contract. But they still need tanning and makeup artists. I told them about you. They've seen how many people have moved up based on your work. They're excited about you. You could always sign on for a single season, then decide from there if you want to keep doing it."

"When does it start? There are two more amateur meets."

"Three weeks. So, you would be able to work one of those and have time to refer out the other. You would clip the last two qualifiers, though. I'm not sure Franklin or Max will get further. Do you have more?"

"Maybe Camille." Only Malachi ever reached that level, and he obviously isn't my client anymore. "But what about Franklin and Max? Have you told them you're leaving?"

"Not yet. I wanted to speak to you first. Do you think your brother is going to move up? I'm not sure he's a candidate."

"Hard to say. He just now got a win. But Max?"

"He doesn't supplement, if you know what I mean. His journey is about to end. You know that."

"He was out-developed last time, but he placed. He has stage presence."

"And they will all have stage presence this weekend. Don't get me wrong. Max is killer and I like him a lot.

But he's in the toughest category and he isn't a career player."

My gut rebels at this, but I can't argue with her without tipping her off.

"Probably so."

"See?" Her face is like sunshine, she so happy. "I would love to have someone I know going with me on this journey. Can you imagine it? All the international meets. Meeting all of the bodybuilders. Italy! Africa! Australia! This is an opportunity of a lifetime. I've always wanted to be able to coach all the way up to Mr. Olympia. If I meet the right bodybuilder and he likes my style, I could get on a real team."

That has been my dream, too. Her energy is infectious. She believes it can be done.

But Amy doesn't know about me and Max. Can I leave him in three weeks? Be gone for months and months? We've barely gotten started with this new relationship.

"I have to think about it," I say. "I do have some things keeping me here."

"You mean that brother of yours?" She sips her glass of tea, eyebrows lifted. I know what she's getting at.

"Is he being difficult?"

Amy shrugs. "He's not the ideal client. I'm sure you know his good and bad points."

"I know."

"I'm telling you. This is the next big opportunity for you. You're single. You're young. What better time to travel around the world?"

Our food arrives, and our conversation shifts to more general, work-related things.

I like Amy, and she's been a constant in the circuit for a long time. I know she's good people.

And this is exactly the opportunity I've been waiting for.

There's only one thing holding me back.

Max.

29

MAX

Three days without Camryn is pure torture.

But with the entire family here, workouts, and planning the fiftieth anniversary, I have zero opportunity to see her.

Even our Friday night tanning session, which I had hoped would be a lot more, is interrupted when my brothers text me every three minutes.

Besides, I have a fresh tan, we can't exactly wreck it getting hot and heavy.

I settle for a long searing kiss and a reminder that my family will be leaving town on Sunday. Then we can get back to our new normal.

Dad has insisted we all stay at the hotel so we can be near each other to plan the event while waiting for the competition. They follow me to the deli and even show up for guest passes at Buster's.

It's a lot.

Anthony is the most curious about my routine, so when I rise and shine at five a.m. on competition day to start my carb loading, he's on a chair in the hallway, waiting for me to come out of my room.

"Hey," I say. "I don't remember you being an early riser."

"Right back at you. Funny the things we adapt to when we start being adults."

"Who are you calling an adult?" I shoulder my bag. "I'm meeting my training partner for an early breakfast. You want to come?"

Anthony jumps from his chair. "Absolutely." He gestures to his jeans and a T-shirt that reads *Pickles are a big dill.* "Am I dressed all right for the day? I assume these aren't fancy affairs."

"Trust me. You're classy compared to what a lot of people will wear to this thing."

"Awesome." We head down the hall.

When we arrive at the diner, Franklin is already there with three members of our gym.

"We have an entourage," he says, gesturing to the other twenty-something guys. "They want to see how the champions do it."

"Good to see you all. This is my brother Anthony. He wants to see exactly how much junk we're going to eat today."

"Let's show him!" Franklin roars, and the sleepy servers glance our way. The diner is empty save for us and a lone table of two elderly men sipping coffee.

The guys whoop it up as they settle at a table, arguing over the calorie counts of French toast versus pancakes.

This day is already going better than the last competition, where I spent most of the day alone. I start to see the appeal of having a crew.

Anthony watches in awe as Franklin and I wolf down plate after plate of high-carb meals. Franklin makes a big show of taking insulin to make sure he doesn't wreck his system with too high a sugar load after weeks of low carbs.

He's never done that before, and I have a feeling it's all for show. But I say nothing. This is his day more than mine. He's been waiting a long time to feel like somebody.

When we finally clear the plates, Franklin and his crew head over to Camryn's for his final tan. I send her a quick text as a heads-up that there will be more than her brother present.

She writes back. *Thanks for the warning. Can't wait to see you later.*

I smile and tap out an addendum, *Naked?*
Always.

"You don't need to tan today, too?" Anthony asks as we load into my Audi.

"I got mine last night. Camryn will touch me up on site."

I'm careful to keep my tone even to avoid the slightest hint that Camryn is more than someone who makes me look good for competition. It seems to work, because Anthony drops the subject and reverts to talk of the various diets I do through different stages of the training.

We have time to kill, so I drop by one of the nutrition shops that open early on competition day. I show Anthony the supplements and superfood that get me through the long hours. He's very thoughtful about the whole thing, and I finally ask him, "Are you thinking of taking up the call?"

"Oh no," he says. "I'm always interested in different ways people eat. This is great."

I'm glad Anthony has come along. Jason is fun, but our nonstop verbal jockeying wouldn't help my nerves as I head into this new level of competition. Anthony is chill, thoughtful, and easy-going, the perfect sidekick for a stressful day.

I spot the chocolate bar Camryn brought me last time. I pick up a couple of them.

"What's so great about those?" Anthony asks.

"Carbs. Fiber. They taste good without making you too thirsty."

"I noticed you didn't drink much at breakfast."

I squeeze my fist to pump out the muscles of my bicep. "See these veins? They don't show unless you're dehydrated. Part of the judging."

"Crazy."

As we check out, he points out a sign that reads, *Anabolic steroids are prescription only.* He leans in. "So, do you do them?"

I pass my credit card to the cashier. "No. Not part of my process."

"But people clearly do. Otherwise, they wouldn't have a sign."

I nod.

"Does your training buddy?"

I shrug. "Not as far as I know. Physique doesn't require the bulk that traditional bodybuilding does. Although, they merge closer every year."

We head out to the car. I could probably confide in Anthony about Cam, but as we head toward the arena, I don't. I know what's happening with Camryn is important and real. But I'm not ready to share it or defend it against my brothers' endless ribbing and nonstop questions.

Anthony stays with me as I check in and grab my pin. He openly gawks at the size of the people around us.

"I thought you were big. But you're looking small compared to some of these guys."

"We're getting to the big-time," I say.

"You think you have a chance?" A female bodybuilder in a mermaid green bikini strides by and Anthony almost stumbles over his own feet.

"I'm going to get stomped."

He drags his gaze back to me. "Really?"

"I'm going to have fun with it. That's all it ever was."

Despite this being a higher-level match, the setup is much the same as all the rest. Bodybuilders in their warm-up suits line the walls of a huge empty room. The women must be going first here, because they are the ones already showing skin.

Anthony is entranced. "They're unbelievable. How do they look like that?"

"Dedication. Nutrition. Workouts. It's simple. But

you need the willpower to do it."

"And you do?"

"So far."

A line of women file by, only a few feet from us. A few glance at us and one winks at Anthony. "I'm down with big pickles," she says as she passes.

I reach over and bump his chin where his jaw has dropped. "Control those salivary glands, brother."

"You think I can meet one?"

"You going to ask them about their food choices?" I punch his arm.

"Maybe."

"I take it you're not dating anybody," I say.

"I did for a while. But she moved on."

"You never mentioned her."

"Wasn't too busted up about it. That should tell you everything." He elbows me. "What about you?"

I choose my words carefully. "The way Dad keeps me hopping with this anniversary thing, I barely have time to bang one off in the shower."

No lies there.

"But you were going to bring someone to dinner the first night."

Shit. Right. "I just started seeing someone. I can't let you all scare her off."

"Now that's totally fair. Dad is on a rampage anyway. For someone who has turned over the franchise, he sure is all over this party."

"It's his last big shindig."

"It's a lot."

Franklin and the entourage arrive, loud and jocular.

There are more of them, four now. Security stops them at the door.

He's forgotten he's only allowed two guests backstage, spots generally reserved for your trainer and maybe a coach.

He chooses two of them, and the others take off.

Franklin grabs his pin, then they all head toward us and plop down on the floor.

"Now, we wait," Franklin says.

I unzip my bag and pull out one of the chocolate bars. I toss it to him. "For luck."

He holds the chocolate in his hands, and his expression sets off my alarm bells. "How did you know I like these?"

My heart skips a beat for a second, thinking I'm busted. But I smooth it over. "Dude, I know when you take a shit. We've been training together too long for me not to know all your brands."

He's not convinced. "Camryn's the only one who gives me these."

I decide I should confess at least that much. "That must be why she gave one to me. She told me you liked them. I offered to get this round."

His eyes pierce mine. "When was that?"

"When I got my tan last night." I hold out my arms. "I'm damn dark, right?"

"Yeah." He shoves the chocolate in his bag. "You want to get a pump on?" He turns to the other two guys. "You have to keep your muscles pumped so they're not flat for the stage."

"I'm gonna wait," I say. I decide not to remind him

not to burn the glycogen stores too early. He's in teacher mode and enjoying his spotlight. I'm happy to let him have it.

Franklin and the other two guys take off for another corner to do some light reps and push-ups. I keep my eye on the door, hoping Camryn will show while Franklin's occupied on the other side of the room.

Otherwise, talking to her seems risky. The way Franklin already suspects something's going on, he'll be looking for any sign he's being lied to.

Which, of course, he is. We'll have to clear this up tomorrow after the competition is over. It can't keep going. It's not right.

The lightweight classes start passing by.

"Those guys aren't built like you," Anthony observes.

"There are weight classes. I'm in the biggest one."

Franklin's group is called, so he strips down to his red shorts to line up. "You guys go on around to the auditorium," he tells his friends." I'll be out there in a bit. I'm gonna dominate." He strikes a pose.

The two guys clap him on the back and head out.

I text Camryn. *Your brother's about to go on stage.*

I'm in the audience. I owe him a watch.

Fair enough.

When Franklin comes back around, he's pumped. "I crushed it," he says. "I'm going to take this qualifier. Bring on Nationals."

Within minutes, Camryn pops in the door.

"Yo, sis! What do you think? Did I kill it, or did I kill it?"

"You killed it," she says with a laugh. "Amy's doing great work with you. You looked confident and strong. And of course, your tan was flawless." She gives him a quick grin.

Her eyes don't even cut over to me. But I can see the tension in how she fiddles with the bristles on one of the brushes on her belt.

He jerks on his sweatpants. "Now we wait for the evening show."

"You guys have to sit here all day?" Anthony asks.

"We usually do," I say. "But today we're going to head out for a quick lunch with everybody and come back."

Camryn finally turns to me. "You'll have time. With the women going first, the physique and male body-building are closer together than usual." She steps up to me. "Your tan looks good. Let me check a few things. Can I borrow him a second?"

Franklin's hand twitches, and I don't miss the tension in his jaw, but he says nothing as Camryn leads me over the corner. "I had to get us away. I didn't think I could hold this disinterested expression any longer."

I almost reach out to tuck a stray tendril of hair behind her ear, but I catch myself. "I'm with you. It's tough."

"Unzip your jacket and let me take a look," she says. "I don't expect any surprises."

I drop the jacket to the floor, and she walks around me, cool and professional. Her fingers never even brush my skin.

"I'm not going to ask you to take your pants off. I know we handled the white patch last night."

"It seemed fine this morning."

"Good."

"Franklin's already got laser vision pointed in this direction. I wanted to tell you good luck. And I'll be watching."

"Thanks. Do you mind taking my brother Anthony around the auditorium? He'd like to see it."

"Glad to," she says. "And I assume it's still a secret."

"I haven't told a soul."

She nods. "Not a problem. Let me get out of here so you can do your last-minute work out. I think Amy's going to stop by, too."

"I'll be thinking about you up there."

"You better not," she says with a warning look. "That might cause things to, um, grow unnecessarily."

"Damn right it will."

She bites her lip to keep from laughing. "Focus on your stage presence. It's the only thing that can get you points, because let me tell you, the heavyweights here today are all monsters."

"I'm just here for fun."

"Good." She walks ahead of me to talk to Franklin again for a moment, then offers to take Anthony around to watch the show. "You can come with us," she says to Franklin.

"I'll hang back here and wait for Max. I want his thoughts on how he did."

"Done." She turns to Anthony. "I will take this Pickle on around to the front."

Franklin frowns, but he lets it go. My brother doesn't inspire a testosterone rush. He's too laid back.

Before they've even left the room, they are already talking up a storm.

I love that. She's fitting right in. And Anthony doesn't even know she should.

30

CAMRYN

So, all the Pickles have decided to show up for the morning prejudging.

When Anthony and I step inside the auditorium, a great roar goes up in the center row.

"They made it," Anthony says. "I wasn't sure they were going to come until the evening."

I knew I would probably meet Max's family today. It's easier to do under the guise of being a tanning artist than showing up as a girlfriend for dinner.

But because I can't tip off Franklin, I had to wear my usual tanning attire, albeit my favorite set of gray floral yoga pants and a matching fitted short-sleeved top. I wish I could find a place to stuff all my gear, but I had to keep up the appearance of tanner-only right up to the last minute.

The judges switch out as they move from physique to classic bodybuilding, so we have a few minutes before the lights will go down again. I tuck as many brushes as

I can into my side pocket, so I look less like a makeup-store Rambo as we approach the family.

The dad is easy to spot, with gray at the temples. He's a dead ringer for the man sitting next to him, who must be Jason. On the other side of Jason is a woman with long brown hair. Jason's fiancé.

Anthony slides into the seat next to his father.

"Who's this?" he asks.

"Dad, this is Camryn. She's the reason Max no longer looks like a fish belly. She's also Franklin's sister. You know, Max's training buddy."

He extends a hand. "Lovely to meet you, Camryn," he says. "Everyone calls me Sherman."

My nerves jangle until I nearly see spots. I'm shaking Max's dad's hand. And Max hasn't even gotten to introduce me.

I try to pull myself together. "Nice to meet you. Did you get to see any of the others compete?"

"Just got here," Jason says. "I had to hurry them up to make it."

The woman leans forward. "He means *I* had to get everyone out the door. I'm Nova, by the way. Jason's better half."

"You got that right," Jason says.

I wave down the row. "It's great you are all here. Max has kept quiet about his competitions."

Jason smirks. "If it wasn't for the *L.A. Times*, we'd still be in the dark."

"I'm sure Max had his reasons," Anthony says.

Sherman leans forward. "Camryn, do *you* know his reasons?"

My heart hammers. I'm not sure what to say.

But Anthony rescues me. "Don't harass Camryn. Her loyalties lie elsewhere. And she's too sweet for you all to hassle."

Sherman's eyebrows lift. He looks between the two of us, and I can see his wheels turning. *Uh oh.*

"Have you asked this lovely young woman to lunch with us? We'd be delighted to have her and her brother."

Uh oh!

I think fast. "Maybe? My brother has a lot of friends showing up, so they may have different plans."

Sherman sits back. "The invitation's open."

The lights go down, and I let out a long breath. Is Sherman trying to hook me up with Anthony? This is trickier than I thought it would be.

The announcer strides onto the stage. "And now for our heavyweight competitors. These twenty athletes will be competing for five slots at Nationals."

"This is exciting," Anthony says, rubbing his hands together. I have to smile. I like this brother.

The first competitor is the winner of last week's meet. He strides out with confidence, perfectly on tempo with the music. He rolls through the poses with the ease of someone who is used to being on stage.

"Dayum," says Jason. "That dude could break me in half."

The competitor steps off to one side and holds a side bicep pose as the next man comes on stage.

"This goes by quick," Anthony whispers.

"There are a lot of them."

This one is not quite as smooth as the first. His symmetry is imperfect, and his calves are underdeveloped. He might have more general bulk than Max, but he's not going to beat him. No charisma.

The next three competitors are similar. They look good, but not great. Still, Max is behind in the physique at this level, like Amy and I predicted during our lunch.

About halfway through the group, Max comes out on stage. The auditorium is fairly empty, as is typical for the morning show. So when all the Pickles stand and start hooting quite a few judges and spectators turn to look.

I stand up with them in solidarity. I get the sense the Pickles do whatever they want when it comes to backing up family.

When I sit down, Anthony leans in. "Were we not supposed to do that?"

"It's fine."

Max runs through the poses. My heart pounds seeing him up there. It's hard not to. He's beautiful and strong. The light hits his tan perfectly. I decide, though, to take him one shade darker next time. His grin is infectious, and when he holds his final pose, the Pickles jump to their feet again.

This time I shout with them.

When we sit down, Anthony asks, "How is he doing so far?"

"Really good."

He turns to his father to relay that message down the line.

I settle in my seat. It's fun being with Max's family, even if they don't have a clue about me.

When all the competitors have posed, and the call-outs are finished, we head back through the arena.

"What did it mean when they rearranged them?" Sherman asks.

"They want to see the different builds next to each other. It's how they score points."

Jason turns to me. "Max seems like a giant to me, but he looked smaller up there. Does he have a chance?"

"There's always a chance. He wasn't the biggest last week either."

I warn the Pickles that the security guys might not let them all go backstage to see Max, but somehow Sherman manages to get through with the whole crew. Max is already back in his warm-ups and sitting on the floor next to Franklin.

I hesitate. I don't know if it will stand out to my brother that I'm hanging out with Max's family.

But Amy is there, too, and the introductions give me a moment to meet Max's gaze and give him a thumbs up. When Franklin catches us standing too close, I quickly say, "When I was looking at the whole line, I felt like we should take you one shade darker. Would that be okay?"

Max nods. "Whatever you think will look good. You're the pro."

I step away to stand next to Amy. The Pickles are all jovial and friendly, and Anthony comes to talk to me again, catching the eye of his father. He smiles and nods, as if Anthony's attention is exactly what he wants.

This is all really weird. The last thing I want is for Anthony to show interest in me.

As much as I want to go to lunch with Max's family, I can't. This is too complicated. And at some point, we might have to lie. And I don't want to do that either.

Anthony turns to me as the family gathers together to head out. "Are you coming with us?"

Franklin's head snaps up.

"No, I need to check on one of my other clients. You guys go on. But I'll be here for the evening show." Thank goodness for Camille.

Anthony's smile is warm. "I look forward to that."

Max catches on. "Should we go find one of those bodybuilder ladies you were gawking at? I might be able to hook you up."

Anthony's cheeks turn pink. "That's okay. I live a long way from here." He nods, his expression suggesting that he's reconsidering everything. "Let's go."

I mouth *I'm sorry* at Max as they head out. He shrugs.

Franklin calms down as the Pickles leave. "I've got all the guys meeting me at a taco shop. I'll see you at the evening show?"

"Yeah. We'll be here," I say.

"I guess it's you and me," Amy says. "Have you given any thought to what we talked about?"

I watch my brother walk across the room. I don't want him to hear. It's a tough decision, and I don't need his interference.

I like Max. And I have a good job here. I like what I

do. Maybe I have grown out of that dream of travel. Maybe I should stay put.

I turn to Amy. "I have to turn it down."

She frowns. "Why? It doesn't have to interfere with your work."

"But I like my time off."

"I think you could really make it. There's no risk. You go do this thing, you come back and do your usual thing." She hesitates. "What's going on?"

I open my mouth, and then close it. My eyes flick back to the door.

"Wait a minute," she says. "Is there something going on with you and Max? Franklin was acting all crazy earlier saying Max gave him a chocolate bar that was one you always gave him, and how did he know because Franklin never told him."

I hesitate too long. Amy's eyes go wide. "There is! You and Max are a thing!" Her face is all smiles. "Girl, I don't blame you. Guys like Max don't come along very often. I assume your brother doesn't know."

"Hell, no. I'm not gonna tell him."

"Good call. Though, I don't know how long you can keep a secret. If I figured it out, it's only a matter of time until he does."

"We plan to tell him after this competition. We don't want to upset him on this big day."

"That's a good sister. But boy, I don't want to be within a twenty-mile radius of that boy when he figures out what's going on behind his back."

Me neither.

31

MAX

I wish Camryn could've come along on our family lunch. I had envisioned this giant outing with Franklin and all his buddies, maybe Amy, too, and taking over half a restaurant to make it easy for Camryn to be there and not set off any suspicions.

But in the end, it's just us Pickles scarfing burgers at the grill owned by one of the chefs my brother met in culinary school.

By the time we return to the arena, I'm dying to see Camryn alone. Despite my insistence that bodybuilding is only for fun, it would be nice to do well while my family is around.

Not that I think I have a chance. I'm easily in the bottom five in size. And there were zero rookie mistakes at the prejudging. No missed poses. No bad timing. These guys all know what they're doing. My nerves are jangling in a way I don't appreciate. A nice long shot of Camryn would do me good.

When we pile out of my Audi sports car like clowns

in a circus, I tell them they ought to go ahead and secure a good seat for the evening show. "It'll be packed. It's not nearly so serious as the prejudging. This is what everybody lives for who loves the sport."

Thankfully, they agree, so as I head into the backstage area, I text Camryn to see if she can meet me.

I don't hear from her, so, once again, I find myself sitting alone by the wall. Even Franklin and the entourage have made themselves scarce.

The scene is a good deal more jovial than the morning. These seasoned competitors know the most important part of their performance is already behind them. They're focused on looking good for the fans.

The words "L.A. Times" stick out in a conversation of several women competitors a few yards away. They look over. More whispers. More glances.

They're starting to put together that I was the featured bodybuilder in the paper earlier this week.

One of the men I recognize as a sponsor who approached me after my first win. He strides purposefully up to the registration table. I watch as I'm pointed out, and I figure I'm about to have company. He hurries over with an outstretched hand. "Max, good to see you again. Adam Hastings. I saw you in the paper."

I jump to my feet to shake his hand. "Guilty as charged. I did nothing but pick the right gym to work out in."

"Oh, I don't know. You're taking the L.A. bodybuilding scene by storm." His smile strikes me as slick as his satin shirt, which I assume he considers a hip look with the suit jacket. To me, he's trying too hard.

But it's irrelevant. I'm not pro material. "I've had a good run. I'll get knocked out tonight."

Adam vehemently shakes his head. "No way. Those judges know star power when they see it. Don't think they don't notice things like articles in the paper. That gets bodybuilding good press. More seats filled at the arenas. They know when they have someone they should run with."

"It doesn't seem right. It should be about athleticism."

"Oh, it is," he says. "Don't get me wrong. But you're there. Combine that with your ability to generate press and you, my friend, are a winner. We should talk about the next steps. You'll be traveling soon. You'll need a budget."

I can make my own budget for travel, but if he's right, there's no point in turning down free money. "What was your product again?"

"Bonafide T." He fishes out a card and passes it to me.

That's right. One of those testosterone replacements. I picture a full-sized cardboard cutout of myself saying, "Got low T?" and grimace. No thanks.

But I give Adam a polite nod. "Thanks for the interest."

He shakes my hand and claps my shoulder. "Good luck out there."

My phone buzzes. It's Camryn. Thank God. *Where are you?*

I quickly tap out: *Backstage by registration.*
I found an empty room.

Tell me where.

I grab my phone and keys and leave my bag by the wall.

But before I can reach the hall, Franklin and his crew show up at the back door. While he tries to convince the security guard to let everyone in, he spots me.

"Max, my man. I brought your trainers." He shoves two of his friends toward me.

"Hey Max," one says.

I'm game with helping them get in. "Come on back."

"Those two are with you?" the guard asks.

"They're with me. We all work out at Buster's Gym."

Recognition crosses the man's face. "I saw that article in the paper. Where's the gym at? I might check it out."

Franklin chats up the guard with the four guys, and since they're clear to enter, I take off in the other direction.

I was hoping to get away clean. But, surely, Franklin will want to bask in the attention and forget about me.

I follow the instructions Camryn texted until I'm at the end of a long hall. Most of the rooms here are shut tight, but one has a small crack.

I push on the door.

Camryn grabs my hand and drags me inside. "Don't be seen," she says with a laugh.

I'm barely inside when she wraps her arms around my neck and pulls me down to kiss her.

This is what I needed.

I relax into the kiss, reveling in the feel of her. All the familiar smells. Tanning oil. The floral scents I now know to be her shampoo and lotion.

"Poppyseed dressing," I whisper against her cheek.

She smacks my back. "Nailed my lunch."

"Who did you go with?"

"Amy."

"I didn't know you guys were friends." Amy has never mentioned Camryn during our coaching sessions.

"We've been talking more since the two of you started advancing."

"We're making a killer team, the four of us."

"We are."

I hold her tight, pressing her head to my chest. My heartbeat slows down. I feel at rest.

"I think you have a shot," she says. "I know you feel underdeveloped compared to them, but only a couple of them had any charisma. It's probably going to be about like last time. I doubt you'll claim the top spot, but you could place in the top five and qualify for Nationals. That's what you're here for."

I twirl her ponytail around my hand. "I don't even care about that. I want to do a good job up there for Dad and my brothers. This might be the end of the line."

"There are plenty of open competitions if you lose here. And you'll be invited to another qualifier even if you don't place at this one."

"Everybody seems to think I'm some golden boy, getting an article in the paper."

"It's a big deal. Bodybuilding needs all the good press it can get."

"I want to hold you for a while."

And we do. I let my anxiety fall away. Bodybuilding brought me to Camryn. It reconnected me to one of my friends. I definitely lost any flab I once had.

It's done its job. Besides, when we confess to Franklin, I may lose my training partner. Today might be the last day it's exactly like this.

"It'll be all right," she says.

"How did you know what I was thinking?"

"It's all in how you grip my waist."

"We have gotten to know each other, haven't we?"

"We have." She pulls away and looks up at me. "I want you to hear this from me first. Amy got me a job traveling with the international bodybuilding circuit. But I'm going to turn it down. I want to be here with you."

I step back from her, holding her hands. "But isn't that what you've always wanted? Travel? The big meets?"

She shakes her head, and I can see she wants me to support her on this. "That opportunity won't go away. Now that I know about it, I can always try again later. Or if you make the international circuit, then I'll go with you. I don't have to take off with Amy halfway across the world when I feel like my world is right here."

I pull her close again. "Promise me you won't let all your opportunities pass you by."

"I won't. I have lots of connections. Besides, I'm attached to the golden boy of bodybuilding."

I thread my fingers through her hair. "I'm glad you

met my family. I think Anthony might have a crush on you."

"It'll all get straightened out as soon as we reveal who we are."

"Tonight, maybe," he says. "At least my family. And then we'll deal with Franklin as soon as it makes sense."

I squeeze his bicep. "Let's not get ahead of ourselves. You could both advance, and you might want to withhold this disruption to your partnership until it makes sense to put it to the test."

"You're right. You're always right."

I lift her chin to mine. She tastes perfect. Sweet and honeyed and warm. I drag her body flush against me. And something starts to stir.

She feels it. "Now don't go tempting that pickle at a time like this. It's less than an hour until the competition."

"Tempt me later?"

She presses both hands to my cheeks. "You've got a promise there."

So, I'm going to pause the story one more time.

Let's savor this moment. Me. Cam. The competition ahead.

Everyone still likes each other.

We're all a team.

Because, friends, everything is about to go belly up.

So, close your eyes, remember a time like this. Maybe you loved somebody. Maybe you had a big, bright moment ahead.

Give a nice long sigh.

Mine is about to end.

Okay, here we go.

I bend for one more kiss before I have to let her go and put back on the ruse in front of Franklin and the gym crew.

But then the door flies open, and it doesn't matter anymore.

Because Franklin is there, shoving his sister aside.

And the next thing I know, his fist is in my eye.

32

CAMRYN

Oh my God. Oh my God.

I catch myself before I hit the ground. My brother is spinning around to punch Max a second time.

I leap onto his back. "Franklin, stop it!"

Max takes a step back to get out of range of Franklin's wild swings. Max's expression is murderous, and I can tell he wants to waylay my brother as good as he got.

But he controls himself.

"You mother fucking asshole," Franklin yells. He tries to throw me off his back, but we've been fighting for a good twenty-five years, and I know how to cling to him like no one else.

He cranes his neck around. "Get off me, bitch."

Max lunges forward to grasp the front of Franklin's shirt. "Call her a bitch again, and by God, I will break every bone in your body."

Franklin swings, but with the extra weight of me on his back, Max easily steps aside.

Franklin stumbles, and I rock him hard enough to bring him to the ground.

I roll away and stand between the two of them. "Listen you two. You both have to get on stage any minute. Max has a black eye I'll have to fix." I gesture to Franklin's hand. "And you're lucky if you didn't break a bone. Get yourself together. You've worked years for this. We can sort this out later. So get your ass back out there, Franklin. Talk to your crew. And let me fix Max. And, by God, don't think I won't tell the judges and get both your asses thrown out of here if I feel like I have to."

Both of them stop glaring at each other to stare at me.

Franklin turns to Max. "This isn't over. We're going to settle this like men."

"I am not property for you to settle!" I yell. "I have my own life. I have chosen Max. Back off, Franklin."

Franklin whirls around to me, his eyes blazing. "You guys were sneaking behind my back like snakes. It's what you both are. Fucking snakes."

He takes a step like he might take another swing at Max. I jump toward him, arms out.

Franklin laughs. "Look at you. So jumpy. Defending this asshole. This isn't over."

"Yes, it is." I give him a hard shove, and he finally steps away and takes off down the hall.

"That went well," Max says.

"I have to fix your eye."

Max envelops me in another embrace. "It will be fine. Are you okay? Did he hurt you?"

"I'm fine. But you are not."

I pull back and check his face. His eye has already shifted in color and is starting to swell.

"This is going to be hard to fix. Let me get some ice."

I take off down the hall and burst into the main atrium toward the concession stand. If my brother has hurt Max's chances tonight, by God, I will never forgive him.

When I get back to the room, Max is doing push-ups on the floor. "I need to get my pump on."

I dump the ice from the cup onto a makeup towel and twist the top. "Where's your bag?"

Back out in the main arena.

"Do you need anything from it?"

"No. It's my snacks and weights. I can do without it."

He switches to a sitting position, and I press the ice pack to his eye.

He doesn't flinch, but it has to hurt. "Are you all right?"

He laughs. "I'm great. I'm glad the secret's out. I could have done without a punch to the eye right before I go on stage, but hey, it's over."

"Hold this. Let me see what I've got to cover it."

I rummage through my makeup. I find a foundation close to his shade. When the light hits, it might be obvious, but that's better than sporting a big purple shiner.

I organize my tools and send a quick text to Amy: *Are you with Franklin?*

She writes back: *He just lined up to go on. Seemed on edge. What's up?*

Franklin found out and punched Max. Trying to stem the damage.

God. You need me?

Can you grab Max's bag and bring it to the last dressing room on the right?

Will do.

"You have a spy?" Max asks.

"Just Amy."

"Did Franklin go on?"

"He's lined up."

"So, I have about fifteen minutes."

"Exactly. Let's get you out of these sweats so I can prep you. It's gonna be tight on time."

We awkwardly work together as I hold the bag to his eye, and he peels out of his pants and jacket.

Amy arrives as I'm folding up his clothes.

She's pink-cheeked and harried. "How bad is it?"

Max pulls the ice pack away from his face.

"Oh, my God. I can't believe Franklin did that."

"Of course you can," I say.

"I'm resigning as his coach. I'm not going to have that sort of behavior between my clients."

"It's okay," I say. "We can sort this later."

"You can get him disqualified for this." Amy sets Max's bag down beside him.

"We're not going to get him thrown out," Max says. "It was a reaction to us lying to him. It's perfectly reasonable."

Amy huffs. "Your definition of reasonable and mine are not the same."

I pull the ice away from Max and pat his skin dry. "I can't wait any longer. We'll have to work with what we've got."

I don't know what it feels like for him as I press color on the discolored skin around his eye, but he's one-hundred percent chill about it.

"That's looking good," Amy says.

I smooth the color, set it with powder, and blend out some highlights and shadows so it looks more natural.

"You think I should do the other eye to match? I'm worried it will be obvious when the lights hit it."

"Less is more," Amy says. "Besides. You're out of time."

She's right.

I lean over and give Max a soft kiss. "Put all this from your mind. Focus on what you need to do up there."

He gives me an easy grin. "I got this. Don't worry. It'll be fine."

Max takes off for the backstage. I collect his things, and Amy and I rush to make it to the auditorium before the heavyweights go on.

We don't bother trying to find the Pickles, and we definitely don't look for Franklin or the gym crew. We slide into the back row and sink low in our seats.

Amy squeezes my arm. "Are you okay?"

"A little shaky. But I'm all right."

We've barely made it. The first heavyweight comes out, the one who won last time.

"Damn, he looks good," Amy says.

"You ever date a bodybuilder?"

"No. I try not to mix business and pleasure." She elbows me.

Yeah, I know.

Max is near the middle again, and his entrance is heralded by a roar from the left side of the audience. I glance over and squint in the dim light. The Pickles and the gym crew aren't sitting together, but they are close. Franklin isn't among them.

I want to know where he is, but I don't dare text.

Amy leans in. "It's not too obvious. I think you'd have to know to see it."

I focus on Max. With the intense lights casting varied shadows, and Max's continuous movement, it isn't super obvious while he's posing.

But as soon as he goes to stand with the other competitors who have finished their routines, I feel like it's perfectly clear that one eye looks different from the other.

My anxiety ratchets up as we get closer to the end. They often hold their form during the final posedown. His eye is going to jump out. Will the judges notice? Will they care?

But when all the competitors come forward on the stage, it's not as bad as I think. He got lucky in the lighting placements.

Maybe we're going to pull this off.

As the judges rearrange the competitors, I realize I don't even know how Franklin did. His scores should have been announced well before we came into the audience.

But I'm not sure I care. After what he did, I'm not even going to tan him anymore. Amy's ditched him, too. If he keeps advancing, or even if he continues to do the opens, he'll have to find a new team.

And pay for his own damn tans.

The judges finally send the men to the back of the stage while they tally the numbers.

Amy sits back. "He looks good up there. He may not be huge, but he's beautiful."

I see what she means. If these were male models instead of bodybuilders, Max would win hands down. He's gorgeous, friendly, charismatic. And built. His skin is taut, veiny where it should be and smooth in all the right places. His symmetry is perfect. And of course, his tan is exactly right.

But this isn't a modeling competition. It's about muscle mass. And he isn't even in the top ten for size.

I have no idea how this will go.

The announcer makes small talk while the music thunders in the background. The crowd starts clapping to the beat, anxious to hear the results.

This is the highlight of the show. The heavyweights and then the posedown of all the winners.

The runner takes a card up to the announcer. He glances at it and says, "In this qualifier competition, the top five heavyweights will have the opportunity to advance to Nationals."

My heart speeds up. He might be top five.

"In fifth place, from right here in Los Angeles, we have Cliff McClellan."

I release my held breath. I was hoping to see Max in fifth. The higher it goes, the more likely he'll be left out.

Amy reaches out to grab my arm and squeeze.

In fourth place, also from Los Angeles, our own Max Pickle!"

I jump from my chair so fast that makeup brushes go flying. I scream. I hug Amy.

He did it!

The roaring goes on so long that the announcer finally says, "I see Max has quite the fan club."

I finally manage to look at the stage. Max is holding a small plaque and waving at his family. He probably can't see me way in the back.

Finally, the gym crew settles down and Max steps back.

I can't even watch the top three receive their medals. Max has placed! He can go to Nationals!

The majority of the bodybuilders, including Max, step back while the three winners pose for pictures. Then everyone walks off stage, leaving the gold medalist to be joined by the other winners for the overall posedown.

I turn to Amy, who has collected my brushes in her lap. "Let's go back. I can't risk that Franklin might be back there waiting for Max."

Amy nods.

We jump from our seats and take off running for backstage.

But when we get there, Max is shaking hands with

the other competitors and smiling. Franklin is nowhere to be seen.

"Are you going to Nationals?" I ask.

"I'm invited. But I don't know. We'll have to see."

He puts his arm around me.

That's the one good thing to come out of today. We can touch each other in public.

"Have you seen Franklin?" I ask.

He shakes his head. "No. But I haven't had a chance to walk around."

"I say let's don't. Let's call your family and get out of here."

He accepts his bag from Amy. "Thanks. A lot of this is because of you."

She blushes. "I don't know about that."

"Do you get to introduce me as your girlfriend now?" I ask.

He pulls me close. "Absolutely."

33

MAX

Dad insists on a huge afterparty to celebrate my fourth-place standing.

We discover from the other members of Buster's Gym in the audience that Franklin did not place in his category. No one's seen him since he left the stage.

I send my dad and brothers to the restaurant while Camryn and I head to my place for a quick cleanup.

I've been to her place a dozen times, but she has never been to mine.

We pull up to the gate of the townhouse complex, and I give her the code to punch in.

"Looks fancy," she says.

"Not too much. But definitely an upgrade from that crappy house I rented with your brother and our friends."

"I'm not sure I ever went there."

"I think I would have remembered meeting you." I give her a grin, but even so, concern edges her features as I guide her to my side of the complex.

"You going to text him?" I ask.

"Eventually. Once he's had some time to cool off."

"I don't remember him being like that when we were roommates."

"He isn't always," she says.

I point out my parking space under a covered awning.

She kills the car. "I told you we raised ourselves," she says, making no move to leave the car. "He doesn't like anything bad happening to me. I think once he sees you're good for me, he will be okay."

"I can wait on that."

"I'm worried that he lost the competition in the same hour he found out about us. That's a lot of blows for someone like him."

"Why don't you text him?"

We get out of the car. "I might while you're showering."

I take her hand as we walk along the path to my front door. "I should warn you, I'm the messiest of the three brothers."

This makes her crack a smile. "I'm a neat freak. We'll either complement each other, or it will be grounds for divorce."

This is better. My shoulders relax, releasing the tension I felt since the fistfight.

"Here goes."

I lead Camryn into my living room, and I see it through her eyes. Weights scattered across the floor. A few towels and, *oh great,* a jockstrap strewn across the back of the sofa. I quickly snatch them up and wad them into a ball.

"It could be worse," she says.

"Don't go in the kitchen."

"Noted."

I lead her to the master bedroom. I use the other bedroom as storage for all my workout equipment and the deli paraphernalia that has accumulated over the years. Thankfully, that door is closed.

My bedroom isn't too crazy. Some clothes tossed over a chair. An unmade bed. Thankfully I have a housekeeper who keeps the dust and grime levels down. It's just clutter.

"Not bad at all," she says. "I can work with this."

I lean over to kiss her forehead. "I'll take a quick shower." I squeeze her arm. "Let me know if you hear from Franklin."

She sits on the end of the bed and pulls out her phone.

I jump in the shower, not even waiting for the water to get hot. I want all the extra oil and color off my body, then we'll go. My eye stings when the water hits it, but I'm okay with the sucker punch. The moment was stressful, but the truth got out. And I still placed. Who would've thought? The sponsor guy knew what he was talking about.

When I walk into the bedroom in my towel, Camryn lies back on my bed staring at the ceiling.

"Any news?"

"He didn't respond. I'm not surprised."

"Hopefully he's licking his wounds with his new

cronies. And if he doesn't want to work out with me anymore, he'll have plenty to choose from at the gym. I can start over at a new place."

She sits up. "So, you're going to do Nationals?"

"Not sure yet. I need to do some research. I don't want to go in there and look like a chump at barely over two hundred pounds when they're all two-fifty of pure muscle. I might drop down to light heavyweight."

"It's not a bad strategy, but you might have to re-qualify in the new weight class. We should ask Amy."

"I didn't think of that."

I open the drawer to grab a pair of boxers, but Camryn comes up behind me, loosening the towel. "So how late can we be before your family starts looking for you?"

The towel hits the floor.

"I say we find out."

When we finally make it to the restaurant, the table is already full of appetizers and drinks. We decide not to cover my eye again.

Jason notices it first. "You guys get in a brawl?"

"I told you he was wearing makeup," Anthony says.

I decide to gloss over it rather than mention Camryn's brother. It's too complicated. "Some body-builders live up to the hype."

"Someone punched you?" Anthony asks.

"Right before we went on."

"Why?" Dad asks.

I shrug. "It's complicated."

Nova cuts in. "Does it hurt?"

"Nah. Makes me look even tougher." I strike a bicep pose and everybody claps. "Now let's eat."

They take the hint, and Anthony passes me a plate. "I hope you can still carb up. Because we got all your favorites."

The table is stuffed with focaccia bread, seasoned oil, cheese and olive trays, and an entire platter of calamari.

I turn to Camryn. "When are Nationals?"

"Five weeks."

"Bring it on."

Dad pulls a chair out for Camryn next to Anthony. "Have a seat, my dear. So glad you could make it."

Camryn meets my eyes and lifts her eyebrows. *Right.* The brother crush.

"Dad, Jason, Nova, Anthony. I'm sorry I didn't get to introduce you to Camryn properly." I put my arm around her. "She and I have been dating for about a month."

My gaze glances off Anthony, but he's clapping heartily. "I knew it!" he says.

"Excellent," Jason agrees. "Now the pressure is off me to provide a grandkid."

Nova smacks his arm. "Jason!"

"What?" Jason says. "Dad's on us all the time. When he isn't, Grammy is."

"You're engaged," Anthony says. "You've got a head start, so the clock is ticking."

"Not you, too." Jason tosses an olive at his brother.

"I want to be a crazy uncle!"

"Perfect," Jason says. "Make me and Anthony crazy uncles first."

"Sorry for this, Camryn," I say. "They get ahead of themselves."

"It's all right," she says with a laugh. I can tell she's pleased to be accepted so easily.

I busy myself with piling up an incredible amount of food. I'm starving.

Dad watches me fill the plate. "You can eat all that and stay as fit as you are?"

"He has to eat all that," Camryn says. "The amount of energy required to keep those muscles in shape is more than you think."

"What can I get for you?" I ask her.

"I'll handle it. You eat." She takes the seat Dad pulled out for her, but Anthony moves down one to make room for me.

I reject any attempts at conversation as I tuck into all the glorious food before me.

Jason passes Camryn a plate. "Served himself first."

"It's fine," Camryn says. "I know when not to get between a bodybuilder and his carb load."

She adds a pile of olives and cheese to her plate. "How long are you all going to stay in L.A.?"

"We're all flying out tomorrow afternoon," Dad says. "We had a great time. Son, you looked great up there. You did us proud."

I shrug. "I was outclassed. But you never know how the judging is going to go."

"Nonsense. It took a lot of work to even get this far."

Dad settles back in his chair, wine glass in hand. He's pleased, I can see it on his face. "You had a nice crowd cheering you on."

I'm busy stuffing food in my gullet, so Camryn says," The gym where he works out sponsored tickets so members could come see Franklin and Max compete."

Dad turns to her. "Where is that brother of yours? He would have been welcome here tonight."

"He took off with his friends," she says.

"They were an enthusiastic bunch. I'm glad to see you so well supported in your new pursuit." Dad takes another glance at my half-empty plate. "This is the wildest thing I've ever seen." He pats his gut. "If I ate all that, you'd have to roll me out of here."

The hollowness of my belly finally starts to dissipate, so I take a breath. "It sounds like I won't be competing again until after Grammy's big shindig. I'm first, right? From what I understand, I kick it off next week, then it's the Austin branch, then Boulder."

"Got it backward," Jason says. "Anthony second, and I'm third. On the actual date of the anniversary, we will all convene in New York for the big to-do."

"Right. Nationals are also in New York." I turned to Camryn. "You up for that? We go to compete, and then this big family anniversary for my grandmother?"

Her eyes meet mine. I don't know if this is too much, too fast. But I want her there. And I want her to know that.

"We'll need to do some planning," she says. "But I think that'll work."

I grab her hand and pull it to my chest. "This is going to be a fantastic summer."

The waiter takes all our orders, and Dad's eyes practically bug out when I order two pasta dishes.

The conversation turns to the anniversary and stories of Grammy, then we rib each other about various childhood exploits. I can tell Camryn is delighted with the whole thing. Even if it means I got a shiner, I'm glad the story is out. Having her here makes the night absolutely perfect.

Dad's phone buzzes several times, but he ignores it.

I ask him, "You're not even going to check that?"

"I don't do business when I'm with my family," he says. "An adage that will save you boys lots of trouble in your marriage if you abide by it as well."

But five minutes later, my phone buzzes, too. Then Dad's again.

"Maybe you should check," Camryn says.

I flip over my phone. The missed call is our family lawyer. What would he want on a Saturday night? "Dad, it's Ted. Look at yours."

He picks his up. "Mine, too. What the hell does he want?" He clicks through. "What's going on, Ted?"

While he's talking, my phone buzzes again. This time it's Andre, my store manager.

I click through and listen a moment, rage thundering through my body.

Dad's eyes catch mine. His lips are pressed tight.

Then I look over at Camryn. When she realizes something is terribly wrong, fear etches her features.

"I'll be right there," I tell Andre and end the call.

"What's going on?" Jason asks.

I hesitate. I know my next words are going to devastate Camryn. Looks like Dad already knows, although he won't know *who*.

I hold Cam's hand as I say it.

"A green truck has driven straight into the front glass windows of L.A. Pickle."

34

——

CAMRYN

*O**h no.*

The flashing red and blue lights wash over us as I stand with the Pickle family in front of Max's deli.

It's Franklin's truck. No doubt about it.

He's not in it. No one has seen him.

The front of the truck has taken out the low border of brick and crashed through the glass windows of the main restaurant.

The power has been cut to the place for safety, so I can only see the register and counter by the giant lights set up to shine inside.

A firefighter walks out, his heavy boots crunching glass. "Nothing wrong inside. Don't see anything stolen, but you will want to check once everything's secure. Probably somebody was drunk and lost control of the car."

Max and I glance at each other. Franklin isn't much of a drinker, although tonight might have led him to it.

This looks deliberate.

The firefighter gestures to the rubble of bricks beneath the front tires. "They probably would have backed out and taken off, but the front end got hung up. Must have left on foot."

"There's no blood or anything inside the truck, right?" I ask.

The police officer standing nearby shakes her head. "No. It doesn't look like the person who was driving the truck got hurt. The airbag did deploy, of course."

I can't get close to the open driver's side door. It's cordoned off with tape. The scene is like a nightmare.

Sherman powers off his phone and shoves it in his pocket. "The insurance adjusters will be out in the morning. I hired a cleanup team to board this up." He pats Max on the back. "It's a building. We'll fix it."

Max stares into the cavern of his open deli. "But Grammy's celebration is supposed to start next weekend. We were supposed to be the first one."

Sherman kicks at a loose brick. "We could rearrange the timeline, give you a chance to rebuild."

Anthony dodges bricks and glass as he steps close. "I don't know, Dad. We've got the whole publicity engine already in place. It might be easier to cancel Max's part of the celebration."

I clutch Max's hand. I feel so responsible. We should have been more discreet. Skipped meeting when we knew Franklin was around. Controlled when he found out, and how.

"Surely there's something we can do," Jason says. "Set up shop in some empty storefront temporarily?"

"We'll figure it out," Sherman says. "Right now, it's all about finding out who did this and why."

I glance up at Max again. So far, we haven't given up the name of my brother.

A young, fresh-faced police officer shouts over the cab of the truck. "I ran the plates. We have the owner of the truck—Franklin Schultz."

So much for that. I let go of Max and step away. "That's my brother," I say.

Sherman turns to us in disbelief. "Why would he do this to Max's deli?"

Max blows out a long stream of air. "He didn't want me dating his sister."

"Oh," the two brothers say in unison.

Sherman's face seems older in the flashing colors. "I guess that explains the shiner on your eye. Camryn, have you heard from him? Is he hurt?"

It's nice he's worried about someone who wrecked his son's business. "I've been texting him all evening. He hasn't responded."

Max's jaw is tight. I've never seen him look so angry. "It's late. Why don't you head back to your place? We're going to be here most of the night to keep the place secure."

I get it. They want to talk about Franklin without me around. "Okay. Does anyone want me to run them by the hotel?"

Nova steps up. "I'll go. I'm exhausted. The brothers can handle this."

"Sherman?" I ask.

He shakes his head. "I'll stay here with my boys."

I lead Nova to my car, and we ride in silence. There's not much to say. My guilt weighs heavy.

As we pull up to the entrance, Nova finally says, "Max is super great. I'm sure you guys will find a way to work all this out."

I don't know how to respond. I feel like my family has directly ruined theirs.

When Nova closes the door, I'm glad to be alone. I try texting Franklin again, then try calling. Nothing.

I drive across town to his apartment. No one's there, not even his deadbeat roommate.

Finally, in desperation, I call my parents.

Dad answers the phone. "It's kind of late, isn't it?"

"Hey, Dad."

"What's going on?" His voice is full of annoyance at the inconvenience of my call. For a moment, I think *why did you guys even have kids?*

But I only say, "I need to find Franklin."

"We haven't seen either one of you since Christmas. Funny how that is, since we live in the same city and all."

I take a deep breath. "He wrecked his truck. But he wasn't in it. I'm worried about him, that's all."

"Was he drunk?"

My mom's voice is shrill in the background. "Is who drunk? What's going on?"

I press my phone tightly against my ear. "I don't think so. I need to find him. Will you let me know if he calls over there, or shows up?"

Dad's tone turns sharp. "You listen here, don't expect us to bail you guys out of trouble."

"Dad, I'm not in trouble. I'm just trying to find Franklin. Your son."

Mom and dad start squabbling about what's happened to Franklin, and why I don't know where he is.

I hang up. That was a wasted effort.

I pull out of Franklin's parking lot.

Where would he go? He'd have to head somewhere on foot or call for a ride.

I think about all those guys who came to the meet from Buster's Gym. Did they ride together? Probably. Did they know what he did? Did they help?

Anger makes me clench the steering wheel on the drive to the gym. Surely none of those friends would have taken part in sabotaging Max's deli.

But when I arrive, sure enough, several cars are parked along the curb. The street is otherwise silent.

I slide in behind a beat-up Camaro and walk up to the blacked-out front glass. The door's locked.

I knock on it several times. No one answers.

Maybe some of them left their cars here and rode together somewhere. I could sit in my car and wait for them to return.

I'm about to walk away when I hear the unmistakable sound of a metal plate hitting the cement floor.

Someone is in there.

I bang harder on the glass.

I text Franklin again. *I'm here at the gym. Open the damn door.*

For a while, there is nothing, and I think about leaving again.

But then the lock squeaks, and the glass door pushes open.

I recognize the man. He was hanging out with Franklin today.

"Is my brother here?"

"Who wants to know?"

Good grief. "I do."

My brother's voice roars from the weight room. "I don't want to see that lying snake bitch."

Oh no, he didn't.

I shove the man aside and storm through the darkened foyer into the weight room. Franklin sits on a bench, his other three cronies nearby.

"What the hell did you do?" I ask him.

"Do you like the new decoration in front of your boyfriend's crappy restaurant?"

The three other men glance at each other uneasily. Good.

"That's a felony," I say. "You could go to freaking jail."

He shrugs. "I don't think so. Your boy won't want the bad publicity. I got it all figured out. Besides, you two owe me."

I storm right up to him and kick him in the shin. "What the hell do we owe you? I think YOU owe US because you're an overbearing piece of shit!"

The other guys step back. "I'm not interested in jail," one says.

Another one punches his arm. "Stand up for your friends, asshole."

My anger reaches a fever pitch. "I hope you know

who you're hero worshiping. Because this son of a bitch is about to get thrown off the circuit. AND I'll get you thrown out of this gym. I hope these new friends of yours have bail money because you're going to need it. The cops already pulled your insurance card out of the dash."

Franklin sits up slowly with a smirk on his face. "You'll do none of those things. Because we're blood. Because I saved you more than once."

He has me there. I close my eyes a moment, my hands tightening into fists. But this is too much. He committed a criminal act.

"What were you thinking, Franklin?" I ask. "You made it impossible for me to date anyone. And when I finally find someone great, you have to wreck it for me?"

Franklin lies back on the bench. "Rack up ten more pounds. I want to push my limit today. I'll come back stronger at the next meet. I got screwed by the judging today."

One of the young men jumps up to add a plate to his bench press.

Apparently, I'm dismissed.

"Call our parents," I say. "I told them you crashed your truck."

Franklin continues to ignore me, so I head back out the way I came.

I knew this was all going to fall apart. My whole life has been based on this teetering stack of bricks, none of them mortared together.

My parents are no help. And the ways my brother

and I found to make our way in the world didn't do us any favors.

He's toxic. And by association, I'm toxic. As soon as this gets out, my career is going to be wrecked. Nobody will want to touch me.

I have to get out. Away from Franklin. Find my own way, far from L.A. As long as I'm near his circles, I won't be free of him.

And how can I face the Pickle family when my brother has wrecked one of the delis and ruined their grandmother's anniversary?

I know exactly what I need to do.

Take the opportunity that has been given to me.

Time to call Amy and get on the road.

35

MAX

My brothers and Dad are up all night. One of the cops hangs out with us, waiting on the insurance adjuster and the cleanup team.

By the time the photos are taken, and the place is cleared of rubble and secured, it's time to head to the airport.

Nova, Jason, and Dad decide to fly home. They have a lot to do for the anniversary.

Anthony chooses to stay behind. He has an idea about doing a tent party in the parking lot, a way to keep my crew hired and hold the party even though it will be weeks before we can reopen the dining room.

He points out that the kitchen is perfectly functional, and we can route customers through the back to the bathrooms as necessary.

I will take a hit, but it's a small setback. We'll fix up the deli and get back to where we were.

I haven't reached out to Franklin, and I haven't gone to Buster's Gym. As the days pass, mostly working outside, marking off the parking lot and figuring out how to set up, I realize I have no time to deal with finding a new trainer or a new gym.

At first, Camryn takes off to help with the work, but I tell her not to worry. We have it well in hand and there's no reason for her to cancel her tans.

I haven't made a decision about Nationals. If I don't go, the person with the next highest points at the meet will take my place. Without a training partner, and unsure about my ability to follow a workout schedule during the rebuild, my bodybuilding career is on pause.

It's family first.

We set up a new curbside delivery system, and within the week, we're back in modified business. By the time Anthony leaves town, freeing me up to see Camryn alone, I can tell things have changed with her. Her responses are short and often delayed, as if she's struggling with what to say to me.

On Friday, I text her from work to suggest she come over but she's noncommittal.

And when she appears at the back door of the deli an hour later, I can tell from her face that she's made some hard decisions.

The staff goes quiet as we walk through the busy kitchen to my office.

Only when the door's closed, and we're both seated, can I screw up the courage to ask her, "So, is this it?"

She won't meet my gaze, so I brace myself for her words. And they're not easy.

"I've decided to leave with Amy. I'm going to finish out one more competition here, but I'm transitioning all my clients to other tanning artists." She gives me a half-smile. "Just not Ride 'em Shiny."

I have to force the grin. My heart is in my shoes. "You don't even want to try to work this out?"

She stares down at her hands, folded together in the lap of her pale-blue sundress, the one she wore when we went to the beach that day. I wonder if she chose it deliberately. I don't know what it means.

"I wish I had a good plan for what to do," she says. Her voice breaks, and I lean forward to take her hand, but she pulls them closer to her body. "It's a lose-lose situation. If I report him to the circuit, what does that say about me as a sister? If I don't report him, what does that say about me as a person? He could go off on anybody, especially where I'm involved."

"You can't be responsible for how your brother acts."

"I know. I need a break from the scene. And this opportunity gets me away, keeps me paid, and gives me some space to figure things out."

Her eyes are cast to the floor.

"I'd like to see you at the end of it. I'll wait."

"I don't know how I'll be by then," she says.

"You'll still be the same Cam to me."

She fiddles with a loose string on her skirt. "I hope you don't give up on the competitions. You're good."

"I need to focus on what's important, too," I say. "Leaving Buster's Gym to Franklin and his buddies is the best thing to do."

"I heard you decided not to press charges."

"Also a hard decision. The insurance people definitely didn't like it."

She does meet my gaze at that. "Franklin predicted you wouldn't. He knows you're a nice guy, and he used that against you."

"The deli will recover. But he's costing me more than I can bear." I reach out to touch the loose fabric of her skirt.

"I'm sorry."

She gets up as if to flee, but this time I grasp her hand. "Can I text you? Can we talk at all?"

She won't meet my gaze. "Of course. I'll do my best."

And with that, she's gone.

I plunk back down and brace my head in my hands over my desk. We took the wrong path, and it cost us. We should've told him from the beginning. I made the wrong choice.

And now I've lost Camryn.

36

CAMRYN

This day is crazy.

I have six bodybuilders to tan from scratch in the next two hours. All of them want shadowing and extra work.

There needs to be three of me.

I dash down the hall of the arena, spotting Amy only in passing. She's also on the run.

We have too many clients to deal with. And many of them are absolute divas.

And I'm talking about the men.

I burst into a dressing room, where two bodybuilders wait for their final tans before their prejudging. Both are monstrous, veiny super-heavyweights with legs that weigh more than I do. Each.

"Where the hell have you been?" one of them booms.

I ignore his tone as I assess the paler one. "You first because I might need to do two rounds."

"But I go on before him," the other yells.

Good God. I force a smile. "I promise I am fast and thorough."

I glance around the room. The rack of tan canisters isn't here.

Great.

I jerk my phone out of my pocket. I quickly text out a question to the runner who's supposed to move the tanning cart from the women's side to the men's.

No answer.

This is too much.

But I force another smile. "Just a second. Let me go locate the tanning solution."

Both men grumble as I take off in the dead sprint down the hall. This is only the second competition we've done in Italy, and I'm already over it. The runners don't speak English, and I've taken to carrying around pictures on my phone to show them what I need.

And despite being told we were recruited because the bodybuilders wanted English-speaking service providers, a good third of them are from other countries and don't speak English themselves.

So, the communication has been painful and difficult, and I'm pretty sure I screwed up the color on at least two clients last weekend.

I can't imagine keeping up this frustrating pace for three more months.

But I signed a contract.

I dash into the women's main dressing area and spot the rolling rack of canisters. I check to make sure all the colors are loaded and begin pushing it toward the other side again.

A job like this is the world's best weight loss program. I may not have a lot to lose, but I am definitely dropping pounds.

If we had time for strolling along the streets of Italy, sampling gelato, and the many pizzerias, maybe I would enjoy myself.

But that is not even within the realm of possibility. The schedule is jam-packed, and the travel is grueling, red-eye flights and train stations before dawn.

But we all keep going. One more day. One more competitor. One more tan.

The only thing good about my life right now is I drop dead asleep every night, and never have time to mourn the loss of Max.

We finally catch a break three weeks in. It's time for Nationals in New York, and even though we're not working the event, the recruiters are expected to market to the bodybuilders who qualify for the international circuit.

So, we descend on the city with forty-eight hours to spend on our own.

Amy and I wander everything that's free. Central Park. Chinatown. We eat hot dogs from street vendors and duck through the museum gift shops.

"One day, I'm going to come here with so much money that I can do anything I want," Amy says. "I'll rent a helicopter and fly over the Statue of Liberty."

We both lick ice cream as we wander down a side street on the Upper East Side.

We're half the island away from the bodybuilding events happening over the next two days. I try not to think about them.

But Amy finally asks. "So, is Max here? Is he competing?"

I shake my head. I haven't talked to him in a few days, but I know he dropped out early to allow the other competitor to make travel plans.

"I think he's taking your advice. Dropping fifteen pounds. Getting into light heavyweight territory where it's not quite so competitive."

"You can't make it big unless you're a heavyweight, though."

We pause at the crosswalk with a dozen other New Yorkers. I feel out of place. My shoes are wrong. My jeans don't have the right cut. But it's all good. The city is busy and alive.

"He's got a new workout buddy. He's not at Buster's anymore."

"That's too bad. He brought them so much publicity."

"It was Franklin's gym first."

"Still sucks. You seeing him when you get back?"

"I'm not sure."

Now that we're separated, it's easier to see the problem stretching out across our entire future. What if we got married one day? Do we invite my brother? Snub the whole family?

Amy punches something into her phone. "Let's go

this way," she says. "Google says there's an interesting stop over here."

"Is it free?" I toss the trash from my ice cream cone into a bin.

"Totally."

We wander along the sidewalk, window shopping, and I notice that up ahead a crowd has gathered outside of a storefront.

Then I recognize the style of the green and white striped awning.

"Amy, you didn't."

She threads her arm through mine. "What's the big deal? It's not like he's here. You said yourself he didn't come to New York for Nationals."

I glance up at the giant sign.

Manhattan Pickle. Max's dad's deli.

"Why are so many people here?" I ask.

"It's a hot place for lunch," she says. She holds up her phone. "Look. Five stars. Average forty-minute wait."

"Wow. They do better than the one in L.A."

"It's the original. And it's huge." Amy lowers her sunglasses and stares up at the building.

"I do love their hot pickles," I say, and bite my lip to keep myself in check. The thought of those moments with Max is hard to bear.

We move forward, and I can almost see inside the place. Only when we get close to the door do I notice the giant banner on the opposite windows.

"Fiftieth anniversary party for Alma Pickle."

Oh no. This is the big event they were planning.

Max said he was going to be here for this.

I take a step back and run into an elderly man behind me.

"Watch where you're going," he grumbles.

"So sorry," I say. "Amy. I can't go here. It's the anniversary. Max is probably here."

She holds on to my arm. "Then we should see him."

I shake my head. "I can't drop in unannounced." I step to the side and almost ram a baby carriage.

"Watch it," the mother growls.

I'm not in California anymore.

And I have to get out of here.

I duck out of line, looking both directions to figure out which way to escape. The line behind me is long, but the sidewalk is clear on the other side of the door.

So I make a break for it.

"Camryn!" Amy calls.

I'm almost past the door when an elderly lady steps in front of me with a tray. "Free sample?" she asks.

I have to stop or run her over.

"No, thank you," I say.

Her eyes twinkle. She wears a bright green satin shirt over navy pants and orthopedic shoes. She's got to be over seventy but the ethereal beauty of her face beneath her cotton-candy gray hair reminds me of someone.

"Oh, I must insist," she says. "We have juicy pickles, spicy pickles, sweet pickles. I'm partial to the hot one." She winks as her long finger points out the pickle I remember well from Max's deli.

"Okay," I say, and lift the clear cup with a slice of pickle inside.

I'll eat one, for old time's sake.

I try to step away, but she moves with me. "We should get you a glass of water for that. It's quite hot."

She neatly sidesteps me, blocking my escape. With the line to my right, the only way to go is into the deli.

"I should wait my turn."

"I'll tell them you're with me." She presses her hand to my back. "Your friend can come, too."

I glance back and see Amy waving. No way. She got me into this.

We head into the dining room. Every table is packed with people, and a long counter four times the size of Max's lines the entire right side. Panic rises as I glance along the row of workers for any of the Pickles. I've met them all.

But they're all employees. Nobody I know.

Along the left side, a big stage is set up. A group of musicians cluster together, the keyboardist plunks a note and a guitar player tunes his strings.

Looks like something is about to happen.

The woman leads me to the drink counter along the back wall.

"I'm fine," I say.

"Nonsense," she says. "Humor an old lady."

We fill a plastic cup with water, and the woman waits patiently for me to eat the pickle.

I hesitate, not wanting my mouth to die like before. "Last time I had this, M— I mean, the person I was with suggested I try it with the dill cream cheese to cut the heat."

Now her eyes practically sparkle. "I bet so. I've taught that trick to many people. Let's get you some."

"Oh, no. I didn't mean we had to do that. I'm nervous it will be hot."

She sees something behind me, and her eyebrows lift up and down like a signal.

I whip around.

It's Anthony Pickle.

Oh, boy.

"Hey," I say. "Fancy seeing you here."

"I didn't know you were in New York!" he says, but I can tell his innocent act is exactly that—an act.

"What is going on?" I ask.

"You tell us," the old woman says. "You're the one who came to our deli. Looking for someone?" Her face lights up with happy mischief and the resemblance settles into place.

This is Grammy Alma Pickle.

37

MAX

It's five minutes until the big ceremony and Anthony has disappeared.

Dad, Jason, Nova, and I crowd inside Dad's office at the back of the main kitchen. We're supposed to be heading to the stage to give our spiel about how much we love the Pickle franchise.

But Anthony left to check on the musicians, then came back, grabbed Grammy, and took off again.

"Should someone go find him?" I ask. I don't know why no one else is anxious about this.

Jason claps me on the back. "For someone who gets up on stage wearing nothing more than dental floss, you sure are nervous about this shindig."

"For someone who grew up in New York, you sure picked up a lot of Texas words. Like shindig."

Jason laughs. "You've been grumpy since you got here. Somebody needs to get this boy laid."

Dad glances up from his phone to pierce us with a stern glare. "None of that locker room talk at work."

To Jason's credit, he shuts his mouth. Though he is right. Not about the getting laid part. But about my bad attitude.

Dad stands up from his chair. "Go time."

I ponder what Jason's said as we file out of the office and through the kitchen. I am on edge. This New York trip looks nothing like the one I once planned. Showing Camryn around New York. Introducing her to Grammy and the cousins.

Whether I did Nationals or not, this would've been an incredible week.

Now, it feels hollow.

I miss her.

The dining room roars with conversation, the clink of utensils, and the twang of the musicians tuning up.

The place is packed. Every table is full, and a line along the counter snakes out the door.

"There's no more seating," I say to Dad.

He shrugs. "Nothing we can do about it. I pick the quietest part of the afternoon for this. I had no idea."

Anthony materializes in front of us from outside a clump of people near the drink counter.

He turns me toward the stage. "Max, you can go first."

"What? I thought you were introducing everyone."

"New plan. Let's get up there."

"Why the change?"

"You're the most comfortable on stage."

He must be nervous. It's fine. He's right. I'm used to this.

Anthony and I pick our way across the stage, avoiding wires and stage lights.

"Anything in particular you want me to say?" I ask.

"It'll come to you." He plants me near the center and points out across the room. "Right about …now."

And I see her.

Camryn.

My heart thuds so hard it could be a drumbeat. My throat instantly goes dry.

She's near the drinking fountain.

And talking to…Grammy?

"What is she doing here?" I ask Anthony.

"I spotted her in the line to get in."

"Do you think she wants to see me?"

"I'm not sure. She's been trying to escape. Grammy's been holding her hostage."

It's true. Grammy has blocked Camryn's way out. She's trapped between the end of the counter and the wall.

Go, Grammy.

Anthony takes a microphone from the stand and hands it to me. "Don't throw away your shot."

"What will I say?"

"You know her best."

"If she was in line, she came here on her own."

"She did."

"Some part of her wants to be here."

"Take it away." He flips on the mic and descends the stairs to stand next to my dad and brother.

Camryn hasn't seen me up here. I have a moment to collect myself and think about what I want to say.

So, hey.

I could use some help here.

You've heard the whole story.

What would you do?

What would you say?

If the person you were absolutely certain you could not live without was trapped by your Grammy and a tray of hot pickles…how would you start?

The light brightens the auburn in her hair to a majestic red. The long silky locks I remember so well flow down her back and across her shoulders, shimmering as she nods to my grandmother.

I can almost smell it. And her.

As soon as I start speaking, the room will quiet down, and all attention will turn to the stage.

To me.

She'll see me.

It will be my one shot.

I'm supposed to talk about my grandmother. Our family deli. This place that supports us and feeds so many people.

How do I say those things but also speak to her?

My hand tightens on the microphone.

And I have it.

I think you guys beamed all your good juju right at me.

I draw in a breath. "Most of us have been lucky at least once in our lives."

My voice reverberates across the room, and I pause, waiting for everyone to quiet down.

Grammy turns to the stage, and Camryn looks up.

Our eyes meet. I haven't seen her face in weeks. I haven't held her close for longer than that.

My arms ache with the very idea.

Her hand flies to her mouth. Her eyes are big, and I think, alarmed.

I have to get this right. She looks ready to run.

"Most of us are lucky at least once," I say again, now that I have the room's attention.

I don't take my eyes off Camryn. I'm afraid if I look away, something will happen to her. She'll dash away. Or maybe evaporate into a mirage.

"When we get that one piece of luck laid at our feet, we find someone who truly matters. Maybe it's your mother, who tucks you in at night. Someone, even long after she's gone, continues to wrap you in comfort whenever you think of her."

I clear my throat. Camryn drops her hand to her side.

"I got lucky with my mother, even if I lost her before her time. But I didn't get lucky only once. I also have a strong and fearless grandmother. When my grandfather died unexpectedly, far too young, she took what she did best—feeding her family—and turned it into a deli in Brooklyn."

The room is mostly quiet, the only sounds the whispered food requests and the muted sounds of the cash register working in the very back.

"Because of that strength fifty years ago, I got to grow up sitting on a stool behind her counter. When my father was ready to take on the tradition, he opened this very store where we celebrate today. He took every dime he had ever saved, every dollar his mother could scrape together, to take out an outrageous loan on this building and open the first Pickle franchise."

The room claps and cheers, but I don't dare let go of Camryn's gaze. I'm afraid she will spirit away like a startled deer. I'm not positive she came here for me. She seems too anxious, too unsteady. It's almost as though a twist of fate brought her here, and she isn't sure she should follow its lead.

"My father and brothers will tell you more about Grammy Alma's impact on all our lives, but I wanted to impress upon you that I got lucky a third time. Back in Los Angeles, where I have my own deli, a girl walked in with hair like fire and earth in equal measure. She believed in me and wanted to make sure I wasn't going to screw up on my path."

My gaze is so intent on Camryn that several people turn to see what has my attention.

Camryn realizes she's been noticed, and her hand moves to her hair. A collective *ahhh* ripples through the crowd as they realize I'm speaking about her.

"She was right of course. I did screw it up." I wait out the chuckle from the crowd. "I'm up here to make sure she knows I made the wrong decision. The way I feel about her should've been out in the open from day one. We should have let it shine."

She bites her lip, so I know she's heard me and understands. What will happen next with her is out of my hands.

So I break her gaze and look at the crowd.

"Not everyone can be a strong as Alma Packwood.

And I'm here to say I'm in awe of what she started, and what she led our family to do. If you find yourself getting lucky with the people the world brings to you, don't be like me and squander it. Be like my grandmother, Alma Packwood, and let everyone's light shine."

I lower the mic and turn to the side of the stage. My dad is already coming up the steps, followed by Jason. Anthony heads to the crowd to collect my grandmother.

My part is done.

I pass the mic to my dad, glancing out to see if Camryn is still in her spot by the drinks.

But she's gone.

It didn't work.

Jason smacks my back as we pass on the stairs. Nova squeezes my hand. By the time I get to the bottom, Anthony has returned with Grammy. She kisses me on the cheek. "That was lovely, grandson."

I stand in a quiet corner between the stairs and the back wall, my hands clasped in front of me. I've made the biggest fool of myself ever.

And she left anyway.

The speeches continue, Dad talking about Grammy's legacy. He jokes about the early days of the Manhattan Pickle. Jason goes on with his jocular self, about how he did his best to run his franchise into the ground but was saved by his brother Anthony.

I should listen more closely. But I feel leaden, as if my veins are filled with concrete. I failed.

I gave it my best shot.

38

CAMRYN

I press my back to the wall behind the drinking fountain, out of view of the stage.

My legs are shaking.

Why did Amy drag me here? I was doing so well, leaving my past behind. Forging a new way.

Oh, who am I kidding?

We know I was flubbing it. My job was terrible. I've been miserable since I left Los Angeles.

Since I left Max.

I have not been as lucky as the speech he gave. No great mom. I only met my grandparents a time or two. Our family is not close.

Perhaps the best person in my life has been Franklin. At least he took care of me when no one else would.

I'm adrift.

Not lucky. Except…

Max.

He thinks he's lucky to have met me.

How can that be, when it cost him the career he'd just begun?

How can he think of me as good when it all went down so badly? His deli, wrecked. His friendship, ruined. His partnership, ended.

He said he was wrong. He shouldn't have kept this a secret.

But it was my decision, too.

He's blaming himself.

But it's *my* brother. *My* lie.

Our lie.

I peek out from behind the water fountain. Grammy is up on stage with Sherman, Anthony, and Jason.

Where's Max?

Grammy turns to the back corner. "Max, I need all my boys up here."

I lean against the cold steel of the ice chamber beside the fountain.

Max runs back up the steps. They look good up there. Such a tight, close family. Jealousy floods me.

Max is lucky. And he knows it.

Max accepts the arm his brother Anthony puts around him.

His eyes go to the water fountain, to me. I don't duck behind the stand. I stay out. Let him spot me.

The relief on his face tells me everything. He thought I'd left again.

Like in L.A.

I walked away. Took the easy route.

I'm not going to leave again.

As the room stands and claps, I push my way through.

I dodge chairs, squeeze through narrow channels between tables, and finally, I make it to the bottom of the stage.

Anthony sees me and turns to the musicians, pointing at them to start playing.

As the Pickles file off the stage, I wait.

Then he's standing in front of me.

Max.

My Max.

"It's like the day we first met," I tell him.

He tilts his head. "I have a bad tan?"

I can't help but laugh. "I see you in a crowded room."

I touch his chin and move his face from side to side. That beautiful face. How I've missed it.

"But, yeah, I don't see much tan action here."

He closes my hand in both of his, holding it to his cheek. "You told me that day you would have to save me."

"I remember."

"And you did. I became the biggest winner in the room."

I know he doesn't mean the gold medal. My heart turns over. "It's your turn."

"To save you?"

I nod. "My new job is terrible. We're overworked. Fourteen-hour days plus travel. People yelling at us all the time. No ventilation for the tans. It's a madhouse. I have to go back tomorrow, and I don't want to."

"I'll help you."

"It'll ruin my reputation. The bodybuilding circuit is cliquish. They'll close ranks if I blow them off. I'm under contract."

He draws me up against him. "I have every faith we will figure it out."

Anthony pops his head over Max's shoulder. "And we have lawyers."

Max nods at him. "Call Ted. There might be a union. If not, some worker's oversight committee or commission."

Anthony puts his phone to his ear. "On it."

The band crashes into its first notes. It's no sweet romantic tune, but a loud, upbeat American march, like a parade.

Max puts his arm around my waist and leads me through a door in the back. The rest of the Pickles work the crowd, smiling and shaking hands.

Sherman glances up and spots us. If he plans to say something, to tell Max to come be with family, he lets it go. He gives a quick nod and turns back to the table of customers.

As we pass through the kitchen, Nova pops her head up from where she's watching two men madly punch floury mounds of bread dough. When we aim for the office in the back, she says, "If you're heading in there, you better lock the door."

"Why?" I ask.

She shrugs. "I know what happens in the Pickle offices." Her grin is unmistakable.

"Now that's a story I want to hear," Max says.

"Jason doesn't kiss and tell," Nova says.

"But do you?" he asks.

She's part of the family, too. How easily they take in outsiders. I felt it from the beginning, sitting in the audience when they didn't even know who I was.

Max pulls me through the office door and closes it. After a second, he twists the lock.

I laugh. "What do you think is going to happen in here?"

He steps close. "I don't know. I keep thinking you're a mirage or a ghost." His fingers thread through my hair. "But you're here."

"It was Amy's doing. She tricked me."

"Then I owe her."

"I have to go back to work tomorrow. Then Germany. Australia. China."

"I thought you always wanted to travel."

I tilt my head up. "I do. But all I get to see is the inside of buses, hotel rooms, and arenas."

"I'll take you anywhere you want to go."

I hesitate. "Even if you get me out of the contract, I think we might both be on the outs in the bodybuilding circuit in L.A."

"I could pose for tips on the street corners of Hollywood Boulevard."

Now I'm laughing. "You'll get arrested."

"You can switch to tanning porn stars."

Oh, Max. "You're crazy."

"Only for you."

Our eyes lock, and it's like I always remember feeling. "I heard your speech."

"I did it for you. Anthony got Grammy to trap you. He made me get up there."

"I had a feeling she was up to no good."

"Grammy's always up to no good."

"But she's the reason you feel lucky."

He touches my nose. "Only one of the reasons."

I'm wearing the rainbow Converse, which don't help me one bit with the height differential. Even on tiptoes, I'm not in kissing range.

But Max knows me. And all I have to do is tilt my chin, and he's there, those miracle lips, that scruffy face I'll have to shave before I can tan him again.

And for the first time in my life, I feel things I've never known.

Faith that everything will work out.

Hope that my future will be easier than my past.

And someone who is completely, unconditionally, mine to *love*.

39

MAX

S *ix months later.*

I pop my head into every prep room along the hall, looking for Camryn.

Clusters of competitors glance my way, getting on their final tan and oil before heading on stage. I'm beginning to think she's dodged me completely when I head into the last door.

Dahlia sees me first. "It's the man candy. I'm terribly disappointed that you don't let me take a lick."

Camryn glances up from her position on her knees, adding a shadow to Dahlia's calf. She lets out a gasp. "You're supposed to be lining up!"

I lean down and kiss the top of her head. "Already done. Only six competitors today."

"I missed it!" Camryn's face is anguished as she moves to the other leg.

"It's all right."

She sighs. "I hope you kicked their butts."

I stick my hand inside the front pocket of my sweatshirt and pull out the gold medal.

Camryn rocks back on her heels. "And I missed it! I was headed there as soon as I finished Dahlia."

"Not a big deal. There's always next time."

"I don't want to miss a single one."

"It's all right." I kiss her head again.

Dahlia steps away and examines her calves. "Perfection."

"You better get going," Camryn says.

She nods and straightens the strap to her shiny silver bikini. "Congrats, Candy Man. You going to kiss me for luck?"

I lean in and give her a quick peck on the cheek.

She rolls her eyes. "One day, hot one. One day." She flounces out of the room.

Camryn shakes her head as she stands up. "She's a pistol."

I wrap my arms around Camryn. "I felt guilty competing in the natural bracket."

Camryn rests her head on my chest. "Why? You're clean as a whistle."

"I'm a monster compared to the others."

"Take it back a notch, then," she says. "But remember, you're showing everybody what is possible."

"Was Dahlia your last?"

"She was. I'd planned to watch you compete and then we would spend the day together. These things never run ahead of schedule!"

"We can have our day."

Camryn unfastens her toolbelt. I take it from her, fold it up and stuff it in my bag. "You want to go watch the women compete?"

"Not today," she says. "I had eleven competitors to manage. I'm wiped."

I wrap my arm around her shoulders as we wander down the halls.

"Sounds like someone needs a hot bath and a massage."

She turns her face up to me, her long hair streaming down her back. "Somebody offering?"

"You bet I am."

We take our time cutting through the guts of the arena, occasionally pausing to say hello to competitors and trainers still working with Camryn. She was both right and wrong about the consequences of quitting the international circuit.

The men's side unilaterally snubbed her. But the women bodybuilders just laughed. "We can totally believe they overworked you," the women's coordinator told her. "The fact that you lasted as long as you did tells us everything we need to know about your longevity in the sport."

The majority of her female clients returned to her, plus scads more. She opted to drop all the men, except for me, of course.

Switching to natural competitions has been a good move. Less pressure. More fun. I've gotten to know several of the leaders, and we work out together at the gym one of them owns. Sometimes I even get Camryn to come over and pump a few weights, although she complains for days about being unable to lift a brush.

This is the first mixed competition we've attended since the new season began. The natural set and the classic competitors don't mingle a lot.

So when we turn the corner and spot Franklin with the crew from Buster's Gym, it's the first time we've crossed paths since the night Franklin rammed his truck into my deli.

Camryn stumbles but recovers quickly. The whole group of them halt in the hallway.

Camryn also draws to a stop, so I stay with her.

She speaks first. "Hello, Franklin."

Franklin tugs on the collar of his jacket. "Sis."

"How did it go today?" She sounds calm, but I can feel the tension in every muscle of her body. I grip her more tightly.

"Silver." He unzips his jacket to show off the medal around his neck.

"That's great. "You headed to the invitational then?"

He glances right and left at his buds and adds a swagger to his next words. "Let the winner through. I'm doin' fine."

I can feel Camryn stifling her laugh. "All right. You look great. Good luck."

We both continue walking. As we're about to pass shoulder to shoulder, my gaze meets Franklin's. His eyes narrow and look me up and down. I consider fishing out my gold medal to flash at him, but I'm not going to do that.

I'm glad he's finding some success. And friends.

Everybody needs someone who has their back. Franklin was that for Camryn most of their lives. He just didn't know where to draw the line.

I almost walk by without saying anything, but at the last second, the words pop out. "Thanks for watching over her. Growing up, I mean."

Franklin's glance shifts to Camryn, then back to me. He thrusts his chin up, and then they pass us and move on down the hall.

Camryn wraps both arms around mine. "You didn't have to do that."

"But it's true. From what I hear, you were a real handful for a big brother to manage."

"I do have rotten taste in men."

"Hey!"

"Present company excluded." She grins up at me, and my world breaks open with happiness.

"I want to ask you something." We pass another acquaintance in the hall, and I wait until they're gone to continue.

"What's that?"

"There's a house for sale in the neighborhood that backs Lucas Street. I could walk to the deli from it."

"That's a nice neighborhood," she says. "And I'll always love the park where we met that time."

"Our first kiss."

She laughs. "Our first very short, very platonic kiss."

I hesitate again as we pass by registration and out to the parking lot. I continue to hold the thought as we stow our things in the trunk and climb into the front seat of my Audi.

Camryn pulls down her shoulder harness. "So, when are you thinking about making an offer?"

I reach over and take her hand. "Just as soon as it meets the approval of the woman I want to live there with me."

Her jaw opens, then closes. "Really? You're ready for a house full of tanning tents and the constant smell of oil?"

"It's one of my favorite smells. It has the best memories."

She bounces in her seat. "Can we go there now?" Her face radiates joy.

"I thought you were tired."

"Not anymore. I have something amazing to look forward to."

She chatters nonstop as we drive across town. "I could set up in the garage, maybe. We could have a room for your medals."

I revel in the sound of her happy voice. She's making plans with me.

We pull up in front of the white stucco with a red Spanish tile roof. A circle driveway sets the house back from the road enough to look classy, but not so much to be L.A. elite.

"Oh, wow!" she says. "Look at this!" She jumps out of the car. "Look at it!"

I glance at my phone. "The realtor will be here in fifteen to let us in."

Camryn spins around to face me. "It's so beautiful!"

"We can peek in."

We peer through the front windows. "Look at that fireplace!" she says. "I've never had a fireplace!"

She runs around the side. "The master bedroom! There's a garden tub!"

The back gate is locked, but I remember the code on it from my visit yesterday, so I buzz it open.

She pulls on the handle and runs ahead.

Ah, so she's going to see the surprise.

She stops dead in her tracks. "Max!"

I hurry forward so I can see everything through her eyes.

A pool glistens, edged with blue and white tile. At the opposite end is a cabana house, the doors thrown open to show the spacious interior.

She hurries to it. "It has a bathroom! People could change in there! I could tan in here!" She whips around. "You picked this for me!"

I nod, and she runs at me, jumping so hard she almost knocks me into the pool.

But I clutch her body, her face buried in my neck. She wraps her legs around my hips.

"I love it," she says, and barely contains a sob.

"I love you," I say. "I want all our dreams to come true here."

She pulls back, her wet eyes holding mine. "They already did."

I kiss her in the backyard of our first house. I want everything of mine to be hers, to wrap her in security, family, and love.

This is a good start.

EPILOGUE: CAMRYN

When I first see Max in his tuxedo, I have to admit, I almost like this version of him better than when he's naked in my tanning tent.

Almost.

He's let his face scruff grow since we're between competition seasons. The natural bodybuilding circuit has fewer meets. But it feels like the right amount. Enough to show off his hard work. But not so competitive or driven that it impinges on his life.

The black jacket shapes his shoulders like a linebacker. The pants are custom fit and accentuate his powerful thighs.

Honestly, I want to take the whole suit right off of him.

But we're out of time. The wedding is less than an hour away.

Max turns in the circle. "What do you think?"

"I think you're too beautiful for this world."

He tweaks his white bow tie. "Funny, that's the way

I've always felt about you. Take a spin in that beautiful dress. I'll try to keep everything in my pants."

"Not your strong suit," I say with a laugh as I take a slow, easy walk on the hotel room's Berber carpet.

Jason's wedding is in an hour. My fitted gold dress is sheathed in sequins. The light from the balcony windows hit it like I'm a disco ball, throwing off bits of light across the walls.

"Perfection," he says. "And those shoes are outrageous. I love them."

I kick up a heel of the six-inch gold platform stilettos. I'm probably going to break my neck. But I have a pair of tiny folding flats tucked into my clutch. The platforms are mainly for the pictures, so I don't look like a Lilliputian in the land of the giants.

I take three long strides toward him, like I'm on a runway. And miraculously, I don't trip over myself and botch the effect. "The better to kiss you with," I say.

"It's true," he says. "Your face is up here."

"It's almost time to meet the photographer for the groomsman shots," I remind him. "We should probably head down."

He takes in a deep breath, and it shudders as he lets it out. He's nervous. About his brother's wedding? That's crazy.

"You okay?"

He widens the gap in the sheers covering the door to the balcony. "Once Jason's wedding is over, everyone will be looking to us."

"That's all right. They know we've moved into the house."

"They do."

"We all seem to get along. I love when we come to New York and get crazy with your big family."

He nods again, and I can tell something is getting to him.

"Max?"

He checks his watch. "Okay. Here goes."

He takes my hand and leads me out into the sunshine beaming down on the balcony. It's a small boutique hotel, so we're only on the second floor. An intricate wrought-iron rail separates us from the busy city.

"Come close," he says, pulling me against his side.

Below I hear music. Classical music.

I peer down. On the sidewalk below, a string quartet has set up and is playing something peppy and upbeat.

"How cute. They're busking right outside the hotel." I lean over to see them better, my arms propped on the rail. "Only in New York."

"They're good."

"Is this what you wanted me to see?" The violinist must have a break in his music, because he looks up and waves. I wave back. It's midsummer in New York and the weather is sublime. If we didn't have the wedding, I could sit out here all day. The violinist sets his instrument back under his chin, and the music takes a quieter, more thoughtful turn.

When I turn back to Max, he isn't standing anymore.

He's kneeling.

"Camryn Elizabeth Shultz," he says, and my hands fly up to my mouth.

"Max?"

His eyes are shiny, and his hands shake. "Some people claim there is no love at first sight. But I know the truth. Sometimes you see someone for the first time and just know."

He clears this throat. "The crowd parts, and your eyes land on someone so perfect, so exactly what you've been looking for, that you know this is it. This is the moment you've been waiting for. That's what it was like the day I met you."

My throat is so thick I can't even respond.

"I know I was a pain in your side that day. I messed up your schedule, I created havoc in your day. And I embarrassed the hell out of myself."

"Not so much," I tell him. "You have no idea how close I came to going back in that room and locking the door."

His smile is ten miles wide when I say that, and his nerves seem to back off. "During the time we were apart, nothing made sense anymore. But thanks to my brother and Grammy Alma, I got one more shot. And today I want to make sure I never have to let you go again."

He pulls a small green velvet box from his pocket and pops it open. "Camryn, will you marry me?"

I want to embrace him, kiss his head. But the stupid shoes are miles too tall so I reach out to touch his uplifted arm.

"Of course. Yes. Yes! I will marry you."

He slides the ring on my finger, and I gasp. It's the sort of ring you see on the hands of celebrities. Princesses.

"Max?"

"Only the very best for you." He stands up, pressing his lips to the back of my newly bejeweled hand.

"Then you better kiss me," I tell him. "Because otherwise, I'm going to assume this is only a dream."

"Maybe it is."

His lips are warm and gentle on mine. In the New York street below, the string quartet kicks the tune up a notch. A few people on the street must notice us, because a cheer rises.

A breeze ruffles my hair and Max pulls back to gaze at me. I imprint this moment on my mind. This man. This kiss. This day. I want to remember it forever.

The song comes to an end, and Max leans over the rail. "Thank you!"

As they play one last song, I say, "You have to get them back for our wedding."

"You want to get married here in New York? Not L.A.?"

"I think so. I want to be with all your family." There will be things to sort out. My brother. My parents. But that's for another time.

"You are already a part of it." His hand closes over mine. "I don't want to detract from my brother's big day." He laughs. "Actually, maybe I do, but I won't. So, should we keep this a secret? One last undercover romance before everyone knows we're together forever?"

I look at the ring one more time. "Absolutely. I love keeping secrets with you."

When we're back inside the room, I pull a long gold chain from my jewelry box and slide the ring through. Max fastens it around my neck, and I tuck it under my dress, right over my heart.

We'll think of a fun way to announce this later, but we're late for pictures. We dash down the hallway to the elevator, hand-in-hand. When we catch up to Grammy Alma, who is also heading down, we share a conspiratorial grin.

"Don't you two look like the cat who ate the canary," she says as Max punches the button to go down.

"I have a question," I say to her.

"Yes, child."

"If you were to name a pickle after Max, what would it be called?"

She peers at her grandson, eyes full of mischief. "Damsel in Distress."

"What?" Max asks. "Why that?"

She shrugs. "You might be the big tough one in our family, but it's the rest of us who keep having to save you."

"I love it," I say.

"Done!" Grammy Alma says. The doors open and Max holds the door for us to step inside. She leans in. "And I say, make it the *hot* pickle."

Max shakes his head as he enters the elevator and presses the button for the lobby.

He pulls me close. "You have secrets with everyone."

When my gaze lifts to meet his, I see nothing but

happiness and joy. That's the way I hope it will always be.

Grammy Alma sighs. "Young love."

Max leans his forehead against mine. It's fun to have this little surprise for his family.

It's a great secret. The best kind.

I hope you'll keep it for us.

Gotta love those Pickles!

You read Jason and Nova's secret boss love story, right? If not, go get Big Pickle!

Anthony is next with Spicy Pickle! Make sure you sign up for emails or texts to know when he arrives in early 2021!

Intrigued by Colt and the MMA fighters at Buster's Gym? They ALL have their own series!

- Colt and Jo's epic love story in Uncaged Love.
- Parker and Maddie's second chance romance in Fight for Her.
- Hudson and Chloe's enemies to lovers romance in Reckless Attraction.

BOOKS BY JJ KNIGHT

Romantic Comedies

Big Pickle

Hot Pickle

Single Dad on Top

The Accidental Harem

MMA Fighters

Uncaged Love Series

Fight for Her Series

Reckless Attraction

Get emails or texts from JJ about her new releases:

JJ Knight's list

ABOUT JJ KNIGHT

JJ Knight is one of the pen names of six-time *USA Today* bestselling author Deanna Roy. She lives in Austin, Texas, with her family.

If you would like to see everything Deanna writes, here are her pen names:

JJ Knight

(Romantic comedies and MMA sports romance)

Annie Winters

(Romantic Suspense — slightly hotter on the scale)

Deanna Roy

(Emotional New Adult romance)

 facebook.com/jjknightauthor

twitter.com/deannaroy

 instagram.com/deannaroyauthor

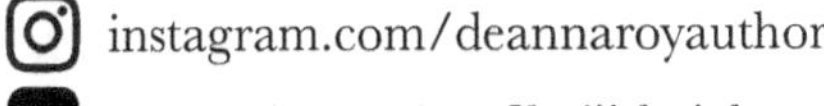 bookbub.com/profile/jj-knight

9 781938 150913